THE BOX

A DEREK REED THRILLER

Victoria M. Patton

Dark Force Press

Dark Force Press
www.darkforcepress.com

Publisher's Note: This is a work of fiction. Names, characters, places, and incidents are a product of the author's imagination. Locales and public names are sometimes used for atmospheric purposes. Any resemblance to actual people, living or dead, or to businesses, companies, events, institutions, or locales is completely coincidental.

Book Layout © 2016 BookDesignTemplates.com

The Box-A Derek Reed Mystery/ Victoria M. Patton. -- 1st ed.
ISBN-13 978-1-946934-15-4
ISBN-10 1-946934-15-1

Library of Congress Control Number: 2019900554

Editor: Judith Bixby Boling
Cover photo by: Karolina Grabowska / Kaboompics www.kaboompics.com.

Other books by Victoria M. Patton
Damien Kaine Series
Innocence Taken
Confession of Sin
Fatal Dominion
Web of Malice
Blind Vengeance
Series bundle books 1-3

Derek Reed Thrillers
The Box

Short Stories
Deadfall

CONTENTS

CHAPTER ONE

Late August
Moorhead Mississippi

The stench of stale sweat mixed with blood wafted around the hot carnival tent. Blood flowed from the cut above Derek's swollen right eye. Every lick of his dry lips coated his tongue with salt and the taste of metal. His hands hung limply in the leather bindings, and his fingertips tingled from the numbness setting in. Both knees rested on the dirt floor stretching his arms to their limits. Craning his head and angling his body, he could see the deep gash on his left side still bled, soaking the top of his jeans. A wave of nausea crested over him as he watched the crimson liquid pulse out to the same beat that thumped in his head.

Derek's stomach rolled as he glared at the disgusting man. Josiah's crooked, yellowed teeth were just the start of his lack of hygiene. The smell of rotting eggs permeated the air around him. The odor in the tent was unbearable.

He turned his attention to the girl. Salty tears stung his eyes, spilling over and down his cheeks as he stared at Chrissy. Her blue eyes pleaded for him to stop Josiah from raping her. "Just keep your eyes on me, Chrissy. Just me baby." Derek choked out the command. Caustic bile hovered at the top of his throat threatening escape.

Derek's stomach tightened as Josiah's grunts filled the tent. He wanted to look away, to shut out the disgusting scene before him, but Chrissy needed him. The rag stuffed in her mouth muffled her screams of terror. Derek kept his eyes locked on the twenty-year-old. Her face was black and blue from the repeated beating by Josiah. "Chrissy," he said. "Keep looking at me, baby."

Opening her eyes, they flooded with tears.

"Mr. FBI man," Josiah Craig said as beads of sweat covered his forehead. "You should've paid better attention." His breath quickened, and he snorted as he glimpsed over at Agent Derek Reed. He pulled out a long serrated blade from the sheath on his belt. He continued his assault on Chrissy. "It's too bad you didn't get here in time—Derek." He grinned at the agent. "It's a shame really. You might have been able to save her." Josiah grinned as he reached out and dragged the edge of the blade across Chrissy's neck as he emptied himself into her.

"No! You fucking bastard," Derek yelled out as blood spurted from the neck wound. All the air left his lungs. "Oh Chrissy, I'm so sorry," he whispered to the dying girl as her eyes remained open and locked on him. For a split-second, Derek saw the girl's face relax as if she was thankful the nightmare she had lived for the last six days had finally ended.

Josiah moved from the makeshift table, zipping his pants. He walked towards Derek, slowing his breathing down. Standing within a foot of the agent, he kicked Derek in the stomach. "Not so tough now, huh?"

Derek grunted as he tried to inhale a searing breath. He coughed, tasting the iron as blood and vomit mixed together. "Kill me and get it over." Derek gagged as he continued to cough.

Laughing, Josiah grabbed Derek's hair and yanked his head up. He punched the agent in the face crushing his nasal bone. "I'm not going to kill you. That would be too easy for you. No, I want you to carry the image of that young girl, all the girls you couldn't save, for the rest of your life. I want you to remember how you—the great profiler—almost figured it out." He leaned back and cackled. "Almost mind you. No, I want you to remember, how me—a lowly uneducated carny—bested the big fancy profiler."

Josiah pulled Derek's phone from the front of his jeans.

"What are you doing, Josiah?" Derek asked as he spat more blood from his mouth.

Josiah smiled at him. "You'll see." He flipped open the phone turning it on. "I'm surprised you aren't using one of those fancy smartphones. This damn thing is ancient."

The pain from his broken nose radiated from the front of Derek's face and reverberated against the back of his skull to the pounding of his pulse. "It's a phone." He looked up when he heard ringing coming from the speaker. "Who the fuck are you calling?"

Josiah held up his finger.

"Derek, Derek? Where the hell are you? We've been looking for you?" an agent on the other end asked.

Derek was about to say something when Josiah kicked him in the stomach again. "Agent Reed is slightly detained at the moment."

"Who the hell is this?"

"This is Josiah Craig. The serial killer you have been looking for."

Silence echoed through the phone.

"Listen, you need to come get your agent, or what will be left of him. He's at the back of the Sunset Circus in the main supply tent. Although, I would hurry. He has a few significant injuries that need attention." Josiah disconnected the call.

Derek's head hung to his chest. He tried to glance up at the sound of his gun being loaded but only managed to raise his eyebrows.

Josiah sneered. "Don't worry, this bullet isn't for you." He knelt right in front of the agent. "No way I'm ever going to outrun the FBI. But I sure as hell don't want to go to prison. I think it's time I meet my maker on my own terms." He reached out and lifted Derek's chin with the barrel of the gun. He hit Derek across the cheek with the weapon.

Derek's head snapped to the side. The crunch of the bone caused starbursts to explode behind his eyes. An agonizing pain spread across his face like splintering wood.

"I hope you think of me once in a while." Josiah turned his head and lifted the gun to his temple.

Derek watched in horror as Josiah blew his brains out inches from him. Brain matter spattered on Derek's face and neck. It was the last thing he saw before he passed out.

CHAPTER TWO

One week later
Phoenix, AZ
3:00 a.m. Monday

Derek's legs hung over the edge of the bed. "What the fuck was that noise?" He sat motionless trying to figure out what had woken him from a deep slumber. He shook the cobwebs from his head. The movement had him seeing stars. Home from the hospital for three days, his head throbbed from the resetting of his nasal bone.

Squeezing his eyes shut, he centered himself, slowing his breathing. He stood on wobbly legs and staggered into the kitchen. He braced himself against the fridge before opening it and grabbing a bottle of water. "Motherfucker," he said as he rested his hand on the counter steadying himself. Dizziness swept over him like a tsunami.

"It's about time you came in here."

Derek's back straightened, and the hair on his neck and arms stood on end. He stared down at the counter and breathed deeply. His body shuttered at who or what was in his kitchen at three a.m.

"Don't pretend as if I'm not here. It's not like I've been trying to get your attention or anything."

Her voice echoed in the sparsely furnished kitchen. Derek lifted his head slowly turning in the direction of his visitor. The hand holding the water bottle shook. His chest constricted forcing him to breathe in sharp stinging breaths of air.

"For crying out loud will you sit down already. We need to talk," she said.

Derek opened one eye and dropped the water bottle, gasping at the young lady before him. Blood ran from the gaping wound on her neck, and her head hung at an awkward angle as if it had been plopped on top of her shoulders. Her eyes were cloudy, and the bright blue color he remembered was now a pasty gray. "Chrissy?"

"Duh. Who else would show up here?" She lifted the cigarette to her lips and sucked in a long drag.

Derek watched in horror as the smoke billowed around her, escaping through the open neck wound. "This isn't happening. There's no way this is real." He covered his ears and squeezed his eyes closed.

"Oh, it's real—Derek. How could you not help me?"

A loud hissing noise made Derek open his eyes. He stepped back towards the counter, gripping the edge. Chrissy's mouth opened, and black flies swarmed out. Her jaw elongated and distorted her face as she levitated from the chair.

Derek ran from the room heading for the front door tripping over his coffee table. He rolled onto his back trying to drag himself across the floor as Chrissy's contorted figure moved towards him. "Go away. I did all I could do. I tried to save you—I tried to save you." Derek curled into the fetal position as she inched closer to his face. "Please go away. Please go. I did all I could do."

"You didn't do enough Derek. You never do enough."

Derek screamed at her, his body shaking. "I did everything in my power to help you...I did everything!" He covered his face and wept.

"Did you Derek? Did you do all you could?" Chrissy asked. "You're lying to yourself. You didn't. You never do. What about Sheila? Did you do all you could to help her?"

Derek shot up in bed gasping for air. Sweaty and tangled in his sheets, he struggled to free himself. He dragged a hand through his dampened hair. The pounding pain from his newly reconstructed nose brought him back to reality. Rat-a-tat-tat, his pulse beat like a machine gun against his temples. His rasping breaths burned his throat. He spun his head around, searching for Chrissy.

He swung his feet onto the cool tile floor. The thrashing behind his eyes added to the flood of nausea that engulfed him. Slowing his breathing, he reached for the pain meds on his nightstand but thought twice. "No fucking way I'm going back to sleep." Derek threw the bottle of pills on his bed as he staggered to the bathroom leaning against the doorframe for balance. His legs slowly gathered the strength to carry him to the sink.

He stood in front of his mirror ogling his face. He wasn't the best-looking guy to begin with, now with all this damage, he was even uglier. Josiah had not only crushed his nose but broke his cheekbone. The facial bruising was still blue and dark purple. A stark contrast to his bright green eyes. The effect of black eyes was made even more prevalent by the still slightly swollen right eye.

The light sheen of sweat coating his body caused goose bumps to form when the AC kicked on. The nightmare of seeing Chrissy seemed all too real. He understood his mind was looking for ways to rationalize what he witnessed, but he wished it would find some other way than scaring the shit out of him.

CHAPTER THREE

9:00 a.m. Monday morning

Derek walked through the lobby of the FBI Building in downtown Phoenix. The walk from the parking garage to the entrance felt as if he had slogged through a mud bog. The amount of energy needed to lift each leg had his head beating like a drum corps. If removing his nose from his face would relieve the radiating pain, he would chop it off right now.

The security guard scanned his ID and his thumbprint, letting him through without making him take off his weapon, bypassing the scanners. Entering the elevator, he removed his sunglasses. A young woman stared at his injuries. Her brow furrowed then softened. Yet, she couldn't look away. When the doors opened, and he stepped out onto the seventh floor that housed the Behavior Analysis Unit, he turned towards her. "You should see the other guy," he smiled at her expression as the doors shut.

Several agents stopped what they were doing as he passed by their cubicles. He nodded, winking at them. He walked with purpose into his unit's section, and all heads followed his every move. Ignoring their ogles, he turned on his computer. As he waited for the ancient machine to boot up, he sensed someone behind him.

"Derek? What the hell are you doing here? Have you been cleared to come back to work?" Agent Davis asked. "Did you already see the psyche doc?"

"Why wouldn't I be able to come back to work? It's nothing more than a broken nose. The gash on my side is stitched up. What the hell do I need to wait for? And who put you in charge?" Derek stood and headed towards the coffee pot in the break room.

Agent Davis followed right on his heels. "Dude, you know the rules. If you're injured during a case, you have to go to mandatory counseling." Davis made the crazy sign. "You know, to make sure you haven't lost your marbles. They don't want you going on some kind of rampage because you have some serious issues." He poured a cup of coffee out of the same pot that Derek used.

"Well, I have a psychology degree, I can do what all those counselor's do. I don't need to go to counseling." Derek started back towards his desk when his boss cornered him in the corridor.

"Why are you here?" Assistant Director Fretz asked.

Agent Davis smirked as he scooted passed the AD. He glanced over his shoulder shaking his head.

"Why wouldn't I be here? I work here. Unless you've fired me and neglected to tell me," Derek said.

"Follow me to my office."

Derek followed. As he walked past Agent Davis, the agent made the crazy sign again. Derek rolled his eyes at the annoying man.

"Shut the door behind you, Derek," AD Fretz said as he sat behind his desk.

"How have you been? Catch the game the other night? Those Diamondbacks might take the pennant, huh?" Derek asked.

"Derek, you hate baseball. And the Diamondbacks don't have a chance in hell of winning the pennant." He folded his hands on his desk. "Why the hell are you here?"

"As I said to Agent Davis, I work here."

"You are a thorn in my side. You know the drill. You need to be cleared by the doctors to get back out in the field." The director took a sip of his coffee.

"Why do I have to go to a doctor? I've seen worse."

AD Fretz's jaw slacked. "Are you serious? You've seen worse than a young girl being raped and murdered in front of you, then have a man splatter his brains all over you?"

Derek shook his head. "You know what I mean."

"No, I don't actually. Can you fill me in?" When Derek didn't answer, he continued. "Listen, Derek, I'm not sure how you see the connections you do when it comes to your cases. That's what makes you one of the best profilers ever to come into the BAU. You seem to have a knack for seeing things that no one else sees. I know you figured out a connection between the carnival and the girls." AD Fretz leaned back in his chair. "You went to the carnival and found Josiah Craig. You didn't follow procedure and almost got yourself killed. Now you need to be medically and mentally cleared to work."

Derek patted his pockets, searching. He stood and checked every pocket of his jeans, twice. "C'mon," he said. He stopped and glanced up to find his boss staring at him. "Got any gum?"

AD Fretz smiled and reached into his desk. "You, of all people should realize you switched one obsession for another." He threw a pack of unopened gum at him. "Quit avoiding this conversation."

He removed two pieces putting one in his blazer pocket, while he stuffed the other in his mouth. "Thanks." Derek tossed the pack onto the desk. "I'm not avoiding anything."

The AD leaned back in his chair. "Have you been contacted regarding your appointment with the psychologist yet?"

"Nope," Derek said, shaking his head. His brow furrowed. "How soon is my appointment?" At that moment his cell phone pinged. He pulled it from his pocket. "Well, I guess it's Wednesday." He shook his phone at AD Fretz. "That was the doc's office." His face was about to implode with every chew of the gum, but he refused to let his boss in on that secret.

"Good, the sooner he clears you, the sooner you can get back to work." Fretz looked at his profiler. His arms looked weighted as if they pulled his shoulders low. Even though he had quick-witted responses, he lacked the humorous gaze that usually accompanied his sarcastic personality. "Derek, I read your report. While you gave a clear and concise break down of events, I would still like to know why you went to the carnival without backup?"

Derek squirmed in his chair. He drew his mouth into a straight line. Biting his bottom lip, he stared at his hands. Why did he think no one would ask him this question? "I didn't think."

"You're a profiler, you've been with the FBI for over twelve years, how can you even use that as an excuse?"

He shrugged as he twisted the watch on his left wrist. "I had been studying the case and saw a connection that—that didn't stand out until that night. I acted on a hunch."

AD Fretz eyed his best profiler. He watched the unease settle around him. Hell, the man squirmed in his chair as if his pants were on fire. "I know you aren't telling me the whole truth. Your report is somewhat satisfactory, but this question will come up again. And the real reason will come out." AD Fretz took a drink of his coffee. "Your one saving grace is you stopped Josiah Craig. That's probably the only thing keeping you from disciplinary actions. That, and the fact that you were hurt.

How are the injuries healing, by the way?"

Derek bristled. The injuries were a constant reminder of how stupid he was. "They're healing."

"Any other residual effects?"

"What? What do you mean? What have you heard?" Derek leered at his boss. "If you've heard something, I need to know."

"Wow! What the hell is your problem? I haven't heard anything. I was just asking." AD Fretz frowned at him. "Listen, maybe you should stay at home until you see the doctor. Get the clearance you need."

Derek straightened in his seat. He tapped the face of his watch. "No. I'm sorry. I need the distraction. I've been at home since my two-night stay in the hospital, I don't want to sit at home doing nothing. It's making me crazy. Just let me stay. I won't work on any active cases." He continued to tap his watch.

AD Fretz dragged a hand down his face. "Oh man. I know this is a bad idea." He sighed. "No active cases. You can work on cold case files. We have several of those. No going out in the field. You hear me, Derek?"

"Yes, Sir. I hear you."

"Go. Get out of here before I change my mind."

CHAPTER FOUR

Late Monday morning – FBI Offices

Derek sat at his desk nursing his third coffee, which wasn't the best idea ever. All that caffeine made his pulse race, making his face throb, and making him want to relieve the pain with a bullet. With every passing hour, the pain intensified pounding behind his nose and cheek. "Fuck," he whispered as he controlled his breathing.

He opened the most interesting cold case he could find. Three couples were murdered outside Phoenix five years ago. The lack of evidence left at the scenes and the fact that all family and friends had been ruled out as possible suspects, left very little to go on. Derek scanned the police reports and the reports from the FBI agent in charge of the investigation.

"This guy is a total dumbass." Derek dragged a hand through his wavy brown hair. "Shit," he said wincing in pain. "Even my fucking hair hurts." He rummaged through his desk and found a half-empty bottle of Tylenol. He swallowed four pills with the last sip of his cold coffee.

He continued reading the file. His skin tingled and a thin line of sweat formed on his hairline. He didn't want to turn around. Instead, he gave sidelong glances while keeping his head still. "No, no, no...." he hissed. He sunk into the chair as he pushed it out from his desk. He peeked around the office. "Please go away. Please go away." He clamped his eyes shut repeating the mantra silently to himself.

"Derek, you know I can't do that," she whispered right next to his ear.

Cool air tickled his earlobe. "This is where I work. You're a figment of my imagination. I'm telling you to go away." He felt the wisp of cool air move across his neck the same time he heard a faint giggle in his ear. "This isn't real. It's just my mind."

"Oh, sweetie, I am so real. Does AD Fretz know how you found Josiah?"

He brushed it away like an annoying gnat. "You aren't real." His knee bounced under the desk. Derek stared at his computer. He resisted the urge to swat his other ear, where the cool air seemed to settle.

"They will find out." She dragged a finger across his shoulders.

Derek had a chill that started on his left shoulder and moved across his back to his right. He shuddered at the sensation. "Stop. If I tell you to stop, isn't there some rule you have to?"

"Hey, Derek, who are you talking to?"

Derek spun around in his chair. "Huh?" His forehead wrinkled. He frowned at Agent Rogers. "Uh, what are you talking about?"

Agent Rogers glanced around Derek's desk. "Who are you talking to?" he asked looking over his shoulder then back at Derek.

"Umm, no one. Just myself. Kind of a bad habit." Derek smiled at the agent.

"What are you working on? You aren't cleared, right?" He angled his body to see what Derek had on his computer.

Derek smirked at the nosy bastard. He pulled the stick of gum from his pocket and stuck the piece in his mouth. "What? Are you checking up on me, Rogers?" His nostrils flared as the pain erupted throughout his cheek. He grinned at the agent.

"No. Of course not." He peeked over Derek's shoulder and glimpsed at the open file on his desk. "Is that a cold case file?"

"Damn, you are so nosy. Yeah, the AD said I could work on cold cases. It's the three murdered couples outside Phoenix. Back in 2013."

"Hey, I knew the agent in charge of that. He had nothing to work with. And when I say nothing, I mean zilch, not a damn piece of evidence." Agent Rogers leaned on Derek's desk. "They looked at clubs, libraries, anything that the couples could have had in common. They didn't find anything. All the family and friends were cleared, co-workers were cleared. He couldn't find any connection, and neither could the local authorities."

Derek nodded at the tiny annoying elf. How he ever got into the Academy, he had no idea. "Well, it beats sitting at home." He turned back to the file hoping Rogers would get back to his own caseload.

"I'm going to get out of here. Going over to the café across the street to have lunch with several other agents. You want to join us?"

Derek shook his head. "Nah, but thanks for the offer." He glanced at his watch, tapping the face. "Shit, not even eleven thirty," he groaned.

"Alright, see ya later," Rogers said as he slapped him on the back.

Derek watched the man walk away with a group of agents, grateful prying eyes and ears had gone. He turned back to the file, also thankful the annoying dead girl was gone. "I may need counseling if I keep seeing dead people." His concentration now lost, he opened a secure browser on his computer. He typed in Josiah Craig, his finger trembled as it hovered above the enter key.

All kinds of articles popped up. "Oh no." Derek gaped at the screen. "Fuck, this can't be good." Scanning several stories, he was relieved that they didn't have any good pictures of him attached to the articles. He didn't want his face plastered all over the internet. He scrolled through more pages landing on one regarding how he found Josiah Craig and stopped him. "Oh, hell. This had to be put out by the FBI. Shit." He scrolled through the article. His hung head and his shoulders curved inward. "How the hell can I ever tell them the truth? Jesus, they all think something else happened."

"You're going to have to sooner or later."

He turned towards the young girl's voice. He sucked in air through pursed lips. He closed his eyes hoping she would go away. Slowly opening them, Derek inhaled sharply. Her gaping wound was crusted with dry blood and maggots had woven themselves between the layers of her skin. Her eyes were dull and pasty, and her face was sunken. "Can you not fix your—you know—wound?" He waved his hand in front of his neck.

"Look, you're the one with the guilty conscience." She fiddled with the pen on his desk.

He watched as the pen spun around. He placed his hand over it. "Stop doing that." He rose to get a glimpse around the office. "People will see this."

"Dude, only you can see me."

Derek rubbed his temples. "This isn't happening." He got up and headed to the vending machine. He fed it a five-dollar bill and picked out three items. None of them would ever make the food pyramid. He started to open the chili cheese Fritos when a draft encircled him. "Seriously, do you have to follow me everywhere?"

"It's your fucking head I'm in...maybe if you didn't feel so guilty about all the lies you've told, you would let me go."

"What the fuck are you talking about?" he popped a Frito into his mouth as he fed the soda machine a couple of dollars.

"You can't be that stupid." Chrissy moved to the other side of him.

"I want some chips." She looked at Derek. "You know, Josiah didn't feed me the whole six days he held me. He rarely gave me water or anything else to drink."

"Why are you telling me this? Are you trying to make me feel more guilty?"

She flinched back. "No. Not at all. Why would I want you to feel guilty?"

"You fucking know why."

"Really, you're angry at me? I think you have issues, Derek, not to mention you're acting a little crazy."

Derek turned around to leave and ran right into the AD. "Hey, AD Fretz. What are you up to?"

"Who are you talking to?"

"Huh?" Derek's brow furrowed. "Umm, I don't know what you mean?"

AD Fretz stepped back with a raised eyebrow. "You were talking to someone. I heard you."

Derek giggled. "Oh, I was running through that cold case I have been researching. Thinking about the conversations they might have had with the killer. I guess I didn't realize I was saying it out loud." Derek smiled. "I'll be getting back to my desk."

Fretz reached out and touched his arm. "Hey, I understand you went through something pretty traumatic. I think it would be best if you stayed at home tomorrow and rested before your psyche appointment, don't you?"

"You know, you're probably right. I'm in a lot of pain. I probably should give my body a rest. Who knew looking at old files would be so hard. Right?" Derek headed back to his desk and watched the clock. He needed the right moment to escape. Hopefully, Chrissy would stay behind.

CHAPTER FIVE

8:30 a.m. Wednesday morning

Derek glanced around the office of the psychologist's assigned to his case. He'd been here before, however not in this capacity. He patted down his jacket, searching each pocket. Standing he searched every pocket of his jeans. "Son of a bitch. I can't believe I forgot that."

The young receptionist, startled by the agent's outburst glanced up. "Agent Reed? May I help you with anything?"

Derek sighed and plopped down in his chair. "No, Shelly," he said pouting. "Wait, unless you have some gum?" he stared at the other clients waiting in the room. "Anyone?" his head turning from side to side. "I'll take anything."

The receptionist rolled her eyes. "Yes. I have some." Shelly bent down and pulled her purse out of her desk drawer. Rummaging through her bag, she found the prize. "Here Agent Reed. Just keep the pack." He took the gum from her putting a piece in his mouth. She was sure she heard him moan as he chewed.

Derek sat back in his seat and closed his eyes. His cheek ached, and with every chew of the gum, a sharp pain erupted through his face rattling at the back of his head. But the chewing calmed him. He tuned out the pain, closing his eyes. His nose twitched as a faint odor drifted around him. He peered around looking for the source of the body odor. No one sat near him, and he was sure no one walked by. He closed his eyes resting against the back of the chair.

Within minutes, his skin tingled, and his pulse sped up as his adrenaline spiked. He cracked open one eye and searched the room. A thin line of sweat ran down his spine. His knee bounced, and every time he tried to stop it, the other one took over.

"Not here. Please not here," he whispered. A slight movement to his left caught his eye. In the far corner, her presence was unmistakable. Chrissy's macabre smile filled her face. Her teeth now outlined with black as the gums had started to recede and decay. The fullness her lips once held was gone. They were cracked and bleeding. Her neck wound had widened and had begun to peel back due to rotting skin. The tendons and muscles looked like stringy old rubber bands. A noise from his right brought Derek's gaze towards the doors.

"Derek Reed?" the young man yelled into the waiting room.

"Oh thank God," Derek whispered as he stood and started towards the open door. Stepping over the threshold, he glanced over his shoulder. Chrissy gave him two thumbs up, and a crooked grin then vanished.

The young man glanced over at the agent. "Are you feeling okay?"

Derek scowled at the man. "Why do you ask that?"

"You look a little pale. Just making sure you were feeling okay."

"I'm fine. Thank you for asking."

The kid nodded. "Sorry about the walk. Dr. Chelsea has moved. I'll show you the way, and then they'll show you where you'll go for your next appointment," he pushed open another door. "And you'll go out a different way."

"No worries." Derek walked down the long hallway. They meandered through a series of corridors. "I parked way the hell back there," he said pointing over his shoulder.

The young man chuckled. "Upon exiting, you'll walk around the building. It only seems far because of all these hallways. It's really a short distance, less than a block. Next time you come you'll park on the opposite end." He pushed open a heavy door after sliding his badge through the key lock. "Dr. Chelsea didn't anticipate his office being done this soon. Next week everyone will have the new address and directions. Like I said, though, it's just the other side of the building complex." He stopped outside an office door. A simple nameplate read Dr. Ronald Chelsea. "Here you go."

He knocked on the door and entered. "Hey, Charlotte. This is Agent Reed."

"Oh hell. I know Agent Reed," she said as she walked around her desk. She gave the agent a long hug. "How you been?" She twisted his head from side to side. "Looks like those wounds are on the mend." She patted him on the face. "Wouldn't want anything to mess up that ugly mug of yours."

Derek laughed and dropped his gum into the trash bin before sitting in a chair. "Nice to see you, too, Charlotte. How's your husband? You kill him yet?"

"Unfortunately, no. I don't want to be a guest in an FBI interrogation room. I liked working for them." She smiled at him. "What about you? You kill anyone lately?"

Derek smiled. "Not recently." His gaze lowered as he shifted in his seat. His chest tightened, and his throat thickened, making it hard to swallow. He has killed before. Once as an agent in the FBI, and once a lifetime ago.

An office door opened and two people stepped out. "I will see you next week, Officer Jones." Dr. Chelsea patted the young man on the shoulder. "Charlotte, hold my calls." He pointed at Derek. "You, in my office."

Derek stood laughing. "Ooh, going to the principal's office." He winked at the secretary. "Stay out of jail, Charlotte."

She giggled and waved him off as she answered an incoming call.

Derek entered the old Doc's office. "I see you moved and you brought all this horrible decor with you. You know you suck at golf. Do you think having all this shit makes you look like you can actually play the game?" He sat in the oversized chair and put his feet on the ottoman. Derek smiled as Dr. Chelsea pushed his salt and pepper hair to the side. "You should get that mop of yours cut."

"It's all about appearances. The golf and the hair...all about appearances. Speaking of appearances, shouldn't you be wearing bandages on that nose, so it sets properly?"

Derek shook his head. "I took those off a few days ago. Too annoying."

"They were placed on your face for a reason."

"Yeah, to annoy the hell out of me."

Dr. Chelsea sighed as he reached for his open can of soda and set it on the table in front of him. He plopped down and let out a heavy sigh. "You want something to drink?"

"No. I don't even want to be here. Why am I here?" Derek asked. He stared at his friend. He'd known Dr. Ronald Chelsea for several years. He was older than Derek by ten years and often tried to take on a brotherly role. He was a bit overweight. Round in the middle with skinny bird legs.

"You know damn well why you're here. It's mandatory after you witnessed what you did."

"I'm a profiler, I witness all kinds of nasty things. Worse shit than

Josiah Craig."

Dr. Chelsea frowned. "All of those other incidents were after the fact, Derek. You witnessed Josiah Craig rape and murder a girl you were trying to save. A girl you spent many nights trying to find. This session is not only mandatory, but it is also warranted. You need to talk about what you saw." He sighed. "When your name came up for a consult, I spoke with my bosses and got them to assign me. I figured you would be reluctant to speak with someone you didn't know, but with our history, I thought it might be easier on you."

Derek glanced around the room. "Yeah," he said looking back at the doctor, "I appreciate that."

"Plus, I wanted information to blackmail you with later." Dr. Chelsea grinned.

"Now that I believe." Derek leaned his head back on the chair. "Okay, let's get this over with. What do you want to know?"

"You know it doesn't work like that. But if it makes you happy, I can play your game. How did you feel watching Josiah Craig rape and murder Chrissy?"

"Gee Doc, I don't know. Happy?" Derek shook his head. "How the fuck do you think I felt. It made me sick." He placed his feet on the floor and leaned forward resting his elbows on his knees.

"That's exactly why you need to discuss it. You can't carry that around. It will eat you up from the inside. Witnessing something like that, if you don't get it out and in the open to deal with it, your mind will find a way to deal with it. And when that happens, it isn't always an easy ride." Dr. Chelsea didn't say anything else. He just waited.

Derek stared at the watch on his wrist. Twisting it and sliding it up and down. "Josiah Craig was a nasty bastard. He took great pleasure in hurting all those girls."

Dr. Chelsea nodded. "That's right. And when you became involved in the case, it was no longer about those girls. It was about you. You and Josiah, the proverbial cat and mouse game."

Derek's eyebrows furrowed. "What are you talking about Doc? I didn't even know who the guy was."

"You're one of the FBI's best profilers. You have one of the most successful close rates of cases than any other profiler. Everyone knows who you are. You didn't have to know who Josiah was. He knew who you were." Dr. Chelsea leaned forward. "Josiah Craig was nothing more than a handyman. A carny. His parents were outcasts and were part of the carnival all their lives. He was raised in the carny. You had to know once you got involved in the case, Josiah Craig would focus on you. He wanted nothing more than to beat the best."

"He didn't care about me. Josiah Craig wanted to kill girls. I wanted to stop him. That's it, nothing more."

Dr. Chelsea cleared his throat. "How long did you chase Josiah?"

"For ten months, four days, and roughly fifteen hours. Why?"

He raised an eyebrow at the agent. "Tell me about the case."

Derek sat back. "When I took it over, he had killed three girls. Over the rest of the case, he killed four more. Including the last one, Chrissy."

"First name basis with the young girl. She meant something to you."

"They all mean something to me." Derek glanced at his hands. "You know that."

Dr. Chelsea nodded. "I do. And after ten months, four days, and fifteen hours of chasing him, what steered you to the carnival? I read the file. I didn't see much evidence leading the authorities to think there was a connection."

"No. They never tied the girls to any of the carnival stops."

"Then how did you come up with it?"

"Huh?" Derek asked looking at the Doc.

"How did you connect the dead girls to the carnival that employed Josiah Craig?"

CHAPTER SIX

Derek lowered his gaze as he shifted in his chair. He rubbed his hands together. They were clammy from the light sheen of sweat that coated them. He wiped them on his jeans. He scrutinized the doctor. "How do you report our sessions?"

Dr. Chelsea's brow wrinkled. "I don't think I know what you're asking me."

"Our conversations are confidential. right?"

"Oh, I see." He nodded. "Yes, I have to keep our conversations confidential. I give a general report to the FBI concerning your ability to return to active duty. Other than that. I don't tell them any of the details concerning our conversations."

Derek adjusted himself in his seat. "I didn't find a connection to Josiah. Well, I mean I did. Let me start from the beginning. When I took over the case, I began to look at where the girls were from and where they were found. The abductions of each girl occurred hundreds of miles from the location where they were found. At first, I thought it may have been a trucker.

"But the last sighting of each girl didn't have them anywhere near a truck stop." Derek twisted his watch. "All the girls were located near large but remote rest stop areas. Eventually, I narrowed in on the carnival. I couldn't find any other explanation as to how the girls could travel so far and not be seen." As he talked, Derek tapped the face of his watch.

Doctor Chelsea waited as Derek stalled in his response. He watched as Derek glanced around uneasily. His repetitive tapping of his watch face announced his anxiety like a beacon. "I'm assuming when you made that connection, that you researched traveling carnivals, and saw that the Sunset Circus was in town."

Derek nodded. "Yeah." He scooted towards the edge of the seat. His head hung low on his shoulders.

"You look like you need to get something off your chest. What is it, Derek? You can talk to me."

Standing, Derek paced the room. "I'm not anything special."

"Excuse me?"

"You, AD Fretz, and everyone else. You think I see things that help me solve cases. I don't."

"Derek, how do you explain all of your solved cases? Cases that other profilers and agents weren't able to solve?"

"I can't. I can only tell you it isn't anything special."

Doctor Chelsea sighed. "Derek, I know you're carrying around a lot of guilt. But Josiah wanted to use you. He wanted to make..."

"You don't understand."

"What don't I understand? Explain it to me."

"I didn't go to the carnival because of what I—figured out!" Derek placed his palms on the side of his head. "I didn't go to the carnival because I'm some kind of super fucking puzzle solver, I went because Josiah Craig texted me. He sent me a picture of Chrissy and told me where she was."

Doctor Chelsea stifled his gasp. "Oh, Derek."

Derek tilted his head back. He rested his hands on his hips.

The doctor shifted his chair to face his friend. "Derek, this only bolsters my original assessment. When the best profiler in the country took over this case, Josiah Craig wanted to match wits against you. You didn't know it was Josiah Craig until the end. But he knew who you were. And he wanted to fuck with you."

Derek chuckled at the profanity. "Is that a real diagnosis Doc?"

"In this case, yes. I explained to you, it ceased to be about the girls. Those last four girls were used to get you where Josiah Craig wanted you. He had no intention of letting you take him alive. He had one of the FBI's best on his trail, and he wanted to make sure you paid the price."

"I was so stupid. I can't believe I didn't see it. If I had, I might have been able to save Chrissy."

"No, you wouldn't have. Josiah planned all along to kill Chrissy, and himself. His whole purpose was to fuck with you. And he has succeeded."

"What the hell am I supposed to do now?" Derek plopped down in a chair. "When everyone finds out, I'm fucked."

Doctor Chelsea chuckled. "No, you aren't. Leave the report as it is. If you are questioned, tell them what you just told me. How you narrowed in on the carnival, and you were stupid, you should have brought back up. Lesson learned."

"You're pretty good at lying Doc."

"The FBI has what they want. No more dead girls. Josiah Craig is dead, and their best profiler is still the gem of the Department." The doctor stood. "I noticed your watch. It's unusual. You also seem to fidget with it a lot. Is it new?"

Derek's brow furrowed. He glanced at the watch. "No. I got it from a friend when I was fifteen."

"It's still working all these years later?"

"I've had a watchmaker keep it in tip-top shape. I know I should buy a new one, but I can't seem to part with this one." Derek wrung his hands. "Umm, so…"

"Umm, what?" Doctor Chelsea scribbled on a notepad.

"Is it normal for someone to…I don't know…umm imagine dead people and talk to them? That's a coping mechanism, right?"

The doctor raised an eyebrow at him. "Is that what you're doing? Talking to dead people?"

"Oh man. I'm sure it's my guilt. I'm rationalizing what I saw. You're right. Watching Chrissy get raped and killed has made me slightly crazy." He grinned at the doctor.

Doctor Chelsea moved across the room and leaned against his desk. "Who are you seeing?"

"Chrissy."

"Derek, our minds have a way of working things out. When we experience a horrible act whether it be against ourselves or someone we know, as you did with Chrissy, the brain deals with that stress in different ways.

"I'm a little concerned. When we begin to manifest imaginary conversations, we're getting into a slippery slope. If you're seeing the dead girl and speaking with her, even in your mind, then you need to deal with the trauma. What you witnessed was horrific, even for someone who has seen some really nasty shit.

"Right now, your brain is trying to process the events. You're still trying to deal with what you saw and the obvious guilt you carry. If you are manifesting Chrissy to deal with it, you need to face this. You need to let Chrissy and Josiah go. You can't do that working."

Derek bristled, standing. He frantically tapped the face of his watch. "What do you mean? Are you going to recommend they fire me?"

"No. Not at all. But I am going to tell them you need an extended amount of time off." He reached around for a prescription pad and scribbled on it. "Here. When you leave here, go see your boss. Give him this. I will rush the paperwork through the channels today. But that note will get you out now."

Derek glanced at the note. "Are you fucking serious?"

"Yes. At a minimum, sixty days."

"I can't be off cases for sixty days. I will definitely go insane." Derek shifted from one foot to the other. "No. This is unacceptable."

"You have no other choice. If you don't take the time, I will recommend that you be moved to another unit. One less stressful." The doctor crossed his arms.

"I really hate you right now."

"No, you don't. All you have to do is enjoy your time."

"Enjoy my time? What the hell am I going to do for sixty days?"

"I don't know. Hell, don't you like photography?"

"Oh, that's genius." Derek paced again. "I'll just become a fashion photographer."

"Why don't you go see your family, and on the way take a bunch of photos. Leave the dead alone for a while. You spend all your time with them. Look at the world through the eyes of the living. Not the dead."

"Yeah. Yeah. Okay. I'll go see my family." Derek headed for the door. He reached out for the doorknob, stopping he turned around facing the doctor. "Hey Ronald, Thanks."

Dr. Chelsea cocked his head to the side. "For what?"

"For doing this and not letting me talk to a stranger."

"I'm straddling the line of ethics by counseling you. But I knew you wouldn't go for talking to anyone else." Dr. Chelsea stepped over to him. He squeezed his shoulders. "You're my friend. And you're damn good at what you do, Derek. Enjoy this time off. Regroup. And remember to let the dead stay dead."

CHAPTER SEVEN

11:30 a.m. Wednesday

Derek sat in front of AD Fretz's desk, chewing on a piece of gum as his boss read over the notes from Dr. Chelsea. He winced with every chew as his broken cheekbone erupted in crunching pain.

AD Fretz turned his attention from the notes to his profiler. "How do you feel about this?"

Derek shrugged. "I guess a paid sixty-day vacay isn't so bad. Although I might go crazy by day twenty."

"Well, I agree with the doc. I think you need this." He pulled a file from his desk drawer. "I guess this is as good a time as any to tell you something."

Derek's eyebrows wrinkled together. "I don't think I like the tone of that."

AD Fretz shook his head. "It's not bad I promise you. I don't think it's bad anyway. Okay, listen. Long before Josiah Craig, the FBI was starting a new unit, the Legacy Unit. My boss put you on the Craig case for a reason."

Derek shifted in his seat. He frantically tapped his watch as his knee bounced at a furious rate.

"They liked the way you handled this case, along with the way you've handled all your cases, and decided you would be a good fit for this unit." AD Fretz smiled at his agent. "Derek, you really need to calm down. I can see the fear in your eyes." He halfway chuckled.

"There is fear in my eyes because I'm waiting to be sent to a Siberian outpost for fucking up the Craig case."

"Derek, I've tried to explain to you, even with your lack of judgment in bringing back up, you didn't fuck anything up. Look, they want you to head the unit."

Derek's jaw fell open. "What?"

"You heard me. C'mon, how could you think this would never happen? You're one of our best, you had to know you would get your own unit."

He balked. "Uhh—no. I didn't."

"It's a great unit. You'll be working on cold cases, specifically the more heinous murder cases. You'll be based out of here, so you get to stay in Phoenix."

Derek sat stunned. He didn't want to be in charge of any unit. It's hard enough working with the living, he preferred the dead. Now, he had to oversee a unit. Sweat beaded on his back causing his shirt to stick to him. "I don't think this is a good idea. I'm not leader material."

AD Fretz roared back laughing. "I think this is the first time I've ever seen you so scared you're about to shit your pants. Oh, Derek, it isn't that bad."

"Where will I work out of? I mean building wise, this building?"

"No. The FBI acquired an old Catholic church, it's a great eclectic office space. Just north of here. You should like it. There are a few rooms that can be used to bunk in, and the main church area has been renovated into an office space." He slid the folder over to Derek. "Inside here you will find ten agents to choose from. I need you to pick seven. I think you will be familiar with a few of these. These people specialize in cold cases, but most of all they are some of the best agents we have."

"I don't understand. Can't you just incorporate the BAU? Make a small unit from this one?"

"No. The higher-ups want this unit to handle only specific cases. Murder. No robberies or theft, or anything other than the most heinous murders that have occurred. Mostly cold cases, once in a while you may be put on a more recent case." The AD leaned on his elbows. "Back in 2009, the FBI started the Cold Case Initiative. This stems from that. You will do most of your research from here, and when needed you will go on-site with your team."

He pointed to the folder on the desk. The agents in that folder are unattached. It will make it easier. At least starting out. Your new unit may be spending a lot of time on the road. It isn't a prerequisite. But I think it will make logistics a lot easier."

Derek shook his head. "I don't think this is a good idea. You really should pick someone else for the job." Derek squirmed under the stare of his boss. "Really, this is a bad idea. I've already proven I don't follow protocol. Imagine what I will do with a bunch of agents under my command. Nope. This is a bad idea."

AD Fretz shook his head. "You can come up with every excuse, but it won't do you any good. For now, you will be under my command.

That should alleviate some worries."

Derek frowned at him. "Pfft. I think you are a little full of yourself."

AD Fretz laughed. "You need to choose your agents within thirty days. I want those names turned in to me ASAP so we can notify them. Some are here in Phoenix; the majority are not. By the time you get back from your vacation, your new unit will be ready for you to take control. I will have the office outfitted with everything you guys will need. Oh, two of the agents in that group are tech geeks. You need to choose just one of them. Do you have any questions?"

"Do I get a secretary?"

AD Fretz raised an eyebrow. "Do you need a secretary?"

"Listen, if I'm going to be running a unit the last thing I want to do is answer my own damn office phone. Plus, if we are doing that much traveling, we need someone back here that can do things for us."

The AD smirked. "Alright. I will throw in a secretary. I will pull someone from one of the offices here. I bet we have a few that wouldn't mind a new unit, away from this building."

Derek sighed, determined to make the best of this. "They need to know how to find stuff and get stuff. They need to know how the FBI works."

"A little demanding now, huh?"

"Listen, I didn't ask for this. But if you are going to give it to me, I want to run it my way. I might as well start it off right. Please, don't give me someone who is green. I don't want to have to train them on anything."

"You got it. I will make sure to give you someone who will be an asset to your team, not a hindrance."

Derek stood and headed towards the door. "Just remember. I told you this was a bad idea."

CHAPTER EIGHT

Derek's packed bags sat on his bed. The last thing he put in was his weapon. He wasn't cleared to carry his weapon on duty, but he would never travel without it. He decided instead of leaving that evening he would get an early start on Thursday morning. Looking at his road map, he picked the most scenic and entertaining route to Nashville, where his crazy family lived. Approximately 1600 miles, he figured he had built in enough sightseeing places to help with the long drive.

He placed his bags on the floor and walked into the living room. Flopping down on the sofa, Derek leaned his head back, hoping his face would quit throbbing. He'd gotten his pain prescription refilled, although he hated taking the damn pills. However, his body wasn't even close to being healed, and he would need those pills at some point.

Derek looked around his sparsely decorated home. He loved this house. Inherited it from his grandmother and moved in when he was transferred to the BAU five years ago. Arched doorways led to a semi-open concept. The domed shape of the ceilings allowed for air flow throughout each room. His grandmother had been smart enough to put in a cooling system when she had the whole house retiled. Couple that with the Adobe rooftops, his home often remained cool without running the AC unit into the ground.

He turned on the DVD player. Episode nineteen of *Star Trek*. He glanced at his watch. "Fuck, I could die of starvation. Where the hell are you?" Moments later his doorbell chimed. Pulling his wallet from his pocket his mouth started watering. "Damn it's about time." He yanked open the door. "Man where have...oh, you're not the pizza guy."

"Nope. I'm not. But I did bring beer." Elizabeth held up the twelve pack and pushed passed Derek heading towards the kitchen. Her boxer, Lola, followed close behind.

"Umm, why are you here?" he asked as he followed her and Lola to the kitchen. "Hey Lola, how is my sweetie?" he asked as he scratched the dog behind her ears. Elizabeth turned to inspect his face. Gently turning his head from side to side, Derek saw her expression soften.

"We didn't have anything scheduled, did we?" he asked.

She flinched back. "Since when do we have to have something—scheduled—for me to come over. I thought we were friends?"

"You know you're one of my closest friends. Practically my best friend, which makes me even more pathetic now that I think of it. But I wasn't expecting you." He took the beer she held out and twisted off the cap handing it back to her. He lifted one from the package, twisted the cap off, and took a long pull. "If you showed up tomorrow you would've missed me."

Heading towards the sofa, a loud knock rattled the front door. "Oh, please be my pizza." Lola bounded towards the door barking and wagging her butt. "Get back, Lola."

"No kidding," Elizabeth said. "I'm starving." As Derek walked back in carrying two pizza boxes, Elizabeth went into the kitchen for two plates and paper towels. "Unless you want me to leave and let you eat alone?"

He waved her off. "No, of course not. You know I love your company. Although I don't think I will be much use tonight. My face may explode if I get my blood pressure up." He winked at her. She had big round hazel eyes, with a ring of gold surrounding each iris. They widened at his comment.

"Is that all our relationship is, a kind of transaction?" she grinned wickedly at him.

"If it were a transaction you would make me pay you." He pouted when she smacked him on the arm. "Ouch."

"Hmm, don't make me hurt you," she said, walking away.

They carried their plates and the pizza boxes to the living room. Lola took up a position directly in front of them, hoping for scraps.

"Lola move, you're blocking the TV." Derek watched as the dog sauntered over to the oversized love seat and settled in, eyeballing them both waiting for her snack.

"Just because most of the men in my life pay for my company, doesn't mean I would ever have you do that." She took two pieces of the pepperoni pizza and crisscrossed her legs at the end of the sofa. Breaking off a part of the crust, she tossed it to her beloved chocolate brown Boxer. "Do you remember when we met?"

"Like it was yesterday." He chuckled. "Wasn't it roughly eight years ago?"

"Exactly eight this month." She took a bite of her pizza. "Why didn't you turn me in that night?"

"I didn't care about you. I was only interested in the man you were entertaining that night. Once he was murdered, I knew you were going to need protection."

"Well, you definitely protected me. Kept my name out of the investigation. To this day, no one knows I was even there." She leaned over and kissed his cheek. "I don't know if I ever thanked you."

"You don't need to thank me. You've become a very good friend. That's thanks enough."

She gave Lola another piece of her crust.

"Are you still hobnobbing with the elite of Phoenix?" Derek asked.

"Of course. Who else would I sell my services to?" she gulped her beer. "Plus, I'm not the girlfriend type. Although, if I were, I would set my sights on you."

"Okay, right. After the lifestyle you have accumulated, I can't imagine you ever settling down." He finished his first two pieces and grabbed two more along with two pieces of the calzone. "You don't sleep with everyone, do you? Don't some just want you to be their escort to high-falutin events?"

"Yes. Actually, I sleep with very few. If I choose to sleep with one, it is because of an attraction, not money."

"Very noble."

"You're such an ass." She laughed when he stuck his tongue out at her. "So, tell me how you are doing. Really doing."

"You see my face. It hurts as bad as it looks."

"Oh Derek, I'm so sorry you were hurt. When I heard you were in the hospital, I was so worried."

Derek cocked his head to the side and raised an eyebrow at her. "How the hell did you hear about me being in the hospital. But more than that, what exactly did you hear?"

"I was out with Congressman Jackson. He told me about..."

Derek's slice of pizza stopped halfway to his mouth. "What the hell are you doing out with him?"

"Jackson, hell I've known him longer than you. I was a regular escort for him when his wife was ill. And before you judge me, she knew."

"I would never judge you. You know that." He scowled at her. "I'm surprised, that's all."

"He's actually a wonderful man. He bought my condo for me, years ago. He's a good man."

"He's practically the head of the FBI. The only thing missing is his name on the door."

She smiled at him. "I also hear you're going to be the head of your own unit. Hmm, are you excited?"

Derek placed his plate on the table. "Let me guess, Congressman Jackson?"

"Of course, who do you think put the bug in his ear?"

Derek turned and gaped at her. "What the hell are you saying?"

She placed her plate on the loveseat, letting Lola scarf down the remaining pieces of her pizza. Elizabeth held up her finger as she took a sip of her beer. Letting out a huge belch she giggled at Derek's expression. "I have won many a burping contest in my day."

"Your talents never cease to amaze me. Now explain what you meant by that." He reached over and paused the DVD.

CHAPTER NINE

Elizabeth stretched out her legs, placing both feet on Derek's lap. Even with the bruising on his face, his boyish charm was still ever present. He wasn't the most attractive man she had been involved with, but his piercing green eyes and wonderful sense of humor drew her to him. His tall, lean muscular frame was also a plus.

He looked young for a man in his late thirties. She couldn't keep from smiling as she looked at him. His wavy brown hair always a mess, yet always perfect. But it was the way he made her feel when he made love to her that tipped the scale. Her insides quivered. She loved spending the night with him wrapped up in his arms. He explored every inch of her as if he was with a woman for the first time, every time. It didn't take long for her heart to choose Derek, but her heart didn't know any better.

"I was out with Jackson, almost a year ago. He was staying the night with me and was telling me all the details concerning the new unit he had discussed with the head of the FBI and Secret Service. He said they were deciding who should be placed in charge of the unit. They originally thought Agent Dillon McGrath, but then her grandparents were murdered. Anyway, all they knew was they wanted a profiler. I suggested they put you in the position."

Derek stopped rubbing her feet. "Wait a minute. That's around the time I got assigned to the Josiah Craig case."

She wiggled her toes. "Yes, I know that. Jackson said he knew of you and wanted to see how you would handle yourself. I guess he was satisfied. Cuz you got the job." She laid her head on the back of the sofa. "That feels so good."

Derek continued to rub as his mind considered what Assistant Director Fretz had said in his office. Lola's barking brought his attention back to the present. He glanced around his home, no one else there and no one at the door. But Lola was barking at someone.

"Lola," Elizabeth shouted. "Stop it. There's no one there." Lola continued to bark. Elizabeth followed her stare to a chair in the corner. "What has gotten into her?" she glanced at Derek. "Hey, Derek?"

Derek turned towards her. He tried to be nonchalant, but his heart pounded against his chest. He hoped Lizzy couldn't hear the thumping. The same putrid odor encircled him. He winced inwardly hoping Lola's sense of smell sucked. He avoided looking in the same direction as Lola. *Please don't show up now.* He said to himself as he stared at Lizzy. "What do you think has her so riled up?" he asked.

"I have no idea. Maybe you have a ghost," she said.

"What!? Why do you say that?" Derek plastered a smile on his face. His gaze still avoiding the corner and the old chair.

"They say pets can sense the dead. Maybe that's what she sees." Elizabeth clapped her hands getting the attention of the dog. "Hey, Lola, stop it. Come here, girl."

Lola broke free from her trance and bounded up on the sofa, snuggling between them.

Derek reached over and patted her head. "I'm pretty sure I don't have ghosts." Derek stood and began to clean up.

Carrying everything into the kitchen in one trip with the help of Elizabeth, he put the empty boxes in a trash bag. "Hey, do you still have a key to this place?" he asked her as she helped smash the empty boxes into the bag.

"Of course I do. Why?"

"Would you come over and put my trash can up tomorrow afternoon. Then come by every few days to pick up the mail. I don't want to stop it, but I don't want it to pile up either. Not that I get that much."

"Sure babe. No problem. I can even stay a few nights here and there, so there is a car in the driveway."

"Thanks, I would like that."

They finished the cleaning and headed back to the sofa. Before retaking his seat, he let Lola out into the backyard to do her business. "If you want to stay tonight, I would like that, Lizzy." He said as he took his seat on the sofa.

She smiled at the use of her childhood nickname. "I would definitely like to do that. And I won't take advantage of you. But maybe some extra care would help you sleep. Hmm?"

He smiled at her grin. "You are an evil woman. You know that?" She sat across his lap, facing him. She ran her fingers through his thick wavy hair. He brushed her bangs out of her face pushing the rest of her long auburn hair off her shoulders, letting it drape down her back. She had a small figure with the perfect curves. More than just beautiful, she was intelligent too. Could carry on a conversation from architecture to football. No wonder she was in such high demand.

Lizzy played with his hair. His bright green eyes almost emerald like. Shimmered in any kind of light. She traced her finger along his square jawline. He had a rugged look, but his boyish charm kept him from looking unapproachable. She could feel his excitement through his jeans. "I love you, Derek, you know that, right?" The words hung between them like damp, heavy wool drapes. She started to pull away when he grabbed her hips. Elizbeth's breath hitched.

"I know you do. You're the only woman I have in my life and the only one I want. You need to remember that." He gently kissed her soft lips. "You really are my best friend."

CHAPTER TEN

4:00 a.m. Thursday

Derek woke to light snoring. He smiled remembering he had a beautiful woman next to him. He turned to wrap his arm around Lizzy. "Oh seriously?" Instead of Lizzy, Lola's nose greeted him. At some point during the night, she had snuggled in between them. He smiled at the scene. Lizzy laid on her side with her arm draped over the dog. Her dark auburn hair spread out around her. He had a sneaking suspicion this was a regular occurrence.

Needing to relieve himself, he stepped into the bathroom, closing the door to keep from waking his sleeping guest. Flipping on the light, he studied his face in the mirror. The bruising was starting to turn yellow-green on the outer edges, giving him a ghoulish look. The swelling around his broken cheek area had gone down, but his nose had a long way to go. The doctor at the hospital in Mississippi had done a remarkable job setting it. Every day that the swelling went down, he could see how straight it was healing. Once he healed, there should be little outward reminder of the damage done by Josiah.

Glancing down at his waist, the large wound on his side was healing better than he expected. The doctors had said no swimming, but showers were okay. The skin still puckered but the surgeon had assured him that as it healed that would go down more and more, eventually smoothing out and leaving little scarring. He brushed his finger over it wincing a bit. The wound was still tender to the touch.

Derek decided against going back to sleep, instead opting for an early start on the road. He jumped into the shower. Hot water flowed out of the massive rain shower head. Steam swirled around him. He placed his hands against the wall allowing the water to run down his back. A sense of doom crept over him. Derek didn't want to take this trip. The last thing he wanted to have to do, was to explain to his family why he was even out there. But more than that, he didn't want to be reminded of Sheila.

Turning off the water, a grin pushed the corners of his mouth upward at the only bright side to this trip. He loved taking landscape pictures, especially those of abandoned buildings. And he was sure the route he picked would allow for just that. He ran through the first leg of the road trip as he dried off. From Phoenix, he would travel I40 to Albuquerque, roughly a six-and-a-half-hour drive. If he didn't feel too tired, he'd drive on.

He stepped out of the shower and wrapped the towel around his waist. He heard a light scratching on the other side of the door. He opened it. "Lola," he whispered. His brow furrowed, there was nothing there. Turning back to the sink, he yelped. "Quit fucking sneaking up on me."

"I'm not sneaking up on you. Why are you so jumpy?" Chrissy sat on a built-in bench that ran the length of one wall. "She's pretty." She nodded towards the bedroom.

Derek stood with his mouth gaping wide. Today Chrissy was some sight. Her neck wound had drawn entirely back exposing rotting muscle and tendons. Their stringy, rubbery look replaced with blackened cracked tissue. The maggots had doubled in number, and large black flies now buzzed around her. The roots of her teeth had been exposed due to the rotting gums.

He lifted his chin and sniffed the air. "Oh my God, you're starting to ripen." He covered his nose stepping back. "Can you not change how you look?" Derek pinched the bridge of his nose wincing in pain. "Fuck I have to quit doing that." He leaned against the sink as the pain spread out through his face. He blew a sharp breath out shaking his head. "I don't want to see you like this. If you're going to insist on showing up, you have to change the way you look and smell."

She crossed her arms. "You do realize you have the power to change me? Not me." She tapped the side of her head. "You have to change what you see."

Derek finished shaving hoping if he ignored his subconscious, it would make her go away. "I need to get dressed," he said as he pulled open the door. Fresh air rushed in. He glanced over at her. "Please show up and look like you did before Josiah killed you. I remember those beautiful blue eyes and the softness of your face. That's the Chrissy I want to see." He waved his hand in front of her. "Not decaying, bug infested, gross, stinky Chrissy."

"Okay," she said. "I guess I'll see you later." She disappeared into a wispy smoke.

Derek sat on the side of the bed. He glanced at his watch, then gently rubbed Lizzy's head. He raised an eyebrow at Lola, who had decided to take his vacated spot. Her head now rested on his pillow. "Lizzy? Hey baby?" he said as he nudged her.

"Hmm?" she stirred before opening her eyes. "Hey, why are you up?"

"I decided to go ahead and leave early. Stay as long as you like. Don't forget the trash can and the mail. I'll text and call to let you know where I am."

"Okay." She reached out and took his hand. "I can't wait for you to get back."

He bent down and kissed her. "I won't stay gone too long. I'm driving to Tennessee and back, that's it." He stood and gathered his suitcase, a large overnight bag, and his computer bag. Before he walked out, he glanced back at the pair. "Not a bad way to wake up every morning," he whispered as he walked out the door.

CHAPTER ELEVEN

Thursday afternoon

"Thank you." Derek smiled at the convenience store clerk. He had filled up with gas and bought some snacks. He looked at his watch, just after two p.m., it was way too early to stop for the night. As he headed out the door, a brochure stand caught his eye. "Well, I'll be." He picked up one of the brochures and smiled. The banner across the top read Ghost Towns of New Mexico. He was a few miles from several old ghost towns that were thriving back in the day of the gold rush.

In his car, he threw his snacks into the middle console and opened his diet soda. He checked his glove box for his weapon. He'd placed it in there that morning before he left his house. Derek picked up the map from the passenger seat. Golden New Mexico was not far up the road, and that was the perfect first stop. After that, he'd get off the main interstate and go down Highway 285 and pick up Highway 54. He'd hit a few more ghost towns in Duran and Ancho.

The junction for the turnoff to Golden was less than twenty-five miles away. Derek longed for a cigarette. A habit he gave up long ago. He reached into his console for one of the many packs of gum he brought with him. Putting two pieces in his mouth, he turned the radio to a classic rock station. *Foreigner* blared out the speakers, he banged on the steering wheel to the thumping of the base. He ignored the pain in his jaw and cheek. The gum was way more important than any pain.

"Wow. You really like this song, huh?"

Derek jumped, yanking the wheel to the left, correcting his mistake moments before he hit the vehicle in the adjacent lane. "Seriously? Are you trying to kill me too?" He closed his eyes hoping she would go away. He concentrated on blocking the rancid smell from making him throw up. The blare of a horn pulled his attention back to the road. He veered this time to the right. "Fuck!" he yelled as he pulled onto the shoulder. Slowing to a crawl, white-knuckled hands gripped the wheel.

He heard giggling as he pulled to a stop. His stomach fluttered then knotted as he turned towards her. He swallowed, squeezing his eyes shut. The back of his throat ached. Not wanting to see the decaying rotten corpse in front of him, the smell was bad enough. He focused on the way she looked before Josiah Craig hurt her. He pictured her beautiful brown hair as it hung over her shoulders. Her blue eyes radiant in his memory, not dull, gray, and pasty. Facing his fear as his pulse raced, he lifted his eyelids.

He sucked in a breath. The insects were gone. That was the only good thing. The neck wound was still gaping but was no longer oozy. Her gums were no longer rotting, but they were still blackened and receded showing way too much of the enamel. Her cracked lips were thinner, almost nonexistent. The iris was cloudy, but specks of blue color seemed to peek through in spots. The sclera was still pasty gray. Her skin was ashen in color yet seemed to look not so—dead. An instant shadow came over him. If he had saved her, she would still be the vibrant young lady she was before Josiah had gotten to her.

"Stop doing that to yourself," she said.

"I'm sorry. Stop doing what?"

"Beating yourself up. He was going to kill me anyway. His whole purpose was to have you there."

His eyes narrowed in on her. "How do you know that's what I was thinking?"

She roared back laughing. "You're such a dork." She made the crazy sign on the side of her head. "Plus, you are a little wacko." She glanced around the scenery. "Where are you heading?"

Derek turned his attention back to the road as he pulled into traffic. "Going to Golden, a ghost town."

"Do you think that's the best idea you've ever had?" she raised her eyebrows at him.

"Well, seems fitting to me. Since you're my new traveling buddy."

She smiled at him. Her rotting teeth on display. "I like traveling. Used to do it with my family." Her mouth turned down. "I wonder how they are doing."

Derek sighed. "I'm sure they miss you every day."

She nodded. "I hope so."

Dead silence filled Derek's restored 2006 Jaguar XJ.

Chrissy adjusted herself in the soft leather bucket seat. "This is a really fancy car. How does a G—man afford this? You on the take, Mr. FBI man?"

Derek gave her a cheesy grin. "No. I'm not," he said winking. "I got it at a government auction. It was in pretty decent shape, but I had it restored to its glory. I love this car." He inhaled a deep breath as he patted the dash. Driving this car always calmed him. It was the one place he felt secure and at peace. The midnight blue color sparkled in the sun. The creamy beige interior was trimmed in dark wood inlays. The seats were buttery smooth, and the two front seats had warmers in each. He had the car's sound system revamped during the restoration, adding in satellite radio and Bluetooth.

"I bet this car gets you all the chicks."

He scowled at her, squinting. "Do you have a boyfriend?" He cracked the window, hoping the rotting smell would be sucked out.

She shook her head laughing. "Uh, I'm dead. So, no."

"Shit, I'm sorry."

She waved her hand around. "No, it's okay." She wrung her hands in her lap. "That's why I went to the carnival. A boy I used to know from high school said he wanted to meet there. Instead, I found Josiah Craig." She swiveled her wrists to make jazz hands. "Lucky me."

Derek started to say something, but she continued with her story.

"It was the last night it was going to be in our hometown. The next stop was two counties over. Maybe a hundred miles away." She gazed out the side window at the passing landscape. "To think I was so close to my home," she whispered shaking her head. Her hair tossed across her shoulders. "Anyway. Let's talk about the pretty lady in your bed. Are you married to her?"

"No. And I don't really feel comfortable talking about her."

"Why? You love her, but don't want to admit it?"

"What do you know about love. You're twenty."

She frowned at him. "I was twenty." She smiled at his expression. "Okay. How do you know her? You seem like you guys are pretty comfortable with each other."

"I've known her for many years." He continued to stare out the window. This scene in the car seemed all too real. He took the exit for Golden. Leaving the highway, he pulled through the almost empty town. What was left, made its livelihood off the tired traveler looking for excitement. He was struck by the desolation. Most of the town had been abandoned back in the 1930s.

He drove through the heart of town and found a place to park. He and Chrissy exited the vehicle. He reminded himself to not speak out loud to her. As he and his mental sidekick roamed the ghost town, he snapped photo after photo. Some of the buildings had been vandalized by would-be thugs, but most stood, having been ravaged by time and weathering.

After about an hour he headed for his car. He didn't see Chrissy anywhere. "Yo, Chrissy," he called out. Immediately scolding himself. "Oh hell, man, you are going to need medication. Keep it up, Derek." His mind did a great job of making her seem real. Even using his olfactory senses.

It was just as well. He needed to concentrate on driving, and the odor of decaying flesh was not making it any easier. He headed back to the highway. Following 256 down to Highway 54, he would arrive in Duran within the hour. The sweltering August heat had his shirt sticking to him. He cranked the AC and set out for the next town.

Duran was uneventful. Derek headed on to Fort Sumner. He had passed Vaughn and was about twenty-five miles outside the city when he drove through a small unincorporated town. He didn't pay attention to the name, but this one wasn't empty and desolate. Small stores lined the two-mile main street. A half a mile past the last store the speed limit increased. He was almost up to speed when he spied an old farmhouse off to the right. He whipped the car onto the old dirt road that led to the homestead. His heartbeat sped up as an uncontrollable draw pulled him towards the house.

"This is a bad idea, Derek." Chrissy stared at him.

He glanced at her then turned back to the road. "Why? It's an old house. I love old farm houses the most. They are both creepy and inspiring. I always feel like I am transported back in time."

"This house is different. You don't want to go inside. Take your photos from the outside then let's get the hell out of here."

He pulled up into the weed-covered drive. The house stood off to the right. An old unattached garage sat at the end of the crumbling driveway. The house had a lopsided staircase that led up to a small covered porch. The old white paint was peeling and chipped exposing the grayed ancient wood.

Derek turned towards his companion. Her color had paled a little. "Chrissy, why are you so worried about this house? It is an old house." He opened his car door. He wiggled his eyebrows at her. "I won't be too long. If anyone comes near my car, scare them like you always do me."

"Derek. This is more than just a house."

CHAPTER TWELVE

Derek stood on the first step of the porch. He glanced over his shoulder at his car. Chrissy sat in the front seat surrounded by a misty haze. Or at least the tiny gnats that surrounded her made it look like a misty haze. He questioned why his mind played such a vivid joke on him.

He lifted his camera and took a few photos of the front of the house. He moved up the stairs, pausing at the top. Snapping a series of photos, he could later turn into a panoramic view, his heart pounded against his chest. "Why the hell am I so scared? And what the hell am I so scared of? Damn you brain."

Derek stepped towards the front door. Reaching his hand out for the knob, his hand shook. He pulled it back wiping his palm on his jeans. Twisting his neck from side to side he opened the door. The hinges creaked as the door swung inward. He stepped over the threshold and entered a time warp. Furniture from another era filled the room. An old, rotted, poop brown colored sofa sat in the center of the room. Boxes of varying sizes littered the floor.

He heard a scratching noise. He angled his head trying to discern where it was coming from. He narrowed in on one of the boxes on the floor. As he moved closer, the rustling noise grew louder. He dug in his front pocket for the small knife he always carried. Looping the camera strap around his neck, he pulled the two-inch blade from its covering. Both hands trembled as he used the edge of the knife to lift one of the flaps. He hesitated, blowing out a breath. Slowly he raised the edge of the flap, keeping his face from the opening. The rustling noise stopped.

Derek breathed in deep through his nose and out from his mouth. As he pulled back the second flap, he peered in over the edge. He sucked in a breath through gritted teeth. A nest of shredded paper lay inside, with four baby rats. The mother looked up and hissed. Derek jumped back clutching his chest. "Shit, I hate rats." His breath came in pants. "Fuck. Why did I do that?" He shimmied his shoulders as if he were shaking off bugs.

Regaining his composure, he walked around the house. Each room was in a different state tof decay. The kitchen looked as if someone had left in the middle of a meal. A plate and glass sat on a lopsided table.

Whatever food was on the plate had rotted and molded into some horrible science experiment. "Yuck," Derek said as he opened the old refrigerator. The smell was putrid, worse than rotting flesh. He gagged at the moldy and decayed remnants of some sort of animal. Not sure what crawled inside and died, he shut the door. Exhaling through his mouth the fiery breath he held.

Back in the living room, he headed towards the hallway. At the first door, he hesitated before opening it. Not sure what may lay on the other side, he almost turned around, but curiosity got the best of him. He turned the nob and pushed it open. The creaking door swung inward slowly. It took a minute to recognize it was a bathroom. This one in worse shape than most convenience stores. He gagged at the smell. The stench of stale piss and hundred-year-old hippo shit seeped out towards him. He pulled the door shut. "Jesus, this place is gross."

He crept down the hallway. A second door beckoned him. He stood in front of it, contemplating how badly he wanted to know what waited for him on the other side. He reached out to open it when cold air wafted around him. His skin prickled. He closed his eyes and pushed through the fear. He turned the knob and the door opened with ease. Derek held his breath waiting for the reveal of yet another dead animal, or worse. He exhaled when he saw a barren room, untouched by father time.

"You're going to give yourself a fucking heart attack." He breathed slow, in through his nose out through his mouth, settling his edgy nerves. He came to the last doorway at the end of the hall. He had his hand on the doorknob when he heard a noise.

He gave a sideways glance, turning his head enough to catch a glimpse behind him. Nothing. Cold air crept across his shoulders as if it engulfed him. The hair on his arms stood on end as goosebumps broke out. Turning the doorknob, he stopped. Chrissy's warning echoed in his head. "It's a house. A creepy old house," he said as he shook his head and proceeded into the room.

An old wooden rocker sat in the corner. One of the armrests was missing. Against one wall, sat a dilapidated chest of drawers. The wood had begun to rot, and a few of the drawers were missing. He noticed a closet door on the far side of the room. As he moved towards it, the floorboards creaked under him. Standing in front of the chipped wooden door, he noticed carvings in the wood. He stepped closer peering at what looked like writing. He dragged the tip of his finger over it, trying to trace it, but he still couldn't make it out. His mouth turned upward, as he thought of some young kid who no doubt pissed off his mother with his vandalism.

Not giving his fear a chance to take over he yanked open the closet door. He yelped as he jumped back falling on his butt. He braced his hands out trying to stop his fall, catching himself at an awkward angle. "Why the fuck do you keep doing that?" he snarled at Chrissy. She stood inside the closet doorway.

"You need to get out of this house. It is a bad place. Bad things happened here."

"You have to quit doing that. You're going to fucking scare me to death." Derek grunted as he pushed off with his hands. He heard the crack, but he wasn't fast enough to stop his arm from breaking through the rotted floorboard. "Ouch," he said as shards of wood scraped his skin. He shifted his weight trying to roll to his side when his hand brushed against something. He yanked it out, rubbing his arm.

He sat on his knees and peered in. The sunlight filtered through a dirty window, allowing enough light for him to see a small metal box wedged about one foot down. He reached in and pulled it out, placing it on the floor.

"Don't open that." Chrissy stepped next to him. "Please don't open that box."

He frowned at her. "Quit wigging. It's a box. You never know, maybe it has a treasure inside. I'll be able to quit my job and retire to Tahiti."

"Derek, if you have ever had that little voice inside you keep you from danger, this is the time to tap into it. If you open that box, your life will never be the same."

He stared at the old rusted metal box. Reminiscent of a '60s lunch pail, it was perfectly square. He reached out and brushed the years of dirt away. An old picture of Popeye and Olive Oil filled the top of the lid. The tin box had been beaten up over the years, but enough color definition remained detailing an old sailor holding a bouquet of roses out to his true love.

"Derek, this is a terrible idea," Chrissy said taking a step back.

Derek waved her off. "For Pete's sake, it's a damn rusty box. I bet we find a shit ton of ruined baseball cards." As he started to lift the metal latch on the front of the box to peek inside, his car alarm blared. He looked up to find Chrissy gone. "What the heck?"

He stood carrying the box from the room. His car alarm blared louder as he moved quickly through the house, which didn't seem as scary now. He shook his head thinking he acted like a chicken. "You're such an idiot, Derek," he said as he pulled the key fob from his pants pocket. He had worked himself into a frenzy. He had to find a way to deal with his guilt about Chrissy and his disgust for letting Josiah get the best of him. If not, he really would need medication. He exited the house and stood on the porch. His car sat alone in the driveway. No gusting winds that may have set it off. He could see no other reason for his alarm to have gone off.

He stepped off the porch glancing around the property one last time, taking a few more photos, as he stood at the driver's side door. The farm was nestled in between mountains on either side. The acreage looked as if it went for several hundred miles.

In his mind, he saw this area thriving long ago with Indian Tribes. He closed his eyes and imagined the rhythmic thumping of the tribal drums carried by the hot summer breeze rolling across the mesa. The breeze picked up. Derek opened his eyes to find the blue sky had turned dark and gray. Thunder replaced the rhythmic drum core as a dark black cloud crept across it, consuming every inch of blue. It wasn't until the first few drops pelted his skin that he noticed the downpour about to start. "Holy shit!" He fumbled with his car door and hopped inside an instant before the deluge of rain hit.

The sky cracked open dumping a sheet of water on the roof of the car. Derek wanted to get off the dirt road before the car got stuck. He pulled out of the driveway and sped towards the main road. A quick glance at the highway allowed him to pull out without stopping. Heading towards Duran, the box sat on the passenger seat. He kept glancing at it. His curiosity was slowly going to make him that much more insane.

His watch said four p.m. but the dark sky tried to convince him evening was setting in. He grabbed the map and quickly divided his time between it and the road. He hit Highway 60 and headed towards Fort Sumner. That seemed as good a spot to spend the night. He was less than an hour away and the early morning start had begun to wear on him. His attention drifted back to the box. He wanted to know what lay inside. The next hour would prove to be the hardest part of the drive.

CHAPTER THIRTEEN

Thursday evening
Holiday Inn, Fort Sumner

Derek sat with his back against the headboard. He had bought a sandwich and a six pack of beer and sat holding the box on his lap. His mind must have left Chrissy at the farmhouse because he hadn't heard anything from her since he took the box from the house.

Maybe she was teaching him a lesson. "Maybe I should seek psychiatric help," he mumbled through his bite of food. He stared at the unopened box, not sure what was keeping him from the prize inside. Maybe his subconscious was trying to warn him. Not sure of what, though. "Okay, it's time to find out what I won."

He pushed his plate to the other side of the bed and propped himself up a little better, getting comfortable. His hands trembled as he popped the silver clasp releasing the lock. "Tahiti here I come."

Derek lifted the dented lid. "Well, what is this?" Several postcards sat on the top of the pile along with a small envelope. He set them aside. Under the pile of postcards, lay trinkets of sorts or what might be called keepsakes. A lock of braided hair. A coral or plastic ring. He picked up the ring and inspected it. "Definitely coral," he said placing the ring in the tin. A bracelet made of some sort of chain or metal with a few charms lay on the bottom of the box. After further inspection, Derek matched the charms to broken hooks on the bracelet.

He set the box aside and picked up the pile of postcards. He looked at the first one. A picture of Clovis, NM graced the cover. On the back was the name of a girl, Margaret Shelling. The second card was from Mount Pleasant, TX. It too had the name of a girl on the back, Julie Richards. Derek's heart sped up. He looked at the third card, Pine Bluff, AR. The fourth card, Greenwood MS. Just like the first two, these also held girl's names on the backs. Lisa Muldare from Arkansas and Liza Parker from Greenwood.

Derek breathed in deep and exhaled through taut lips. His hand trembled as he reached for the small envelope. Opening one end, he dumped the contents on the bed. His heart stopped beating for a split second. A heaviness formed in his chest. "Oh no. No. This isn't good." He tried to breathe in but his chest constricted. Each intake harder than the last.

The first polaroid photo showed a young girl. Derek estimated her age between sixteen and nineteen, possibly twenty. Her eyes were bulging and devoid of life. But that wasn't what cued him into the fact that she was dead. The hair ribbon around her neck was a pretty clear giveaway. The photo still showed enough detail that Derek could see the hair ribbon had been pulled tight enough to indent the skin.

The girl had been posed nude with bruising on her shins, chest, and arms. Derek narrowed in on the girl's hand. He rummaged through the tin box. "Motherfucker." The same coral ring the young girl wore was in the box. These were mementos. Mementos a killer kept.

The second picture showed another girl. This girl looked as if she had been beaten. Her face was bloodied, but she had also been posed, naked. Arms outstretched like the last one. Her head turned towards one side. Each of the other photos showed the remaining girls had also been strangled. One with what looked like a flower belt, and one with a pink shoelace.

Derek sat back and looked at the photos. Each girl looked like they had been brutalized before their murders. He assumed they had been raped because they were all nude. All but one of the girls were strangled with items that could be theirs. The ribbon, the shoelace, the belt. Except for one. He studied the photo. The girl's neck looked as if it had a slight discoloration, indicating she may have been manually strangled.

The picture wasn't clear enough to make out a definite handprint, but it looked different than the others. Assuming the killer manually strangled this victim, Derek had to ask why. The other girls' murders had a level of detachment. The use of an instrument showed that. Although killing someone through strangulation indicated an up close and personal method, manual strangulation goes much further. It has a deep level of intimacy.

No names were written on the photos, leaving Derek to match up the pictures of the dead girls to the names himself. He moved to the desk and his computer. "Fuck, I don't remember the name of the damn town." He pulled up the closest town he remembered, but he still couldn't find the one with the house. "Okay, that doesn't matter." He pulled the roadmap from his computer bag from under the desk. He marked each of the cities.

"Okay, okay," he rolled the chair over to the bed and reached for the postcards. Each one had a date. On his map, he marked the date next to each city he circled. "Clovis, June 1986. Mount Pleasant, February 1986. Pine Bluff, October 1985. Last but not least, Greenwood, May 1985." Derek sat back and looked at the trail.

"Over the course of a year, someone killed these four girls," Derek murmured. Studying the map, he realized he was at the end of the murder trail. He accessed the FBI Violent Criminal Apprehension Program (ViCAP) database. He found only information on Lisa Muldare. He searched the other girl's names but found no listed case information. He didn't open the ViCAP file. He didn't want to risk letting anyone know what he was up to.

Instead, he ran an internet search for each name. He was able to find information on the missing girls. Local papers had run stories about their disappearances. The information within was scarce, but it was enough for Derek to match up the photos with each dead girl.

Going in order of the young girl's abduction dates, Derek charted out where they were abducted. The date of their disappearance, where they were found, and when. He scribbled the information on his notepad:

1. *Liza Parker—taken from Greenwood MS, June 1985. Found— September 1985, in Clarksdale MS.*
2. *Lisa Muldare—taken from Pine Bluff AR, October 1985. Found—January 1986, in Hot Springs AR. (Only one entered into ViCAP)*
3. *Julie Richards—taken from Mount Pleasant TX, February 1986. Found—April 1986 in Garland TX.*
4. *Margaret Shelling—taken from Clovis NM, May 1986. Never found.*

Derek tapped the face of his watch. If he contacted the individual police departments, they would expect more information from him, from the FBI. He didn't have any information to give. "Shit, I'm not even supposed to be on this case. Fuck." He didn't want to run any searches, that may cue someone into what he was planning. And if his boss found out, Derek would be stopped for sure.

Turning back to his computer, he researched each town the girls were abducted from and where they were located. He wasn't going to get the case files unless he called these municipalities and that was out of the question. Derek had no idea if he could even solve these cases. But he also knew that he would need help. He closed his eyes leaning back in the desk chair and tapped the face of his watch.

"Why do you do that?"

He jolted almost toppling the chair. His breathing came in pants as he sank into the chair. Derek wanted her to go away. Even if he escaped, he had nowhere to go that she wouldn't find him. Hell, she lived in his head. He continued to tap his watch. Without looking up, he asked. "Do what?"

"That. Tap the face of the watch?"

"It's a habit." He held his breath as he lifted his chin.

"Where did you get that watch?" She grinned at him.

"Why are you so nosy?" He squinted at her. The blue of her Iris was more—blue. The whites were almost white. He frowned at her. "Can't you wear a scarf or something?"

She chuckled. "Yeah, I'll look into that." She moved to stand behind him so she could see his computer. "Are you going to answer my question?"

"Again, why are you so nosy?"

"I guess Sheila wasn't going to miss it. Being dead and all, huh?"

He gritted his teeth. "What the fuck..." he spun around and cringed. Chrissy was inches from him. He could see all the way through the wound to the vertebrate. The smell emanating from her wound made him gag. "Jesus, that's so gross." He looked away turning back to the computer. "Just drop it, will you?"

"Okay. For now. I'll let you slide. But eventually, you're going to have to talk about it. If you're ever going to get over this whole guilt thing that keeps me hanging around." She moved back to the bed. "I see you have figured out who all the girls are. The new obsession begins."

He sighed. "I'm not going to be obsessed."

"You already are. I tried to tell you to leave the box. I think I even said it was a bad idea. But you didn't listen."

"You're dead. I don't listen to most living, why would I listen to a dead girl." He smirked at her. "I don't know. I want to solve this case." He turned back to his computer. "Plus, I'm taking over a cold case division after my vacation is over. This can technically be considered on the job training."

The pad with all his notes spun towards the edge of the desk. He turned and glared at her. "Really? Do you have to do that?"

Chrissy fanned him off. "I see from your notes that the last girl wasn't found."

"Margaret. Yeah, she wasn't. I don't like that. I want to find her."

"How are you going to do that?"

"I don't know yet. But I have roughly fifty-eight days to figure it out."

CHAPTER FOURTEEN

Early Friday morning

Derek rolled into Clovis New Mexico. He found a Days Inn and went inside. He carried his bags with him, not sure if they even had a room. As he approached the counter, a young girl smiled at him.

"Hi, what can I do for you?"

"Do you have a room available?"

She tapped out a few commands on the keyboard in front of her. "How many nights?"

Derek's brow furrowed. "Well, one night for sure, but my plans may keep me here an extra night. Can I book one and if I need it for another night I can just swing by the desk?"

She nodded at him. "Oh, that shouldn't be a problem. We have plenty of vacancies. I'll go ahead and book you in for one night, and you can change if you need to." She typed away on the keyboard.

Derek paid for the room and took the keys from the desk clerk. Following the hallway to the elevators, he headed to his room. He used his computer to search for online newspapers containing archived reports from May of 1986, the year Margaret Shelling was abducted.

He scanned the digital papers, finding what he was looking for, Derek read the article. Denny's Diner was the name of Margaret's workplace. He quickly looked it up online and found the diner was still in business. Sticking his wallet in his back pocket, he plugged the address into his phone. Lucky for him, his hotel was a ten-minute drive away.

Stepping out of his car, Derek skimmed the parking lot of the strip mall. He assumed that it had been built up over the last thirty years, but without a reference picture, he had no idea what had changed.

He walked around the building. The diner sat on the corner taking up one-third of the strip mall. The outside façade didn't entirely butt up against the rest of the building. Derek was sure it was once a stand-alone entity and the rest of the strip had been added later.

At the back of the building, sat two large dumpsters. A back entrance to the diner allowed for easy disposal of waste. The drive followed the length of the strip. Derek presumed each business had access to the back from the respective stores.

He walked back to the front and counted three entrances into the parking lot. If this building was a stand-alone thirty years ago, Derek surmised that it probably had one maybe two entrances into the diner's parking lot.

Derek stood on the walkway, directly in front of the diner. He didn't notice the patrons staring at him. He stepped back and stared at the front entrance. He reached for the front door when a gruff old man walked out.

"May I help you with something?" he asked.

Derek smiled at the man. His apron was covered in the day's specials, and he had a dish towel stuck in the belt of the apron. "Hi, I'm Derek Reed. I'm with the FBI. Do you own the diner?" The man visibly stiffened at the mention of the FBI. "You aren't in any trouble. I'm hoping to speak with someone who might have been around about thirty years ago. Back in the mid-80s."

"I own it. I'm Frank Wallace." The man extended his hand. "You want to come in and sit at the counter? It's too damn hot out here."

Derek nodded. "Yeah, that would be great." He followed the burly man into the diner. Several patrons glanced up at the stranger among them. Derek nodded at several and continued to the far end of the counter where no one sat. The stools were retro in style. Round silver pedestals covered in fire engine red vinyl. The counter itself looked like something out of a 1960s era diner. Shiny silver with white granite countertops. Beyond the counter, the wall was laden with all kinds of soda pop bottles. As well as bottles of various flavorings that Derek assumed went with the malt machine that sat off to the right.

The entire diner put you in the heart of the past. Booths were silver with the same red vinyl coverings on each. Located against the wall of each booth in the center of the table was an old jukebox looking machine that held the menu. Several families sat eating and laughing.

"So, what can I get for you?" the old man held out a menu. "You want breakfast or lunch?"

Derek looked at his watch, ten thirty. "I think I'll have breakfast. What do you have?"

"You really hungry?"

He shrugged. "Yeah, actually I am."

"I got you covered." The owner turned towards the cook. A tall counter lined with heat lamps separated the kitchen from the dining area. "Jimmy, make one sampler," he turned back to the agent, "fried or scrambled."

"Scrambled, please."

"You hear that?" he asked turning back to the cook.

"Sure did. Coming right up."

"That won't take too long." Frank pulled up a chair and sat across from the agent. "You gonna tell me why you're here?"

Derek glanced around. No one was really within earshot. "Do you remember Margaret Shelling?"

Frank grabbed a pot of coffee pouring two cups. He sighed hanging his head before he looked back up. "Yes, I do. I won't ever forget Margaret. She had just turned nineteen. She had been working here for about two years. Right after she graduated from high school."

"Can you tell me what you remember about that day she went missing?" Derek asked as he took a sip of the black coffee Frank had set in front of him.

"Let's see. She worked that day. She wasn't feeling too well, and she asked if she could leave earlier than normal. I let her. We weren't too busy, and I could tell she didn't feel all that good." A bell dinged on the counter behind Frank. He stood taking the plate that had just been placed under the warming lamp. He set the first part of Derek's order in front of him.

Derek stared at the massive plate. "You weren't kidding when you said sampler, were you? Is one of everything on this plate?" Staring back at Derek was two scrambled eggs, at least he thought it was two. Two pieces of bacon, two sausage links, two pieces of toast, corn beef hash, and the largest mound of hash brown potatoes he had ever seen.

"That's not even the whole order."

"Order up, Boss."

Frank winked at Derek. He spun around and picked up a bowl and another plate of food.

Derek's mouth fell open. The bowl had grits, and the plate had one giant biscuit covered in gravy and three pancakes. "Seriously?"

Frank laughed heartily. "Try a little bit of everything. Especially the grits and biscuit and gravy. You won't find anything better."

Derek set out to sample the sampler. He moaned the minute the biscuit touched his tongue. "This is good."

"What else you want to know about Margaret?"

CHAPTER FIFTEEN

Derek swallowed a bite of food. "Do you remember anything specific happening that day? Anyone stick out in your memory? Someone you thought didn't belong?"

Frank sipped on his coffee. "I don't remember anything like that. This area wasn't as built up as it is now. I own this land and this strip mall. But that didn't happen until the mid-nineties." Rising from his chair, he walked towards the wall at the end of the counter and removed a photo.

Coming back to his seat across from Derek, Frank handed it to him. "That was this place in 1983. I inherited it from my father. That is the day I took it over. I had been working for him for years. I was practically running it anyway.

He waved his hand towards the window. "Up the road, those gas stations you see, there was only one of those, and it wasn't as big as those are now. The others came shortly after I developed this strip mall. You know Clovis is known for our annual music festival. Back in 2016, we celebrated the 29th anniversary. It started in 1987. Before that, we had a lot of Indian festivals, still do. We've always been a big tourist draw."

Derek drank his coffee. "It wasn't uncommon, then, to have a lot of travelers come through here?"

"Not at all. But I don't remember seeing anything unusual the day Margaret went missing. I don't remember any strangers coming into the diner. We were all interviewed by the police. I don't remember anyone mentioning a suspicious person."

Derek sighed and pushed his plate away. "I ate as much as I could, Frank. I may pop any minute."

Frank's smile pushed his cheeks up high. "You wouldn't be the first person to overeat in my diner."

Derek watched as Frank hung the photo back on the wall. He filled Derek's coffee cup. "Thank you. Can you tell me if any of Margaret's family still live here?"

Frank shook his head. "No. That's an unfortunate story."

"How so?"

"Well, shortly after Margaret's disappearance, the mother and father started having bad luck. If you want to call it luck. The mother was diagnosed with cancer, I think five years after her daughter's disappearance. But by then she and her husband had divorced. They remained friends, but the loss of Margaret was too much for the marriage. The mother, Shirley, ended up dying a year after her diagnosis. It was a very progressive pancreatic cancer."

The waitress came to the end of the counter and filled Derek's coffee mug. "Thank you," he said.

"Hey, Janie, do you remember Shirley Shelling?" Frank glanced at Derek. "She has lived here all her life. She knows everyone. She's like a hundred years old."

Janie swatted Frank with her towel. "You shut up old man. You got me beat by two years." She stuck her tongue out at him. She turned her attention to the man across the counter. "I knew Shirley and her husband. They were a mess after Margaret's abduction."

"Do you know what happened to the husband?"

She sighed. "After Shirley died, he moved up north. I think he took a new job. He needed a fresh start."

"Do you know where by chance?"

"No, I don't. But it wouldn't matter anyway. He died in a horrible car wreck. His family brought him back here. Both Shirley and Joseph wanted to be buried by their daughter's empty grave. I think they hoped one day she would be returned to them and they could have a proper burial."

Frank nodded. "It was the saddest thing. They had a funeral for Margaret after the fourth year. Half the townspeople thought it was odd, but then the other half thought they needed to do it to try to move forward."

Derek glanced between the two. "Do you know if any of Margaret's family members still live in the area?"

Frank's forehead wrinkled. "Janie, doesn't the nephew still live here?"

She nodded. "He sure does. He lives out past the main highway junction. Runs that junkyard."

"That's right," Frank said snapping his fingers. "His name is Jeffrey Shelling. His dad was Joseph's brother."

Derek removed his little spiral notepad from his back pocket. He pulled the small pen from the coiled metal ring and scribbled down the name. "Do you think he will speak to me?"

Frank watched as Janie went off to help one of her customers. "I think so. He's a really nice guy." Frank pulled out a phone book from under the counter and looked up his number. "Here is the number." He flipped the book around and pointed to a line.

Derek quickly jotted it down. "Thank you."

Frank zeroed in on the man before him. "You look like you were in a fight recently. Get those injuries while you were on the job?"

"You could say that."

"Looks painful."

"It is. Trust me."

An awkward silence filled the space between them. "Why are you investigating a thirty-year-old murder? Is the FBI looking into the case?"

Derek glanced around. "We might be. I would really appreciate your cooperation in keeping this under wraps. It's an old case, and I don't want to get anyone's hopes up unless I can come up with some concrete answers."

Frank raised his hands. "I won't say a word. I hope you find something that brings Margaret back. I think the parents would like to have her buried next to them."

CHAPTER SIXTEEN

Derek sat in his car as the AC kicked in and cooled off the interior. He pulled up the GPS on his phone and searched for a nearby junkyard. He found it. He checked his notepad against the number listed on his screen and saw they were the same. He clicked on the link to dial the number.

"Hello, Digger's Junk Yard, what can I do for you?"

"What are your hours today?" Derek asked.

"We are open till six. But we will be closing at noon for ninety minutes."

"Okay, thank you." Derek glanced at his watch. It was ten till noon. "Great. Now what am I going to do for ninety minutes?" he stared out his side window trying to imagine the area the year Margaret was abducted.

"You should be driving to Tennessee. Not chasing this case."

Derek jumped. He clutched his chest and tried to slow his pulse. He turned towards her voice. He readied himself for what she was going to look like today. Chrissy's hair hung stringy around her shoulders. Her skin was still pasty but not as gray in color. Her neck wound didn't seem as wide, still no maggots, but the edges were darkened with dried crusty blood.

The tendons of her neck were blackened with decay and looked as if they were ready to snap. He moved up to her eyes. The whites were brighter, and more of her blue color came through the dull haze that covered her entire eyeball.

He frowned at her. "I see you couldn't cover up that wound. At least you don't smell as bad."

She glared at him. "I couldn't find a Walmart to buy a scarf."

He halfway chuckled at that. "I thought maybe you had decided to leave me alone. I haven't heard from you for the last several hours. Actually, almost twelve hours."

"Your new obsession is keeping your mind occupied. You do realize, I can't leave till you release me, right?"

"I don't understand that. I am not keeping you here." A vein throbbed in his neck.

"Yes, you are. You need to let me go, and you can't do that with all the guilt you're carrying around."

Derek pulled into traffic. He wasn't sure where he was going, but it was as if something drew him in this direction.

"Ignoring me won't do any good either."

"I'm not ignoring you. I'm just not sure what to say." Derek glanced at her, then turned back to the road. He made a right-hand turn and continued down a two-lane highway. He had no clue where he was.

"Where are you going?" Chrissy asked.

"Not sure. Just killing time, I guess." Derek turned down a side street. The road had a sharp bend. As it straightened out, a cemetery came into view on the right. His hand tightened on the steering wheel as his heart rate sped up. He broke out in a clammy sweat. His arms prickled as the AC blew cool air over his skin. He avoided looking at her. Instead, he concentrated on the road.

The entrance to the cemetery was ahead. He pulled in and parked near a row of headstones. Unable to avoid Chrissy any longer he turned towards her. She grinned at him. His body shuddered at the sight. The stark white enamel against the decaying outline of her gums gave her a demonic appearance. He closed his eyes and pleaded with himself to make her go away.

"Funny you should end up here, huh?" Chrissy reached out and touched his arm.

Derek's hair on his right arm stood on end as goosebumps broke out. He brushed his hand over his skin where the cool air lingered. He glanced over at Chrissy. "Why do you say that?"

"Did you know this place was here?"

"No," he said as he exited the vehicle. Chrissy followed him as he walked along a pathway. He glanced from right to left and back. Searching, but not really sure for what. The path meandered and came to a split. Derek followed the path on the right.

"You seem to know where you are going."

"Not really." Derek walked a little further then stopped abruptly. He glanced over at Chrissy who stood with her arms crossed. Her hair blew slightly in the breeze. Her face was tilted upward, and she looked— peaceful. If he hadn't been able to see the silhouette of the church through her torso, he would have thought she was a young girl at a cemetery.

Derek's brow furrowed as he glanced around the area. Headstones filled row after row. He imagined this cemetery held the dead from several counties. "What the hell am I doing?" he asked himself as he turned to head back to his car when something caught his eye a few rows ahead of him. Something shiny.

CHAPTER SEVENTEEN

Derek walked with purpose towards the shiny object. The sun glistened off its surface bouncing reflections of light like a prism. His swallowing increased as an ache formed in the back of his throat. His chest tightened as he neared the tombstone where the object rested. A simple silver ring sat before him. He reached out with trembling fingers and picked it up.

"What you got there?"

Startled he jumped, dropping the ring into the dirt. He turned towards her voice to find her right next to him. "Why the hell do you sneak up on me all the time?" He bent over and retrieved the piece of jewelry. Brushing it off against his jeans, then blowing the remaining dirt off.

"I don't sneak anywhere. I followed you from the car. What is that?" she pointed to his hand.

"A ring. Duh." He held the dainty ring in front of her as he examined it. A small silver ring, with a green stone in the middle surrounded by what looked like two small diamonds on each side.

"Umm, you shouldn't have picked that up."

Derek sighed, frowning as he stared at Chrissy. "Why?"

She lifted her hand and pointed to the tombstone.

Derek followed her outstretched arm. He had to take a small step back to see the name. Shelling. Margaret Shelling. Derek's heart raced, nearly exploding in his chest. He panted, unable to stop his body from trembling. His grip tightened on the ring. "Oh," he said.

"You should've listened to me." She squinted at him. "I bet you never listen, do you?"

Derek squeezed his eyes together. The pain from his injuries intensified as the pounding in his head increased. He couldn't blame his mind for this one. He stared at the ring in his hand. For a split second, he started to place it back on the tombstone. Instead, he pocketed it and headed for his car. Leaving Chrissy behind.

Back in the safety of his vehicle, he rested his head against the seat. "Anyone could have put that there. Her mother, before she died. Her father after the mother passed away. One of the remaining family members," Derek said as he pulled out of the cemetery. "I don't for one minute believe some damn dead girl put a ring on a fucking tombstone for me to find. Hell, I don't even believe it's her ring."

He pulled onto the main road and quickly tapped his phone pulling up the directions for the junkyard as he headed towards the main highway. Derek ignored the voice in his head. The irritating voice that sounded a lot like Chrissy. The one that kept telling him he should leave this case alone. He couldn't do that. Not now. Not after learning what happened to Margaret's parents and that they were buried next to an empty grave that shouldn't even exist.

"What the hell?" he yelled when a semi whizzed by rattling his car. "Slow down asshole," he screamed as he pulled through the light. He could see the entrance to the junkyard ahead on the left side of the service road. He rolled into the lot, parking next to a red double cab truck.

Exiting the vehicle, Derek saw a man come out of the office.

"Hey, what can I do for you?" he asked.

A thousand things ran through Derek's mind. The restaurant people already knew he was an FBI agent, he had to figure they would eventually talk to Margaret's cousin. He opted for the truth this time. Derek held out his hand. "Hi, I'm Derek Reed. I'm looking for Margaret Shelling's family."

The burly man took off his baseball hat and wiped his brow with a rag from his front pocket. He placed his hat back on his head and leaned against the truck. "Who are you?"

"I just introduced myself to you. Derek Reed."

"Why are you looking for Maggy's family?"

Derek smiled. "I'm an FBI agent. I recently became aware of Margaret's abduction, and I'm looking into the case."

The man's shoulders relaxed. He reached out his hand. "I'm Jeffrey. Maggy's dad was my uncle."

"Nice to meet you, Jeffrey," Derek said.

"Tell me why you are investigating Maggy's disappearance all this time later?"

"I have a thing for cold cases. You mind answering some questions?"

He wiped his brow again with his oily rag. "If it will help bring Maggy home to rest with her parents, I'll answer anything you ask me. But let's get out of the heat." He turned and headed into the office.

As they walked through the door, a blast of cold air hit Derek in the face. A woman sat at a desk, preoccupied with a customer on the phone.

"Martha, take messages for me until I'm done. I don't want to be interrupted."

She waved them off as she returned to her call.

Jeffrey led the way down a short narrow hallway to an office. Once inside, he closed the door. Derek watched the man grab two cold sodas from a small fridge in the corner. Jeffrey handed one to him. "Thanks."

"It's too damn hot this year." Jeffrey sat behind a large wooden desk. He narrowed in on the agent before him. "What do you want to know?"

Derek set his drink on the edge of the desk. "Tell me about Margaret. Maggy."

A smile tugged at the corners of Jeffery's mouth. "Maggy and I used to pal around together. We were inseparable. Our parents, my dad and Maggy's dad, were brothers. I am—was—two years older than her. Anyway, our dads used to drag us on every fishing and hunting trip they went on. Maggy was a damn good shot, but she really didn't like 'killing Bambi' as she used to say. She did like fishing though. She wasn't your typical girl. She was more a guy than a girl." Jeffrey grinned. "She was pretty too. All my friends wanted me to set her up with them."

Jeffrey reached into his desk drawer and pulled out a small folded frame. He handed it to Derek. "That was on one of our camping trips. It's my favorite photo of her."

Derek looked at the photo. Staring back at him was a beautiful redhead with the bluest eyes he'd ever seen. He recalled the photo in the tin box back in his hotel room. Margaret's eyes weren't near as bright in that photo. "She was beautiful," he said handing it back to Jeffrey. The hair on the nape of Derek's stood on end. He shuffled in the chair.

Jeffrey stared longingly at the photo before putting it back into the drawer. A long sigh pulled his mouth downward. "I miss her."

"Tell me about the few days before the disappearance. Do you remember anything out of the ordinary?" Derek scribbled in his small notebook he had pulled from his back pocket when he sat down. A cool blast of air settled near his right side. He adjusted his right shoulder, trying to shake off the hand he felt resting there.

Jeffrey leaned back in his chair. Agent Reed squirmed in his seat. A thin line of sweat beaded on the man's upper lip. "You okay?"

Derek glanced up from his notepad. "Yeah, why?"

"You look a little pale."

Derek shook his head. "Nah. I'm fine. Continue, please."

"I remember school was getting ready to let out for the summer. Margaret and I were out of high school by then. I worked here at the junkyard for my dad, and she worked over at the diner. Frank's place." He guzzled the last of his soda. "Like I said school was getting ready to be done, which meant a lot of summer parties. Maggy and I were thinking of putting together a camping trip down to the river. We had a bunch of our friends excited to go."

Derek sat and waited. Jefferey struggled with his trip down memory lane. The loss of Maggy was still raw all these years later.

Jeffrey leaned forward placing his elbows on the desk. "Maggy was pulling some extra hours at the diner, she wanted to take the whole weekend off, but she didn't want to miss out on the pay. I remember that week she had been feeling a little sick." He smiled. "She said there was no way, she would let any kind of summer flu keep her from this trip. I know the night she went home she wasn't feeling well at all. She had called me to tell me she was leaving work early. I remember telling her something like, feel better we leave in two days...something like that."

"When did you guys realize she was missing?"

"I called my uncle later that evening. I asked how Maggy was feeling, and he had no clue what I was referring to. He thought she was still at work. When I told him she left the diner sick, the phone went dead. I yelled out to my dad, and he and I drove over to the diner. We found Maggy's parents and the police there." He rubbed his face, pinching the bridge of his nose. "I'll never forget the looks on their faces. I was gutted, I couldn't even imagine what they were feeling."

"What do you remember about the investigation? Do you remember hearing anything regarding what the police may have in the way of leads or evidence?" Derek asked.

Jeffrey shook his head. "I don't know what the police had. I know that Maggy's parents went on TV, held as many press conferences as they could. They put up flyers, everywhere. I think they covered over five counties with those damn flyers."

"You never heard anything about a suspect?"

"Nothing. I think this was too big for this town. At least back then. The only thing that ever got bantered around was that a trucker or a traveler took her from the parking lot."

"Was Maggy the friendly sort, to strangers I mean?"

Jeffrey chuckled. "Hell yeah. She would help anyone who needed it. I used to tell her to not talk to strangers, but she could see no wrong in people."

Derek scribbled in his notebook. He swatted his right ear.

"Ask about the ring," Chrissy said in his ear.

"No," he snarled back. Brushing an invisible fly away from his head.

"Excuse me?" Jeffrey asked.

Derek's head shot up. "Huh?"

"You said no. No, what?"

"Oh, I'm sorry, I was writing a thought down. I must have said part of it out loud." He smiled at Jeffrey. "Do you know if the police in charge back then, are still on the force now?"

Jeffrey's eyebrow wrinkled. "Dang, I don't know." He rested his head in his hands. "Back then I think Jason was a deputy...Jason Riggley...But he died in a car wreck two years ago. I can't remember who else worked the case. I'm sorry."

"No need to be sorry. I can go down to the station and find out. I was hoping to avoid letting any more people know I'm looking into this case. I want to gather more information before it gets out of the bag, so to speak."

Jeffrey nodded. "I understand. I'll keep this meeting between us."

"I appreciate that." Derek stood. He pulled a business card from his wallet. "If you think of anything else, even if you think it isn't important, you can call or email me. You'd be surprised what can blow a case open."

Jeffrey stood and walked around the desk. He took the business card from the agent. "I will do that." He placed it in his back pocket. "Can you promise me something?"

"I don't know if I can promise anything, but you can ask."

"If you find her, will you call me. I want to bury her with her parents. They were a wreck after Maggy was abducted. Their lives were never the same. I believe it ultimately killed them. I want them together. I want them to be with each other."

A thin smile flashed across his face. "I can promise you that. I want her buried with her parents, too." Derek walked through the office and out the door.

Jeffrey moved back to his desk and pulled the photo of Maggy back out. Tears filled his eyes and crested over as he stared at the face of the best friend he ever had.

CHAPTER EIGHTEEN

Derek headed out of the junkyard driving down the frontage road. Stopping at a light, he used his GPS to locate the police department and started towards the station. Halfway there he thought better of that decision. Instead, he reversed his direction and drove to his hotel room.

Back in his room, he sat at the desk and ordered a pizza. He reached into his satchel and removed the file his AD had given him. Scanning through the list of agents, he found the two tech geeks. One worked at the FBI office out of New Orleans. The second guy worked out of the Dallas office. A smile crept across his face while he scanned their bios. He set the Louisiana agent aside and focused on Dallas.

Derek read through Agent Kyle Marcum's file. As he read, his smile broadened. "This is my guy." He glanced at his watch grabbing his phone and dialed the man's number.

"You got me, what do you want?"

"Agent Marcum?" Derek asked as he sipped on the soda he purchased on his way to his room.

"Yes, this is Agent Marcum, what can I do for you, and who are you?"

"This is Derek Reed, Agent Reed from Phoenix. I…"

"Oh, hey man. I was hoping you would call me. Please tell me you want me to join your new cold case team?"

"That's exactly why I'm calling you. Are you sure you want to leave Dallas for Phoenix? It's way fucking hotter than Texas and much more boring."

"Yes, I am. I'm so ready for a change," Agent Marcum said.

"How long have you been on the geek side of the Bureau?"

"Oh hell, I have been a computer geek most of my life. After I received my degree in computer engineering, it made sense for me to apply to the Academy."

Derek smiled at his choice. "Great, then I think you are the man for the team." He heard a howl like scream on the other end and chuckled at the young man's reaction.

"Oh, this so freaking cool," Agent Marcum said.

"Okay, listen. The team isn't being assembled for another sixty or so days. I'm sure you will get a call from my director with the exact dates you need to be at the new unit. I'll be turning in your name pretty quick so he can get the ball rolling. However, I need your help now with a case I'm working on."

"Sweet. Is this a case for the new unit?"

"Umm, not really. See, I'm on vacation, and I've sort of stumbled across a cold case. But very few people know I'm investigating it." Derek paused, drinking his soda.

"I gotcha man. You need some help on the down low. No problemo, what do I need to do?"

Derek let out the breath he held. "I'm investigating a case that's roughly thirty-three years old. I don't want to involve any more people than I have to, especially if I'm not even sure if I will be able to give the families any closure."

"Hey, I gotcha. Families start getting all buggy when they don't have answers, and if they find out you're looking into that old of a case, they will be swarming you like maggots on a dead body."

"Seriously?" Derek asked chuckling.

"Sorry. What do you need me to do?"

"How hard is it to get information from police files? Without asking the police for the file?"

Silence. Derek was about to ask Agent Marcum if he was still on the line when the agent responded.

"If the case was put in ViCAP, not hard at all. They would have put all the case notes in a file that could be accessed by other agencies. In the hopes that if another murder was found with similar attributes, the cases could be linked."

"And, if they didn't do that?"

"A hell of a lot harder."

Derek sighed into the phone. "That's not what I want to hear."

"Ah, but all is not lost. If the jurisdictions in question didn't put the information into ViCAP, hopefully, they have it on their local systems."

"Okay, here's the deal. I have four girls, three were found, and one was not. I'm looking for the original case files, on the abductions and when their bodies were discovered. How can you get them?"

"Asking for them would be a start," Agent Marcum said as he giggled into the phone.

"I'm trying to avoid that." Derek started to pinch the bridge of his nose, then remembered it was broken and pulled on the ends of his hair instead.

"All right. How about this, give me the cities the abductions took place, the cities the girls were found, and all their information. I will see what I can do. I have a few skills that may get us in. I can't guarantee that thirty-year-old cases will even be on the local systems. You got to remember comps were just coming on the scene back in the mid-eighties. That's when this case took place right?"

"Yeah 1985-1986."

"Okay, that's what I thought. Back to the computer issue, it would be years before they were used to their full capacity. Several municipalities began putting their old cases into the computers. And often that was one main computer, with access to all departments. As the internet and cloud storage came about, more jurisdictions joined this movement to get paper reports out of storage units and into the computers. Ultimately uploading to cloud storage. You never know, we might get lucky."

Derek nodded, then realized Agent Marcum couldn't see him. "Yeah, okay that's at least somewhere to start." He had a good idea that his new geek was going to hack into the systems. His stomach knotted asking the kid to do something that could end his career. "You know what, I'll call these departments. I don't want you to do anything you shouldn't be doing."

Agent Marcum's laughter bellowed out. "I won't get caught."

"Alright, how about this. I will give you all the information I have on the victims and the cases. You dig out what you can without crossing any lines. If you find the only way to get information is to hack in, we will make a decision then."

"No problemo, Agent Reed. Whatever you want me to do."

Derek recited the information to Agent Marcum. Giving him the rundown on each girl.

"Okay, Agent Reed. That should give me enough info to get what you want, or at least most of it. Is there anything else you need me to do?"

Derek thought for a moment, "No. Not right now. Hey, but I do need to know one thing."

"Yeah? What is that?"

"Would you ever have a Tribble as a pet?"

Agent Marcum cackled with laughter. "Oh man. That was by far the best Star Trek episode ever. You had cute furry creatures infesting the

Enterprise and Klingons trying to overtake the Federation. Best thing ever. You know that spawned like two more episodes? Anyway, to answer your question, hell yeah I would have a Tribble as a pet."

Derek smiled. He had definitely picked the right guy. He hung up, and his skin broke out in goosebumps. His back was towards the room, and he had to work on slowing his breathing. He let his eyes drift close as he brought his heart rate down. Breathing in through his nose and out through his mouth the rhythmic pounding of his pulse in his head slowly decreased in intensity.

"Whatcha workin' on?"

Derek bit back the urge to scream at her. A few more deep breaths and he finally answered her. "Nothing."

"Really? Sounded to me like you were making plans."

Derek spun around and braced himself. He sniffed the air around him. "You don't stink anymore."

"Well, I guess that's a good thing."

Derek frowned at her. "Quit talking to me when other people are around. They're going to think I'm crazy."

She tilted her head to the side. "Uh, you kind of are, dude. You're talking to a dead girl. Don't get much crazier than that." Chrissy sat on the bed. "Why didn't you ask Jeffrey about the ring? You could've shown it to him. See if he placed it at the grave, or if he knew of someone from the family who might have put it there."

Derek watched as the tin box slid across the bed. Chrissy's hand seemed to go right through the box, yet it still moved. Her neck wound seemed smaller. Derek noticed her lips, weren't as thin or as cracked as before. Her gums were no longer blackened and had begun to fill in around the teeth. Her eyes were brighter and more transparent. "You look different."

She winked at him. "You're finally getting the hang of this then. I bet you have me almost put back together in no time. You still have a long way to go before you get rid of me though, but we'll work on that. Now back to the ring. Why didn't you ask about it?"

"He isn't going to know if it's her ring. Hell, I don't even know if it's her ring. I noticed a freshly dug grave nearby, maybe someone from an earlier funeral placed it on the tombstone by mistake."

Chrissy wiggled her eyebrows at him. "You have the answers right in front of you." The tin box spun around as Chrissy smiled. "I think you don't want to face them. You know, Derek, putting your head in the sand, won't make things go away."

A knock at the door stopped the cryptic conversation. Derek paid the pizza guy grabbing the two-liter soda bottle and pie. "Thanks," he said as he smiled at the young kid. He closed the door and turned when he stopped abruptly. The contents of the tin box were overturned on the bed. He stepped into the bathroom and grabbed a glass from the counter.

Derek sat and opened his computer. Pulling a piece of pizza from the box, he took two bites. He glanced over his shoulder at the mess on the bed, then quickly turned away. He poured some soda into the glass. Derek puttered around on the Internet, reading the news and checking email. Every few minutes he glanced at the bed.

He shook his head. "I'm going crazy. That's all there is to it." He continued eating, avoiding the emptied contents of the box. After an hour or so, and bored with the Internet, Derek turned on the TV. He moved to the chair in the corner. Landing on a movie, he purposely looked past the bed. "Fuck," he said standing.

Taking two steps, he looked down. All the pictures of the girls had been strung about. He would have thought it was haphazard except Margaret's photo was front and center. "I guess this is what you want me to see?" Derek called out to an empty room. "I wish you would go away. You know that, right?" He reached out and lifted the picture of Margaret off the bed. He sighed heavily as he scanned it. He wasn't sure what he was looking for, then he saw it.

His hand trembled as he focused on Margaret's right hand. Her ring finger was easily seen in the photo. A slight sheen of sweat beaded on his back and neck area. Derek closed his eyes and exhaled slowly, hoping to get his beating heart under control.

On Margaret's finger, he could clearly see the ring he had found at the tombstone. The diamonds and the emerald sparkled as the light source in the photo caught the stones at the right angle. "It still doesn't mean she put it there, you know?" he said in a huff.

He gathered everything and placed it in the tin box. He took one last look at Margaret's photo. She was a beautiful girl, and he held on tight to the memory of how she looked in Jeffrey's picture of her. That's how he would remember Margaret from now on.

CHAPTER NINETEEN

Saturday morning

Derek rolled over and glanced at the clock on the nightstand. It was five thirty a.m. He closed his eyes hoping he would go back to sleep for a few hours. After twenty minutes, he rose, showered, and packed to leave. His next destination was Garland Texas where Julie Richards was found in April of 1986. Before he packed up his computer, he typed out an email to Agent Marcum asking him to give him Julie's information first. Derek was about to shut down his laptop when Marcum responded.

Agent Marcum promised he would have something for him later that day before Derek arrived in Garland. Yawning and stretching, he packed up his computer. He'd rested well enough to drive and could see no reason to stay in Clovis any longer. Grabbing his bags, he gave one last walk through of the room checking to see he had left nothing behind. Reaching into his pocket, he fingered Margaret's ring making sure it was safely tucked away. He'd packed the old tin box in his suitcase.

Seven a.m. had him beating the traffic. He drove in silence wanting to clear his head. He decided to follow Highway 84 until he hit Abilene where he would pick up I20 and follow that until he reached I30. It was the most direct route and would take him on the outskirts of Dallas, hopefully bypassing the heavy city traffic. At a distance of 445 miles, he had close to an eight-hour drive ahead of him. Even in the early morning hours, the late August heat gave the road a rippling effect. As if the asphalt was buckling as he drove.

He glanced down at his dashboard and found the outside temperature read 108 degrees. He imagined the temperatures were even deadlier when standing on the road, let alone in the sun. "Shit that is hot," he said grimacing as he reached over and turned down the AC.

The flat plains of Texas rolled by. Derek was struck how desolate this area seemed even though the route was littered with small towns. Two hours outside Abilene, he stopped at a truck stop for gas and snacks. His tank was a little under half, but he topped it off not wanting to stop in Abilene. Making his way to the restroom, Derek felt that familiar coolness surround him. He stopped outside the men's room. "If you're thinking of following me into the bathroom, please don't. That is one area I don't think you should go." He heard a soft giggle. "I really don't think this is funny."

"Excuse me?"

Derek glanced up to see a burly truck driver staring at him. He pointed to his ear. "Sorry man, on the phone." He followed the man in and quickly entered a stall. Once back in the store Derek purchased his items and headed towards his vehicle.

He sighed as he opened the bottle of soda and the bag of nuts. He placed the ten packs of gum in the console between the seats and was about to pull away from the pump when Chrissy materialized in the passenger seat. "How do you do that?" he asked squinting. Her hair had a glossy, healthy sheen. No longer stringy. The blue in her eyes had all but returned except for the small ring of gray that surrounded the iris. Her skin was still pale but the pasty plastic color now gone.

"Do what?" She asked.

"Just pop in like that."

"I don't just pop in. You make me sound like I'm stalking you."

"Uhh, you kind of are. And do not ever follow me into the bathroom again. That is my space for me only. It's bad enough I have to share the public restrooms with truckers. I refuse to share it with you."

"Then stop thinking about me."

Derek took several gulps of his soda. Pulling onto Highway 84, he fell into the flow of traffic. Although it was heavy, it flowed at a nice rate of speed. Tired of the silence, he turned on the radio. He glanced over at Chrissy. She winked and smiled at him. He noticed her gums had filled back in covering the exposed roots. The black decay resembled specks of pepper caught in one's teeth rather than the disgusting rotting look she once had.

"Why are you staring at me?" She wiggled her eyebrows at him.

"You look, better." He motioned his hand in front of his neck. "I see your wound is healing." It had shrunk in size and the edges of the wound where Josiah's knife had sliced through her skin, were no longer rotting. They were glistening with what looked like fresh blood lining the wound track.

"Well, that's all you. I have no control over how I look." She opened the mirror on the visor and looked at herself. "I do like this look much better than a few days ago. I will give you that."

"You and me both," Derek muttered. They sat in silence for a few minutes. Classic rock filtered through the speakers. Derek's head bobbed slightly to the beat of the music.

"Tell me about Sheila." Chrissy turned to face him. She leaned her back against the door curling her legs under her.

Derek's back straightened. His hands tightened on the steering wheel. Adjusting in his seat he changed lanes, increasing his speed.

"Avoiding this conversation isn't going to help you, you know that, right?"

"Why are you so damn interested in Sheila?"

Chrissy's eyes widened. "You can't be serious. She is the reason we're here. The reason why you're the way you are. She is why you do what you do."

"I don't understand. She has no bearing on my life now. None whatsoever."

"Derek, you can't be that stupid. I know you understand the connection to her and why you do what you do. You have to know what happened all those years ago is what makes you so good at your job. The reason you pay such close attention to details most people skim over. Why you see connections no one else sees."

Derek dragged his hand down his face. The broken bones not fully healed, the movement made his face throb. He blew out a breath through taut lips.

"Talk to me. No one else will know. Plus, you need to get it out. Off your chest, so to speak." She leaned towards him, "I keep secrets, you know?"

"There isn't anything to talk about."

"Isn't that her watch?"

He twisted the timepiece on his wrist. Sliding it up and down as he concentrated on the road.

"I know you have taken great pride in keeping it working, and in perfect condition, I might add. Tell me how you got it."

His eyes narrowed into slits as he glared at her. "Leave it the fuck alone."

Chrissy held her hands up. "Fine. You'll have to talk about this. If you ever want to be free of me, you'll have to face what you did. But more than that, you'll have to forgive yourself. For her, for me, for Margaret.

You have to learn to let go of all that guilt."

Derek maneuvered around a few eighteen-wheelers. Weaving in and out of traffic. They were on the outskirts of Abilene and traffic had picked up. His mind went back to that night. He had done a damn good job of burying that whole moment in time so far deep down he hadn't even given Sheila a second thought, until Chrissy.

"My mother used to tell me, you can't change the past. You can only move on from it, learn from it, and do better. She used to try to explain to me that guilt and regret can eat you alive. I had nothing to be guilty about, c'mon I was a young girl. I never really understood what she meant. But now, after having met you...I understand exactly what she meant."

"Were you and your parents close?"

Chrissy sighed. "Yes. We are all close—I mean we were close. My two older brothers and me. We hung out and played games. My parents made us go to church weekly. But I didn't mind that. I wouldn't say I was overly religious, but I found Sunday church comforting." Chrissy chuckled at the memory. "The pastor of our little church was a drinker. Not like drunk as a skunk drinker, but he'd been known to have one too many glasses of wine at the mixers."

Derek smirked. "I bet that made for some interesting gatherings."

Chrissy nodded. "It sure did. One time we had a potluck at the church, and then we all played bingo. We had prizes and all kinds of stuff. The younger kids went to the gym to play, and the older kids and adults played bingo. I stayed with the adults," she said wiggling her shoulders. "I was seventeen. I didn't want to be in the gym with the little kids.

"I remember several of the widowed ladies had an extra glass of wine. They were laughing and flirting with everyone, having fun. Well, Pastor Nichols had had way too many beers that evening. He and another woman were very chummy all through dinner. It was pretty obvious they had forgotten they were at a church function. I know after the dinner, he and that lady seem to always be at all the functions together. I'm pretty sure they had a relationship for a while after that."

Derek frowned at her. "Wasn't he married?"

"No. Oh no, he wasn't married. He wasn't that kind of guy. His wife had died two years prior to this. That probably accounted for his extra drinking. I know it wasn't a year or two after that get together that he resigned as Pastor. Don't know where he is now. Left the church and the state. Our new pastor was very rigid. He took all the fun and joy out of Church. Every Sunday it seemed like we were going to theology class. It was awful. It wasn't too long after that, my family quit going."

"I'm not fond of organized religion."

She sniggered. "Religion isn't meant to be organized. Church isn't meant to be organized. It's supposed to be a soft place to land. A place where you go each week and rejuvenate your soul, so you can face the next week and whatever life throws at you. After a while, it became a chore." She gazed out the window. She sighed as she looked down at her lap. "I would give anything to be able to go back to church."

Derek glanced over at her. Her eyes were closed, and she rested her head on the seatback. He could see the passing terrain through her silhouette. He shook his head as if that would make the vision go away.

"Did you and your family go to church?" Chrissy asked.

Derek frowned. "No. We weren't that kind of family." He grabbed a pack of gum from the console. He held it out to Chrissy. He sighed when she raised an eyebrow at him. "Sorry, I forgot."

"What kind of family were you guys?"

"My dad worked a lot. He worked for the city where we lived. A small town in Northern California."

Her eyes widened. "Did you live near Hollywood? I always wanted to go to Hollywood."

Derek smirked. "Hell no. All the crazy people live in LA and Hollywood. The northern part of California is where the normal people live. Hard working people who don't think shit should be handed to them." He added a second piece of gum to his mouth. "My mom stayed at home. My dad worked all the time. He was the attorney for our small city. It was me, my brother, and my sister. When I was in eighth grade, we moved to Tennessee. Where they all live now." He searched for a piece of paper. He found the gum wrapper and placed the gum in it, wadding it up.

"Didn't you just put that gum in your mouth?"

He nodded. "My cheek isn't healed yet. I keep forgetting and chewing gum. But can't do it for long, before the achiness is too much to handle." He pouted as he glanced over at her. "I miss chewing gum."

"You have managed to swap one obsession for another."

"What are you talking about?" he asked.

"This case is your new obsession. It will take the place of your gum chewing. Either until you solve it, or your face heals." She shifted in the seat. "I gather you don't go home much. Don't you miss them, your family?"

Derek frowned as he shrugged. "Sometimes. I guess not enough to go home."

"What does your family do in Tennessee?"

He nodded. "When we were in Cally, my father had the opportunity to purchase a business from one of the guys he worked with. An accounting business. Taxes, estate taxes, all that kind of stuff. That's what moved us to Tennessee in the first place. He and my mother still have the business. Both my sister and brother work for them. I left for college. Never really wanted to work for my dad."

"Are you the oldest?"

"No. I'm the youngest."

"Where did you meet Sheila?"

"After we moved to Tennessee. But I didn't meet her."

"How could you not meet her if you have her watch?" Chrissy tried to hide her grin.

Derek glared over at the wispy figure. "You won't give up, will you?"

Chrissy leaned her head back and barked out a laugh.

"What the hell is so funny?"

"You. Your mind has really fucked with you over the years, huh?"

"I don't know what you mean." Derek stared out the windshield. His foot pressed down on the gas pedal accelerating the car.

"You have to face what happened back then. You have to let her go, and all the regret and guilt you carry. If you don't, I may be a permanent attachment to you."

"Uh, no. You can leave anytime you want."

"Oh Derek, when you forgive yourself, you will understand. Until then, you and I will be hanging out for a while longer. Probably longer than you think."

Derek stretched his back as best he could. Glancing at the dash clock, he realized he was over two hours from Garland Texas. He had no idea where the time had gone. "Hey, I think..." Derek's phone chirped through the Bluetooth, silencing the '70s music flowing through the speakers. Thankful for the change of subject, he pushed the answer button on the steering wheel. "Derek here."

"Agent Reed, this is Agent Marcum, you got a minute?"

"Yeah, you got something for me?" Derek glanced over at his passenger to see she had vanished.

"I do. I've been looking into Julie Richards murder, after your email this morning. I was able to get the police report regarding where her body was found."

"Please tell me you didn't do anything to get yourself in trouble."

Agent Marcum's laughter filled the car. "No. I didn't do anything to get me into trouble. They would have to catch me first."

"Oh man..." Derek said sighing heavily.

"Quit worrying. I didn't get much anyway. Julie was located outside Garland, on the 190 spur off I30. This is the Lake Ray Hubbard area. There are tons of bait shops and boat rental places all along that route. A huge parking lot now covers where her body was initially found, just off 190 in a ditch.

"I pulled up old images of the area from the 80s off the web. Some came from the city of Garland's website. Wasn't much of anything else around that area back then. I've included the GPS coordinates that should get you very close to the dump site. Unfortunately, you will only be able to get an idea of the area with the help of the images."

"Can you send me everything?"

"Already sent to your email. They found her body after a massive rainstorm, so there wasn't much in the way of evidence. They identified her pretty quick though. The reports of her being missing had been circulated throughout that entire region."

"I'm pretty sure that will be the story with all these girls, no evidence to go on," Derek said.

"Now, regarding her abduction, Julie worked at a convenience store off I30 on the outskirts of Mount Pleasant. According to what I read in that police report, they didn't have much information on her disappearance. It's like she poofed into thin air."

"That's not the best news, Kyle."

"Hey, man, I'm doing the best I can. I do have some information that may help. Her parents still live in the same area. I have their address and their phone number for you."

"Now we're talking. That is good news. I might be able to get something from speaking to them. Send me everything you have on her parents, including any interviews they may have given. You got anything on the other two girls yet?"

"I've got a little on both. Let me get everything I can, and I will send you that too."

"Okay, Agent Marcum. I'll be sending an email to my AD regarding you and this unit. Please don't mention this to him when he calls."

"I promise you I won't, Agent Reed. I know you don't want to say anything to anyone unless you think you can get somewhere with this. I'll keep it between us. I'll talk to you later Agent Reed."

The line went dead. Music filled the car again. Derek frowned. He wanted to see where Julie Richards had been found and seeing what the dump site looked like. But why he even thought that would be possible over thirty years later, he didn't know. Hopefully, Agent Marcum found a few photos of the scene to include in the file.

"Oh, what am I doing? I should have listened and not taken that damn box," Derek said as he exited off the freeway. Needing to stretch and wanting to fill his tank so he wouldn't have to stop again, he pulled into a gas station. Once loaded up with snacks and a soda, he pulled up the email on his phone from Agent Marcum, scowling as he read. He scanned the original police file regarding Julie's body. He wondered how Agent Marcum had gotten the file from the police department.

His chest constricted hindering his breathing. He shouldn't have put the young man in any compromising position by asking him to do something like this. But the file kept him from having to speak with anyone in the department associated with the case. And the fewer people who knew he was investigating this cold case, the better. More than anything, he wanted to solve these cases. That desire outweighed any guilt.

Before he placed his phone into the cradle, he downloaded the GPS coordinates for the site, then headed towards the freeway entrance. He glanced at the dashboard clock. Since he wouldn't have to speak with the police in Garland, after he did a quick drive-by of the location, he could drive on into Mount Pleasant. "What's another couple of hours on the road." Derek took a drink from his soda and turned up the radio.

CHAPTER TWENTY

Saturday late evening

Twelve hours after the day had started, Derek walked into his hotel room in Mount Pleasant Texas. He placed his suitcase on the chair next to the bed and slowly undressed. His body ached, and his head pounded out a beat behind his eyes. He reached into the interior pocket of the suitcase and pulled out his prescription pain pills. He stopped short of opening the bottle and questioned whether he should take one or tough it out. "Fuck it. I can take one, that's what they're for," he said as he unscrewed the top.

He stripped and walked into the bathroom. Cupping his hand under the faucet, he washed down the pill with a gulp of tap water. One of the only rooms they had left was a handicap room, giving him a spacious bathroom.

Derek peeked behind the shower curtain. The shower was large enough to accommodate a wheelchair. A large rain shower head extended from the ceiling in the center of the shower. "Nice," he said as he turned on the hot water. Steam wafted out above the shower curtain.

He placed the palms of his hands against the wall and leaned forward. Hot water ran down his back helping to relax his muscles after being in the car for way too long. He stood up and tilted his head back letting the water pound his forehead. He was careful to keep his nose and cheeks from taking the brunt of the pelting drops.

Thirty minutes later, Derek turned off the water. He stood in the center of the shower, steam swirling around him. A noise from the other side of the curtain made his skin prickle. "Hello? Chrissy?" He called out. "We talked about the bathroom thing." No one answered him. He gulped in air swaying slightly as if his legs could no longer support his weight.

Derek held his breath as he yanked back the curtain. Steam billowed out filling the room, fogging the mirror. Droplets of water streaked its surface. His eyes darted around the room searching for a hidden intruder. Fumbling with a towel from the adjacent rack, he wrapped it around his waist. He turned towards the sink and froze. Scrawled across the mirror was one word—*Josiah.*

"Chrissy? This isn't funny," Derek hissed. Stepping up to the sink, he rested his palms on the vanity. His breath burned his lungs. Something seemed different, darker. He closed his eyes. "I'm tired that's all," he said softly. "I drove too long. That was stupid." His body was still healing, and he knew better. Derek stretched his neck by turning his head side to side. He tried to relax as the fuzzy feeling brought on by the pain meds slowly kicked in.

He inhaled a deep breath, pushing the air out through pursed lips. He reached up and used the side of his hand to wipe the mirror. Derek's heartbeat pounded in his ears. His jaw clenched, and his posture went rigid. "No!" He gasped. Josiah Craig stood behind him. An evil sneer pulled the corners of his top lip upward. The crown of Josiah's head was missing, and blood flowed down the man's face. He pulled a knife from his waistband and licked the tip. Derek searched for anything to use as a weapon. He reached for a glass on the counter and spun around.

No Josiah. Derek's hand shook as he pulled back the half-open shower curtain. "Where the fuck did you go, Josiah?" He ran from the bathroom. Scanning the hotel room, he saw no evidence that anyone had entered the room, or that they were still there. Derek grabbed the door and yanked it open. The hallway was empty.

His face throbbed to the same beat as his pulse. Leaning his back against the steel door, he sank to the floor, resting his forearms on his knees. Tremors ran through his body. Derek balled his hands into fists trying to make the shaking subside. "Why is this happening?" His mind scrambled for reasons to explain what he saw. Josiah Craig was dead. He watched him die. Pressing the palms of his hands against his eyelids, starbursts erupted in a dazzling array of light.

Derek stood and leaned against the wall to steady himself. The light from the bathroom filtered into the room. He eyeballed the open doorway. Readying himself for what he might see, he rounded the corner and stared into the bathroom. The steam was gone, and so was Josiah. Derek took a step towards the open doorway and then retreated to the bed. He removed his towel and crawled between the crisp sheets.

Grabbing the TV remote from the nightstand, he turned on ESPN. He angled his back to the bathroom. He peeked over his shoulder as he started to fall asleep. He pulled the covers up, almost covering his head. His mind jumbled the events of the evening. As the full force of the pain meds kicked in, Derek was pulled into the abyss with scores and highlights from the day's baseball games.

CHAPTER TWENTY-ONE

Sunday Morning

Light filtered through the partially opened blinds. Derek turned over and covered his face with a pillow. He had no desire to get up. He snuggled in, pulling the covers up tight under his chin. He started to drift back to sleep when his phone pinged. Groaning he pulled the covers over his head.

The residual effect of the pain meds left him lethargic and sleepy. He had really no place to go, at least nothing that warranted him getting up at the butt crack of dawn. His eyelids were thick and heavy. The cool air of the room and the warmth between the sheets that surrounded him lulled him back into early morning slumber.

Derek bolted upright. His heart raced and a thin line of sweat beaded on his brow. "What the fuck is that?" The cloud that filled his head slowly dissipated as the alarm from his phone continued to blare. "Jesus man." He groped for his phone shutting off the alarm. He swung his legs over the edge of the bed letting the last remnants of sleep fade away.

Making his way to the bathroom, he stopped short of entering. The vague memory of Josiah crept into his mind. He shook his head. "Those fucking pain pills. I can't take them anymore." He remembered after Chrissy's murder, the pain pills gave him a disturbing dream of her at his kitchen table. He had to wonder if the pain meds allowed his subconscious to use Chrissy and Josiah to deal with his trauma.

Once shaved, Derek got on his computer. He opened the file from Agent Marcum and put Julie Richards' parents address into his phone. According to the file, both parents were retired school teachers. Derek glanced at his watch, "If I were retired, I would be at home on a lazy Sunday morning."

He checked the mileage from Mount Pleasant to Hot Springs Arkansas. He was 179 miles away from his next destination. "Nice. No repeat of yesterday," he said, closing his computer. "I should roll into Hot Springs by early afternoon."

Happy with the travel plans he laid out, Derek packed up all his stuff and headed to his car. Stepping into the hot morning sun, he imagined Hell wasn't too much hotter than Texas. He loaded his suitcase into his trunk and quickly checked his pocket. Satisfied Margaret's ring was where it should be, he cranked the AC down and followed the GPS directions to Daniel and Martha Richard's house.

CHAPTER TWENTY-TWO

Derek maneuvered his car into the wide driveway of the Richard's home. Located in a quaint upper-middle-class neighborhood, the yard had two huge oak trees framing the ranch style home. He had considered being honest with the family and telling them exactly who he was and what he was doing. But he didn't want to give them false hope on the FBI being able to bring closure to their daughter's abduction and murder. He opted instead to tell them he was writing a book about unsolved murder cases.

He exited his vehicle to the sound of barking. A dog glared at him from behind the sizeable square picture window at the front of the house. Derek made his way to the porch and reached out to ring the bell when the door swung open.

"Jasper, settle down." Daniel Richards smiled. "What can I do for you?"

Derek waved and stepped closer to the closed storm door that Daniel Richards stood behind. "Hi, Mr. Richards? I'm Derek Reed. I'm an investigative true crime author. I was wondering if you could take a few minutes to speak with me regarding your daughter Julie's disappearance and murder in 1986?"

Daniel yelled over his shoulder as he unlocked the storm door. "Martha, Martha...get in here." He pushed the door open and gestured for the stranger to come in. "Come on in, Mr. Reed. Please."

Derek stepped inside to the scent of clean, fresh linen. They stood in a foyer that had a large round table in the center. A large bouquet of what looked like fresh cut flowers filled the view with spectacular vibrant colors. "Thank you for this."

Daniel shooed the little fluffy dog away. "Forgive Jasper. He thinks anyone who enters this house is solely here to pet, scratch, and rub his entire body. Go, Jasper, get on out of here."

The dog sulked away, settling down on a chair in the corner of the open living room. He stared at Derek as if he bided his time, waiting for the right moment to make his move. Derek smirked. "I have a friend who has a dog. Thinks the same thing, that we're here for her enjoyment."

"We have always had a dog. We got Jasper five years ago. He was a stray in the neighborhood. Once cleaned and fattened up, he decided this was his castle." Daniel smiled as his wife entered the room.

"Daniel, I was in the middle of cooking lunch. What could be so important?"

Derek saw Julie, except this was an older version of her. He could see where Julie's big round eyes came from, along with her blonde hair. "Mrs. Richards, I'm Derek Reed..."

"Martha, he's an investigative writer, a true crime writer. He's doing a story on cold cases. He wants to talk to us about Julie." Daniel took his wife's hand and led her to the sofa. "Let's hear him out."

Derek noticed at the mention of her daughter's name, Martha Richards slumped. "Nice to meet you," Derek said as he extended his hand.

"Oh my. I wasn't prepared for this," she said, wiping her hands on her pants before shaking his.

Daniel patted his wife's shoulder. "The police here and in Garland have nothing to give us. Every few months we call and ask for any news or updates. We always get an officer who seems to work a desk. None of them ever know anything. Occasionally we've managed to talk a detective and have him look up the file, but even then, we don't get any new answers."

"Most small jurisdictions won't have a dedicated cold case detective. Cold cases take an enormous amount of time and resources. I understand your frustration as parents. Not having answers is another dig in an already gouged out wound. That's why I'm doing this book. I want to see if my research and investigation can help parents like you." Derek was sitting across from them on a separate sofa. He leaned in, "If you two are willing to speak with me, I can do what I can to help nudge the police departments to look into the disappearance and murder of your daughter. I'm actually hoping my investigation will yield some answers."

Daniel nodded at his wife. "Martha and I would welcome any assistance you can offer. What do you need from us?"

Derek pulled out his notepad and pen from his back pocket. "Let's start with the day Julie disappeared. It was February of 1986, is that correct?"

Martha Richards took in a deep breath. "Yes. After Valentine's day.

She had been out of school for about a year." she glanced over at her husband, who nodded in agreement. "She was working at a convenience store off the freeway." She snapped her fingers. "One of those giant truck stop stores." A little yelp escaped her lips.

A faint smile tugged on Derek's mouth. "I know this is hard. All this time later, it still feels like it happened yesterday. Take your time."

Martha sucked in air and blew it out tersely. "She had been working there for eight months. She was taking courses at the local junior college, she wasn't ready to go off to a major university."

Derek jotted some notes down. "Did she ever feel threatened or scared when leaving her shift?"

Daniel shook his head. "No. She didn't work nights. We didn't want her doing that, plus most of her classes were in the evening. The management back then wasn't corporate like it is now. It was much smaller and owned by a mom and pop couple. Anyway, she usually left work by three p.m."

"The day she disappeared, she was working?" Derek asked.

"No actually, she wasn't. She had gone in to get her paycheck. One of her best friends worked with her. When she didn't come right home, we didn't think much of it. We figured she had stayed to visit before heading to her class." Daniel reached his arm around his wife and pulled her close to him.

"Then it was hours before you realized she was missing?" Derek asked.

Daniel nodded. "It was. She didn't come home from her class that evening. We called the gas station, the manager said she picked up her check earlier that day. Then he checked the lot, and her car was still there. We met the police at the truck stop."

Derek scrawled in his notebook. "Did the police find anything? Any witnesses or clues?"

"No," said Martha. "We never heard of any witnesses coming forward with information. As far as we know, no one even saw her leave."

Derek leaned into the couple. "Did you find out anything? Something you may have mentioned to the police?"

"Her best friend later described a young man that had come into the store around the time Julie had been there. She didn't have much of anything to tell the police, and they said they would add it to the file. But when we spoke with her, she was sure that he followed Julie out of the store."

"Did she see the vehicle he drove or anything?"

Daniel glanced at his wife. "Sandy said he drove a truck, not like an eighteen-wheeler, but she said it looked like a really big van."

Derek's brow wrinkled. "I don't understand. A big van, like a panel van?"

Daniel shook his head. "No. She had never seen one before, so she had a hard time describing it. She said it looked like a weird supply van. Bigger than a pallet truck but smaller than an eighteen-wheeler."

"One last thing, can you tell me her best friend's name? I'd like to speak with her."

Daniel and Martha shared a glance between them.

"Am I missing something?" Derek squinted at them.

"Sandy died a few years back. Some kind of cancer."

Derek closed his book, threading the pen through the coiled metal rings, and placed it in his back pocket. "Is there anyone else, besides the police, that I should speak with? Anyone still at the store where Julie worked?"

"I'm afraid not," Daniel said standing. "The store and station were sold years ago. No one from back then is even in this area anymore. At least I don't know of anyone."

Martha nudged her husband. "Ask him, go on. Ask him?"

"Ask me what?" Derek asked.

"Julie was wearing a necklace the day she disappeared. We were hoping to recover it. It was an emerald pendant. Tear shaped surrounded by small diamonds. We bought it for her high school graduation."

Martha walked over to a shelf that held several pictures. She picked up a small frame and removed the photo. "Take this. That is the pendant." Her hand shook. "If you ever find out who did this—I know it's stupid to even think this, but if we could ever get that necklace back..." her voice trailed off.

Derek took the picture from her. He studied the photo. "If I can find her necklace, I will make sure you get it back."

"Thank you, Mr. Reed." Daniel led him to the door. "We will be here waiting to see if you find anything out. Please call us with any news."

Derek nodded as he stepped onto the porch. "I will. I promise." He waved at them as he got into his vehicle and pulled away, leaving Martha

Richards clinging to her husband.

CHAPTER TWENTY-THREE

Derek stopped at the gas station where Julie worked all those years ago. He pulled into a parking spot near the end of the building. Getting out of his car, he pulled the tin box from his bag in his trunk. He searched the box for Julie's picture. No emerald pendant around her neck. The only necklace Julie wore in the photo was a ligature mark. He placed both photos in the box and tucked it back into his bag. Closing his trunk, he leaned against his vehicle and surveyed the area. Walking around the building, Derek tried to imagine what the area looked like so long ago. An old trucker walked past him, nodding at him.

The man stopped and turned around. "Howdy," he said.

"Hey, how are you?"

"Fine. Is there something I can help you with?" he asked.

Derek flinched back. "Why do you ask?"

The old man crossed his arms. "I run this place. I don't own it, but I run it. Saw you out here and I was wondering what you were up to."

Derek smiled at the man. "I'm an investigative writer. I'm currently looking into a cold case from the '80s. I was trying to get an idea of what this place looked like back in 1986."

"Well hell, follow me. I can help you with that." The old man headed towards the entrance of the building.

"I'm sorry," Derek said as he followed him, "I don't understand how you can help me see what this place looked like thirty years ago. Unless we are going to jump into a time machine."

"I got something better than that." He led Derek into an office at the back of the building. He opened the door and stepped inside to a nice spacious area. Each wall held pictures of the property going as far back as the 1970s.

Derek's mouth hung open. "Holy shit. You weren't kidding."

The old man laughed. He held out his hand. "I'm Jethro. My dad owned this place back in the day. He sold it to some big conglomerate for a lot of money. But they wanted to keep him on to run it. He got to do what he loved but didn't have all the headache of having to pay for everything."

Derek shook the man's hand. "I'm Derek. Nice to meet you."

The man walked around an antique metal desk and sat. "When he died, I had just come back from college, and they asked me to take over. I did. And here I am."

Derek moved around the room, looking at the evolution of the property through the years. He found the year he needed. He studied the old picture. The property was laid out a little differently. The main building was now bigger, but the property looked basically the same.

"What exactly are you looking for?"

Derek faced Jethro. "Back in 1986, Julie Richards was abducted from this place. Her body was found months later in Garland Texas. I'm trying to find anything that will lead me to her abductor and killer."

"Damn. I haven't heard that name for a while." He rubbed his chin. "I was away at college when that happened. My Dad felt horrible. It was after that incident that he installed security cameras that cover the entire front area."

"Do you remember any of it?"

Jethro leaned forward on his elbows. "Not much. My dad called me and told me about it. No one saw her leave with anyone. This place had been expanded, and we had a lot of truckers coming through. I wish I had more to give you."

"Thirty plus years is a long time ago." Derek pointed to the pictures. "Do you mind if I take a few photos?"

"Not at all. If it helps solve that case, I'll give you what you need." Jethro leaned back in his chair. "I remember Julie. She was two years behind me in school. She was a pretty girl. Super nice. A little protected. Her parents hovered around her. Kept her on a short leash."

Derek snapped a few pictures. "Did you guys have regulars that you saw several times a year? You know truckers that ran the same routes, anything like that?"

"A lot of truckers came through this place back then, and a million more since. If there were any regulars, I didn't ever meet them. My dad probably did."

Derek pocketed his phone. "Well, Jethro, I really appreciate this. Having these photos gives me a little more insight into Julie's disappearance."

"Hey, no problem. If I can help, please call me." Jethro handed him a business card.

"I will do that," Derek said as he took the card. The two men headed towards the door and walked out into a bustling lobby. Derek studied the traffic in and out of the building. Tons of people must travel through those doors on a daily basis. He figured that's why the killer chose places like this. A person could get lost in the crowd, literally.

CHAPTER TWENTY-FOUR

Derek took a few pictures from the outside before getting into his car. He placed his phone in the cradle stuck to his dash. He rested his head against the seat and pictured the scene in 1986. Julie would have walked out of the store and headed to her vehicle. Within a fifty-foot radius, she would have been taken. The killer would have had to be quick and parked close to the building. But if he had a large van like vehicle how could he get that close? Derek glanced out the window. Several eighteen-wheelers were parked on the diagonal. No way a trucker could get his rig close to the building.

"Wondering how he got her, huh?"

Derek jumped in his seat, grabbing his chest. "Seriously? Can't you ring a bell or something, letting me know you're about to pop in."

"I don't pop in."

"What do you do, then?"

"I don't know." Chrissy shrugged.

Derek ogled her. A smile crept across his face.

Chrissy turned to look out the window, then back to Derek. "Why aren't we driving? And why are you smiling at me? You're kind of creeping me out."

"Really, you're dead and telling me I'm creeping you out?"

"Why are you smiling?"

"You look good. I mean, your wound is dripping. But other than that, you look almost normal."

Her cheeks pushed upward with a smile. "Normal? Is that the best I'm going to get?"

"Well, when your wound closes, you'll be..." Derek glanced out the window then back to her. "You'll look like the Chrissy I want to remember."

"I'll take that," Chrissy said.

Derek drove onto the freeway. Classic rock filled the car. He removed two pieces of gum from the console and stuffed them into his mouth. He winced with every chew.

"Why do you keep chewing if it hurts so much?"

"I need to chew gum. If not, I may start smoking again."

"I can't believe you used to smoke. Such an icky habit." She squinched up her nose.

Derek clenched his jaw. "I know," he said as his nostrils flared. "That's probably the main reason I quit. That and I couldn't smoke at crime scenes, and that was when I needed a cigarette the most."

"So you switched to the lesser icky habit, but just as annoying, gum-chewing one?"

"Yes. But it hurts too much right now." He rolled down his window and spit out the pieces. He heard light humming and turned to see Chrissy mouthing the words to a *38 Special* song. "I didn't think you knew any classic rock songs."

"My dad listened to this kind of music all the time. He used to say the best music came from the '60s, '70s, and '80s. Oh and classic soul. He would blare soul music every Sunday." A sweet smile crested her lips. "He and my mother used to dance around the living room, laughing and holding on tight to each other." Her smile faded, "I think I miss that most of all. Those moments watching them together. Wondering if I would ever find someone to love me like my father loved my mother."

Derek stared straight. His throat ached from the lumps forming. "I'm so sorry Chrissy." The statement came out as a whisper.

"Why are you sorry?"

"If only I hadn't been so selfish, and asked for help."

"I don't understand, Derek."

Derek sighed dragging a hand through his hair. He had alluded to the circumstances surrounding Josiah Craig with Dr. Chelsea, but he never said the whole story out loud.

"Derek, tell me what's bothering you so much. Why are you saying you're sorry? My death isn't your fault."

"Yes, it is." He maneuvered the car around a slow eighteen-wheeler. As he came around the truck, he saw another rig stranded on the side of the road, along with a mechanic's truck. "When I took over the Josiah Craig case, we, the Bureau, didn't know it was Josiah doing the killing. We had no clues at all. I mean we had evidence but nothing leading to a suspect."

"How many girls had he murdered before me?"

"You were his seventh victim."

"Oh."

"By the time I was assigned the case, four girls had been murdered. None of the other investigators found a pattern between the murders. My AD at the Bureau hoped I might be able to spot one and see if the cases were connected."

"And did you?"

"Not at first. It took me several months to see a connection between the abduction and disposal sites. Josiah Craig made it his mission to taunt me. He knew all about me, I didn't know who he was. I was chasing a ghost."

"But why do you think my death or the other girl's death was your fault? Derek, you stopped him from killing more girls. You said it yourself that you saw a pattern no one else did."

"I didn't see it in time." Derek's heart raced. He wiped the sweat off his upper lip. His breathing sped up. "I had no clue where he was holding you. It was only a day or so prior to my finding you that we tracked down a couple of carnivals that our killer could be with."

"I don't think I'm connecting the dots, Derek. I still don't understand why you feel so responsible."

Derek squirmed. "I am, though. You don't get it."

"Then help me get it. Explain it to me."

"I didn't know for sure if the carnival Josiah Craig worked at was the one that I chose for the team to track. Another carnival was going on a few counties over. It was pure luck that I picked his. But I never would have found you. He called me. He told me where he was holding you and to hurry if I wanted to save you."

Derek sat in silence for a few minutes. The realization of his actions hit him all at once. He inhaled a deep breath and blew it out slowly. He glanced over at Chrissy. Cool air brushed over his arm as she reached out to him.

"Tell me."

"I left my hotel without telling anyone. I was so focused on getting to you, I didn't gather the troops and bring back up. I went by myself. I ran into the tent and saw you on the table. All I could think about was saving you. I hadn't been able to save the other six girls before you. I didn't want another girl to die on my watch."

Chrissy sat quietly. She waited for him to say the things he needed to out loud. Things he had been holding in for way too long. "Go on."

"I ran through the entrance. Ran to you on the table, without clearing the room first, and Josiah was able to knock me out and tie me up. My stupidity got you killed."

"You didn't get me killed. Josiah Craig had no intention of letting me leave alive. Based on what you just said, he had every intention of making you pay for being a profiler. He wanted to win. And making you suffer, was his way of doing it."

Derek turned towards her, keeping an eye on the road in front of him. "I'm so sorry Chrissy. I should've brought other agents with me. I should've taken the time to clear the tent and do things the way you're supposed to." Tears rolled down his cheeks. "I'm so sorry."

Chrissy smiled at him. "You were there with me. I didn't die alone, Derek. You will never understand how important that was to me. You need to forgive yourself. For me, for the other victims of Josiah Craig. You need to let us go, or Josiah Craig will continue to use it against you. Think of all the girls you kept him from killing by stopping him. I don't blame you, Derek. You should give yourself a break too." She paused wringing her hands together. Chrissy glanced over at him. "You also need to let Sheila go. You were young, and it was an accident."

He wiped the moisture from his face. He opened his mouth to say something at the same time, his ring tone blared through the speakers of the car. "Oh no. This can't be good," he muttered as he pushed the talk button on his phone.

CHAPTER TWENTY-FIVE

Derek calmed himself before speaking. "Hey, Assistant Director Fretz, what's up?" He slid his watch up and down his wrist, tapping the face.

"How is the vacation going? You close to Tennessee?"

"I'm outside Hot Springs, Arkansas. Kind of been sightseeing. Not really in a rush to see my family."

"I hear you there."

"I'm sure you didn't call to check on my travel plans."

"No. I see you chose a new team member. I guess you like him, huh?"

Derek adjusted himself in his seat. "What do you mean by that?" The GPS rattled off instructions to take an exit in a couple of miles.

"What do you mean, 'what do you mean by that'?"

"Huh?"

"Derek, what are you up to?"

"I'm not up to anything. Why? What have you heard?"

"I haven't heard anything. Is there something for me to hear?"

"No. No, of course not. I'm traveling to see family."

AD Fretz sighed into the phone. "I called to see if you had picked anyone else off the list. I like the tech geek you chose. I think he will be a great fit."

Derek relaxed. He glanced over to an empty passenger seat. He cocked his head to the side, wrinkling his brow as he tried to figure out the moment she left.

"Hello, Derek?"

"Yeah, I think he will fit great, too."

"Okay. What about the other agents? Have you chosen any of those yet? You know I need those names before you come back from your vacation."

"Forced vacation."

"Whatever. I want those names."

"I promise I will get you some names within a week or two. At the most." Derek followed the GPS directions to a local hotel. He pulled into a parking spot.

"Alright. Enjoy your drive. Don't push yourself, Derek. You need time to heal."

"I won't." The line went dead, letting music filter through the speakers. He had made good time and wanted to get to the disposal site as quickly as possible. He was about to exit the vehicle when his phone rang again.

"Derek here."

"Hey, Agent Reed. This is Agent Marcum."

"Agent Marcum. What's going on?"

"Are you in Hot Springs?"

"Yeah, I just got here. You got something for me?"

"I do. Lisa Muldare. She was found on the side of the road off State Highway 70. I sent you a file that has satellite photos of the area. Not much has changed around the dump site. Her body was found on the outskirts of Hot Springs National Park. Although the area has been built up, the particular stretch of road hasn't changed much. I also included the original police file regarding the discovery of Lisa's body."

"Do I even want to know how you got that?"

Agent Marcum laughed. "You worry way too much, man. You know, some of this case was put into ViCAP?"

"Yeah, I found it in there, but I didn't pull the case information. I didn't want it to trigger anyone to the fact that I was looking into the case."

"Good thinking. Anyway, I have a buddy who works for the Hot Springs Police department. He got me the file..."

"What? Please tell me you didn't tell him anything about me working on the case?" Derek's heart pounded against his chest. He tapped the steering wheel at a frantic speed.

"No. Not at all. He and I have known each other since high school. I mentioned I was doing some research on unsolved cases and this was one of them. He pulled the file and emailed it to me."

"What if his bosses want to know why he did that, and they ask you questions. I can't have any information leak out yet."

"Agent Reed, I promise you, my buddy won't say anything. You got to trust me on this."

Derek sighed into the phone. His gut told him to trust Marcum, but his brain raced a thousand miles a minute, telling him this was a bad idea. "I guess I got no choice now." He paused glancing out the window at the hotel he was going to stay at. "I guess the file has all the information regarding her body and any evidence?"

"It does. Unfortunately, there isn't much to go on. No eyewitnesses. Her body held very little in the way of physical evidence. By the time she had been found, she had been a victim of the elements for nearly four days."

"Crap. I was hoping I might get lucky with at least one of these girls having some evidence, even something small that would give me a direction to go in."

"Well, I might have something for you. My buddy's dad knows the guy who investigated her abduction in Pine Bluff."

"How does he know the investigating officer?"

"My friend's dad used to be a sheriff in the area, he knew the man from his time in law enforcement. He gave me his phone number. I included it in the email I just sent you. I thought you might want to use it and talk to him. He's a good man, Agent Reed. You can trust him to keep what you and he discuss quiet."

Derek's knee bounced as he fidgeted with his watch, tapping the face. Maybe talking to the investigating officer would give him some insight. "Okay. I will head that way. I don't think I have any reason to stay here in Hot Springs. Hopefully, the investigator out of Pine Bluff will have more information for me."

"I hope it helps, Agent. I'm still working on the fourth girl out of Mississippi. I should have something for you in the next few days. I'm finishing up a case here. It's my last one before I transfer to your unit."

"I appreciate all your help. Don't do anything to get yourself in trouble. You are still attached to your unit. Do what you need to for them."

"Don't worry Agent Reed. I won't do anything to get you or me in trouble."

"Alright. I'll read that file now. Thanks again."

"Sure thing, Agent Reed."

For a second time, the line went dead, and classic rock pushed out through the speakers. Derek opened his email on his phone and quickly read the file. The dump sites for all the girls were not yielding much information. He scanned the email and found the number for the investigating officer who worked the abduction of Lisa. A few rings later, someone answered.

"Jerry here, what can I do for you?"

"Jerry Pickford?"

"Yeah, who is this?"

"This is Agent Reed, from the FBI. I'm a profiler, and I'm working a case I think you were involved in."

"What case is that?"

"The Lisa Muldare abduction." Derek pulled up the map showing the best way from Hot Springs to Pine Bluff.

"Damn. Never thought I would hear that name again. Why are you investigating that case?"

"Listen, I'll explain everything. I'm in Hot Springs right now, and I'm not that far from you. Could we meet in person and have this conversation then? Say in two hours?" He glanced at his watch, "That should put me in Pine Bluff around three thirty or four p.m."

"I don't have a problem with that. Dick's Diner is located out on Route 65. Meet me there."

"Great, I'll see you then." Derek disconnected the call and plugged in Dickie's Diner into his GPS. Less than two hours away. He drove out of the hotel parking lot.

CHAPTER TWENTY-SIX

Sunday late afternoon

Pulling into the parking lot of the nostalgic diner, Derek checked his phone for a hotel nearby. Finding a Holiday Inn, he booked a room online. He stepped out of the car and stretched. His brow wrinkled as he realized he hadn't heard from Chrissy. Maybe after his confession, she was done stalking his subconscious.

Upon entering the diner, he spotted Jerry. The former sheriff sat in a corner booth facing the doorway observing all persons who entered, something Derek figured all law enforcement officers did. The man's salt and pepper hair stuck out under his fishing hat. The former sheriff had muscular arms and broad shoulders. He may be retired, but Derek thought the man could probably hold his own in a scuffle. He nodded in the man's direction as he headed towards him.

"Jerry?" Derek asked holding out his hand.

"In the flesh. Agent Reed, nice to meet you." Jerry shook his hand then waved over the waitress. "Shirley, another coffee for me, and I will have the chicken fried steak dinner." He raised an eyebrow at Derek, "You eating?"

"Yeah. I'm starving." Derek smiled at the older woman. Her hair was pulled up in a loose, messy bun, and she looked like she was ready for her shift to end. "Shirley, I'll have the same."

"What would you like to drink?"

"A coffee and a water please."

Jerry waited for the waitress to be out of earshot. "Why are you working on the Lisa Muldare case all these years later?"

Derek started to answer when Shirley showed up with their drinks. He smiled at her as she placed them on the table. He glanced over his shoulder making sure she couldn't hear their conversation before speaking. "I'm currently on leave from the Bureau. I'm going to be taking on a new unit in about two months. We will specialize in cold cases. I happened onto this case, and I'm exploring whether there is any viable chance that we could get this case solved. No one knows I'm working on this, though." He cocked his head to the side.

Jerry held up his hand. "No need to worry about me. I will do anything to help you, and I'll keep it between us." He took a long sip of his coffee. "Lisa was one of my early cases. I knew her parents. We weren't super close, but I knew who they were."

Derek nodded at him. "Thank you. I need the utmost discretion. I don't want the families getting wind of me doing this if I can help it. Especially if I can't get them any closure. I hate opening their wounds all over again."

"I'll never forget that case. First, let me tell you about her." Jerry's expression softened. "Lisa was a bit on the wild side. She didn't sleep with a bunch of boys or anything like that. But she had a rebellious streak. She had run away a few times. Usually for a day or two, and it usually coincided with her parents telling her she couldn't do something."

Shirley came up to the table, laden with two plates on one arm and one in the other hand. "Here you go, gentlemen." She set the plates on the table. "I brought you extra rolls. If you need anything else just holler at me."

Derek stared at the mound of food on his plate. "Wow. This is a meal, huh?"

"This place is known for their chicken fried steak." Jerry took a bite and a sip of his coffee before he continued. "Back to Lisa. The day she went missing she had gone up to the truck stop off of I30. She worked at the fast-food restaurant located there. Her parents reported her missing late that night. But earlier that week she had asked to go to Daytona, for fall break with her boyfriend. Her parents had said no.

"When she didn't show up later that evening, the parents contacted the police asking for help in tracking her down. They explained the situation asking for help in hunting down the boyfriend, they were sure she had disobeyed them and ran off with the boy for the long weekend." Jerry took a few bites of his food.

Derek ate as well. "This is fantastic. I don't think I have ever had a chicken fried steak this good."

Jerry's eyes danced. "Wait till you have their apple pie."

They both enjoyed their meal for a few more moments before continuing their conversation.

"I'm assuming, when the parent's contacted you, there was no reason for you to think an abduction had taken place."

Jerry shook his head. "Not at all. The parents didn't have the boyfriend's information. They just wanted to make sure she was safe. Since she was under eighteen, we had authority to contact the police in Daytona and hunt the boy down. His parents gave us his hotel, so we had the local authorities go over to check on her."

"How many days later did that occur?" Derek asked.

"Took us two days to find him. He said he hadn't seen Lisa since that week. His buddies confirmed that Lisa didn't travel with them."

Derek drank his coffee. "Any witnesses at the truck stop?"

"None. By the time we realized she was missing, we assumed she had been abducted, we had no witnesses. The clerks at the store were all we had."

"Did they give you anything?"

"One girl who worked with Lisa had stated that she witnessed Lisa speaking with a young man. She couldn't give us a description, unfortunately. Now, this particular truck stop had surveillance cameras in place."

Derek's fork stopped halfway to his mouth. "Please tell me you got something off those?"

Jerry sighed. "Not really. It showed Lisa speaking with a young man who looked to be in his early twenties. But we couldn't get a clear picture of his face. Couldn't see what vehicle, if any, he was driving. Only one clue ever surfaced. However, I don't know if it is connected or not."

"I don't understand." Derek finished the last of his chicken fried steak and pushed the plate to the side. Shirley showed up as if she had been summoned, filled their coffees, and removed their empty plates.

"We will take two pieces of apple pie, Shirley. But there is no hurry."

"I don't think I..." Derek began.

Jerry waved him off. "You may be full, but the moment you take your first bite, you will find the room."

They waited until Shirley left their table to continue.

"What was the one clue?"

"The girl that worked with Lisa said that several of these 'cool vans' stopped at the truck stop."

"Umm, cool van?" Derek raised his eyebrows.

"Yeah. I was confused at first, but then she explained, and I realized what she was talking about. Mobile service trucks."

"Wait, like mechanics on wheels?"

"Instead of eighteen-wheelers being towed and then worked on, these mobile repair trucks were deployed and could work on the truck on the side of the road. They have been around since the '70s, but back then they were mostly used for farmers. You couldn't take a tractor the size of a house to a local mechanic, so they went to them. Incredible for the time. Now they are everywhere. They carry almost anything to fix an eighteen-wheeler, except for an engine."

"Did anything lead you to think that one of these drivers was involved?"

"No. That's just it. Nothing in the way of evidence. But I would bet my pension one of those guys was our suspect. See, some of those mobile repair trucks had sleeper cabs. Not as large as the sleepers in the big rigs, mind you. However, it helped keep the drivers mobile and always on call. That's a perfect cover to hide a girl until the killer could dump her. It was one of the reasons I put the case into ViCAP later on."

"I saw that."

Jerry shook his head. "The FBI didn't open it up for local law enforcement until 2008. Can you imagine how many cases were put into that thing in one sitting? My bosses only wanted the most recent unsolved cases put in first. Eventually, they would've put Lisa's case into the system, but I knew I was going to retire soon. I did it before I left. No one knew, either."

Derek recalled the conversation with Julie Richards' parents. He was sure the description the young friend of Julie's had given was of a vehicle like this one. His mind began to spin at how he could hunt down the company. "By chance did you guys investigate any of the mechanic companies?"

"No. No way my superiors at the time were going to give me clearance for that. We had no probable cause to request a warrant for any company. Hell, we didn't have a company to investigate. Absolutely no way in Hell I would be able to get a roster of employees and their whereabouts."

"Shit. I have a description from one of the witnesses in another girl's abduction. She describes the same kind of vehicle."

Jerry's jaw hung slack. "You mean more girls were murdered?"

"Yeah, four that I know of. This is a huge break. The problem is it's thirty years later."

Their apple pie arrived. In usual circles, this would be considered two slices. Derek ogled the plate. His mouth instinctively watered. He glanced up at Shirley. "This looks fantastic."

She patted his shoulder. "Wait till you take the first bite. It will be like a heroin addict chasing the dragon. It will never be the same, but always delicious." She refilled their coffees before leaving the table.

Derek took a bite, and for a split second, he was in nirvana. All of his taste buds erupted in pure bliss. He closed his eyes and tried to think of any other time a piece of pie had almost given him an orgasm. The apples were perfectly soft but not mushy. Cinnamon and nutmeg, along with brown sugar hit his tongue at alternating intervals. Just enough of each that left him wanting more. "This is better than sex," he said out loud, not meaning to.

Jerry roared back in laughter. "Well, I never heard it described like that. But I think that's a pretty accurate description, my friend." Jerry took two more bites before speaking again. "Can't you get the information about the trucking companies and which ones were in this area at that time? Surely you have a database that has all that information?"

Derek shook his head. "No. Not without some kind of warrant to probe into a company's records. I'm not that far yet." He hesitated before he continued. "I only have basically two descriptions of a truck. Not much to force a company to give me information about employees."

"I get the feeling you are holding something back."

Derek raised an eyebrow at him. "Really?"

"Yeah, really." Jerry pushed his plate to the side. "I know about Josiah Craig. How are you doing since then?"

"Are you questioning my ability?"

"Are you a little defensive?"

Derek smirked at that response. "I'm doing okay. How do you know about Josiah?"

"I did my research this last two hours waiting for you."

Derek recoiled. "It was a pretty awful experience. I'm on medical leave because of it."

Jerry looked quizzically at the agent. "How did you find this case?"

"You would never believe me if I told you."

"Try me." Jerry watched the man. He had read articles about Josiah and knew that Derek had suffered several massive injuries and he was sure the agent may have healed physically, but the mental healing had yet to begin. "Look, I'm not going to tell anyone what we discuss. I promise you. You look like you could use an ear. Talk to me, Derek."

Derek sat back and sipped on his coffee. He could use a fresh perspective. And talking to Chrissy or himself wasn't always working. He sighed, "I was forced on medical leave. I'm on my way to Tennessee to see my family. One of my hobbies is taking pictures of abandoned buildings. I came across this old farmhouse in New Mexico. I found this box under the floorboards."

"A keepsake box?"

Derek nodded. "I'm not supposed to be working on anything."

Jerry's eyebrow lifted. "Rogue, huh?"

"I wouldn't go that far." Derek grinned. "I'm merely seeing if this case should be considered once my new unit is in place. That's it."

Jerry squinted at the agent. "What are you going to do? I'm assuming since this is off the books, that you can't employ the resources of the FBI?"

"No, I can't. However, I may have a few tricks up my sleeve." He sipped his coffee before he continued. "I have a tech geek that will be in my new unit, he can hunt down the companies. But like I said, without warrants, I can't get any type of employee list."

"But, if you can narrow down what companies and where they traveled for services, you could track them and see which one had a driver covering the area where all the girls have been abducted from and dumped. That will be more than I had thirty years ago."

"Can you tell me about Lisa's parents? Are they still in the area?" Derek motioned for a refill of his coffee.

"No. After Julie's body was found, it wasn't eight months, and they divorced. I wasn't close with either one of them. Saw them around town, talked pleasantries. I knew about the trouble with the daughter because the father always cornered me and ask for my help. Last I knew, the father moved to California, and the mother had moved to Michigan."

Derek's leg bounced up and down under the table. He stared into his coffee mug.

Jerry studied the man in front of him. His research indicated Derek was one of the best profilers in the FBI. But he had someone that could run circles around the FBI. "Listen," Jerry said. "I know what it's like to want to solve a case and not have a damn clue to go on. Right now, you got this lead on these mobile repair trucks. I understand that the laws we fight to uphold often bind our hands and keep us from doing our jobs. It's one of the reasons I retired from my sheriff's position. I couldn't stand the fact that we had rules and the damn criminals had none."

Derek sat back and nodded. "I respect the rules. I don't always play by them. I don't want to put my tech guy in any more trouble than he may already be. I got him working this case now, and he shouldn't be."

Jerry cocked an eyebrow at him. "I think I might be able to help you. I know someone, who can find the information you want. Or at least point you in the right direction."

Derek's back straightened. "I can't have any more people knowing what I'm doing. I'll be fired before I have a chance to bring closure to these families."

Jerry shrugged. "You don't have to worry about anyone finding out what you're doing. But I'll need some information."

"What do you need?"

"I need the names of all the girls. I need to know where they were abducted from and where their bodies were found, and the timeline. I need to know if you have anything else that you're holding back. Anything you haven't told me about this case."

Derek's forehead wrinkled. He shook his head. "No. I have nothing else. I talked to the family of the last girl abducted. Her parents are now both dead. I spoke with Julie Richards' parents, they gave me the first sighting of the repair truck. I can't talk to Lisa Muldare's parents unless I call them, and I don't think that's a good idea. At least not until I have some actual information to help give them closure. I got one more girl on the list, out of Mississippi. That's it. You know what I know."

"Alright." Jerry slid over a notepad. "Write it all down."

Derek did as he was instructed. A knot formed in his stomach. He could use the help, but the more people who knew what he was doing, the harder it would be to keep this investigation hidden. "At the end of the day, I want this fucker caught. And because of that, I want all the help I can get. However, I can't express to you how important it is your guy doesn't say anything to anyone. If my investigation gets out into the news, I run the risk of this guy going underground and me never finding him."

"Trust me. My guy won't say anything. I was in the service with him, and he now runs a security company. The guy can find anything on anyone. If he weren't a good guy, he would be a hell of a bad guy."

Derek handed the notepad back to Jerry. "I appreciate all your help. If I can ever do anything for you, all you have to do is ask." He held out one of his business cards. "I mean it, Jerry. Call me with any information you find out. You can reach me at that number any time of day."

Jerry stood and shook Derek's hand. "I want to be able to tell Lisa's family her killer has been arrested. I want the case closed. I go to bed with Lisa every night. That case ruined two marriages."

"Thank you for your help." Derek waved over his shoulder as he headed out to his car.

Jerry pulled his phone from his pocket and dialed a number. "Hey, friend. How's it been?"

"Damn. I haven't heard from you for a hot minute. How are you?" The man's warm, friendly tone filtered through the phone.

"I'm okay. I need a favor."

"Anything for you. What do you need?"

"I need Kainetorri Security to work their magic and help me solve a thirty-year-old murder."

CHAPTER TWENTY-SEVEN

Sunday evening

Derek rolled his suitcase into his room. Leaving it untouched, he placed his computer on the desk and opened the file on the Lisa Muldare case. He reread the initial report on the abduction. Nothing new popped out. Jerry had covered everything listed in his original notes. Derek had no idea who the man was going to bring into the fold of the investigation, he only hoped he could be trusted.

Glancing at his watch, he called Agent Marcum.

"Yo, what's up Derek?"

"Are you at work?"

"No. I do take Sundays off."

"Crap, man. Kyle, I'm sorry. I really shouldn't be bothering you. I'll call you Monday morning or sometime Monday."

"Hey, don't worry about it. I was going through some of my things. I don't want to take a bunch of shit with me to Arizona. I'm decluttering. Tell me what you need."

"I spoke with that guy, the retired sheriff. "

"Oh yeah. Did he give you anything that might help?"

"Yeah, he did. He mentioned a report of a particular van at the Lisa Muldare abduction. Julie Richards' parents had explained a weird vehicle had been seen around the time of their daughter's abduction. It took me a bit to figure it out, and it really wasn't until I spoke with Jerry, that I realized the witnesses were referring to the same vehicle."

"No shit. What were they talking about?"

"You know those mobile mechanic repair trucks you see on the side of the road repairing eighteen-wheelers?"

"That's what two different people reported over thirty years ago? Damn, that's fantastic."

"Yeah, it is. The first real lead in any of the cases. But no way in hell I'm going to get any kind of warrant to get an employee list. Hell, I don't even have a company."

"I have the abduction and disposal sites. I can do a little digging here and see if I can find what companies might have been in that business."

"Don't do anything to draw attention to yourself. I don't want to have to explain to anyone what you're doing."

"No worries. My current boss knows I'm heading to your unit. I put in for a couple weeks of vacation before reporting. He knows I have spoken to you, but he doesn't know about what."

"Okay, that's good. If you can find out anything, I might take it to my boss and see if I can get him to approve a search on the company's records. But I need proof to go down that road. I have no idea how I'm going to get that."

"Look what you have gotten in a short time. Something will break that will give you another lead. That's how all cases work. Especially cold cases. One piece of evidence pops up and blows the case open."

"Well let's hope that happens soon. I'm heading to Clarksdale tomorrow. Do you have any information about Liza Parker?" Derek heard shuffling on the other end of the phone. "Listen, it's okay. I'll let you go."

"No, man, you're fine. I have a cat that thinks he's helping me. Actually, all he's doing is shredding paper and batting anything that moves all over my house. Squeakers, damn it."

Derek laughed. "He sounds like a handful."

"He is a pain in my ass. Always into shit. Sometimes he sits next to something on the table and slowly pushes it off the edge. Then he looks at me like he's challenging me to do something about it."

"Call me Monday. I'll be on the road fairly early."

"I can do that. I didn't bring anything home with me. I was working on it at work so that I could access the databases. I'll call mid-morning."

"Sounds good. Thanks, Kyle."

"Later."

Derek stared at his computer. The hole was opening up a little more in this case. He could feel the demons tugging on his ankles. Trying to get a grip on him and drag him to Hell. His face throbbed, but he refused to take a pain pill. He rummaged through his bag and pulled out some Tylenol. He took four tablets and stripped as he made his way to the shower.

Steam filled the small room. The days were getting longer. The closer he got to Mississippi it felt as if a straitjacket tightened with every mile.

His mind drifted to Chrissy. As the hot water pelted his back, he wondered why his subconscious used her. He had no problem talking to himself. He really didn't feel he had to conjure up a dead girl to hold a conversation with. He shut off the water and stood in the swirling steam. He pulled the curtain back grabbing a towel from the rack. He started to wipe the mirror, but not before looking over his shoulder. No Josiah tonight.

Fifteen minutes later he crawled into bed and turned on the TV. Skimming through the channels, he landed on a movie. His eyes drifted shut. The drone of the TV helped him relax. Halfway asleep his ringing phone jarred him awake. "Derek here," he said without looking at the screen.

"Hi, babe."

Elizabeth's sultry voice filled his ear. An instant boner at the sweet sound. His hand drifted under the sheets. "Hey." Derek smiled into the phone. "How is my house? Still standing I hope."

"Of course. Lola has decided she loves it here. She may have to come stay with you when I'm gone. She has decided your half of the bed is her new spot. And the backyard was built for her. Hey, what are you going to do with that little bungalow in the back?"

"I might rent it out. I've been thinking about it. Just not sure if I want a stranger in my backyard. As for Lola, I don't have a problem with her at all. I love Lola."

"Yeah? What about me? Do you love me?"

He cocked his head to the side. Contemplating the correct response. His head tried to answer, but this one time his heart took over. "Yeah Elizabeth. I love you. You have to know that."

"I do. I just like hearing it from you."

"I'll say it more often."

"How's the trip? You almost to Tennessee?"

"No, I'm outside Mississippi. I've been sightseeing."

"Have you spoken to your family? Are they excited to see you?"

It dawned on Derek that he hadn't called his parents and updated them. He shook his head. He probably should call them tomorrow. "Yeah, they are."

"Well, I'll let you go. I miss you, Derek."

"I miss you too. Goodnight Lizzy." He placed his phone on the nightstand in the charger. His hand remained under the covers, but the minute she hung up he lost interest. He did love her. One day maybe she would stop what she did. Maybe if he asked her to, she would. But to be honest, he wasn't ready to find out. He turned down the TV but left it on, not really wanting to spend the night alone.

CHAPTER TWENTY-EIGHT

Derek struggled against the restraints. His wrists hurt where the binding dug into his skin. The cries echoed in the recesses of his mind. He tried to open his eyes, but he couldn't. No, something covered them. It was tight around his head and dug into his face.

He heard muffled cries but couldn't tell which direction they were coming from. His head twisted from side to side. He tried to loosen the blindfold by shaking his head. He rubbed his face on his shoulder. After several attempts, the blindfold fell around his neck. He blinked his eyes adjusting to the bright lights of the room.

Not sure where he was, he focused on the muffled cries. Derek's eyes cleared, and he saw Josiah Craig standing next to a table. The evil man turned and sneered over his shoulder at Derek.

His heart pounded out a rhythm that thumped against his skull. Derek's eyes narrowed in on the girl laying on the bench. Something about her seemed too familiar. He yanked against the leather straps that held him. "No. Please, not her. Don't hurt her," he cried out as Josiah stepped to the side.

The beautiful woman turned and stared at Derek.

"Why did you let this happen?" she asked him. Her eyes had been gouged out. Blood flowed from the empty sockets.

"I didn't. I didn't know he had you."

A cackle filled the room. Josiah Craig turned and cocked his head to the side. A swarm of black flies buzzed around him. Maggots weaved their way through layers of flesh. What was left of his brain had rotted and oozed out the opening on the side of his head. The gaping wound where he had shot himself had rotted and caused part of his face to cave in. The other side of his head looked almost untouched.

Bile inched up, burning the back of Derek's throat. Saliva filled his mouth as he swallowed rapidly. He turned his attention to Lizzy. Her head lay facing him. Tears rushed down his cheek, dripping off his chin. "I'm so sorry, Lizzy."

She opened her mouth to speak, but roaches and maggots flowed out instead of her sultry voice.

Josiah leaned his head back and shrieked. He walked across the dirt floor of the tent carrying a long-bladed knife in his hand. He stood in front of Derek using the tip of the blade to lift Derek's head. Josiah grabbed his hair yanking his head back. "You didn't really think death would keep me from ruining your life, did you?"

Derek's eyes widened. He opened his mouth to scream just as Josiah dragged the blade across his throat.

"Christ!" Derek yelled as he shot up in bed. His hands covered his throat and applied pressure. Realizing there was no blood, he swung his legs off the side of the bed. His hands continued to shake as his breathing returned to normal. Grabbing his phone off the nightstand, he punched in Lizzy's number but stopped short of placing the call, thinking he would look like an ass.

"It was a fucking nightmare. That's it. Nothing more. Josiah is dead." He blew out his breath through his mouth. Inhaling through his nose. Repeating the process over and over until he got himself under control. He glanced at the clock on the nightstand—seven thirty a.m. "What the hell is happening to me?" he hung his head in his hands. The vision of Lizzy filled his mind. He shuddered at Josiah touching her. "He's dead Derek, let it go." He closed his eyes slowing his breathing, even more, pushing the vision of Josiah Craig out of his mind.

He stood and gave his legs a minute to steady his weight. In the bathroom, he splashed water on his face and brushed his teeth. After dressing, he packed his bag. He used his computer to check the mileage to Clarksdale, Mississippi—roughly a three-hour trip.

He started to pack up his computer but stopped. Something poked his brain. Needling him. He went back over his notes. He located each city where the abductions took place and disposal sites. He plotted them out on a map. He sat back and studied all the distances between the cities where one girl was dumped, and the other was picked up. Each pickup and drop off point had no more than three hours between them. Except for Clovis. There were seven hours between Garland, Texas and Clovis, New Mexico. Derek's brain kicked in. "Why is that?" he asked as he double checked the mileage. "Son of a bitch. That has to be it."

CHAPTER TWENTY-NINE

Early Monday morning

Derek stood at the trunk of his car. He searched his bags. "Mother-fucker. Where the hell is that damn ghost town flyer?" He remembered he left Duran and traveled through Vaughn. If he could remember the name of the small town, he could get a good idea of where that damn farmhouse was located. "Shit. I can't drive back now." He slammed the trunk and yelped. "I'm buying you a fucking bell," he said as he stomped to the driver's door.

"You are awfully jumpy today. What happened Derek?" Chrissy said from the passenger seat.

Derek's brow furrowed. "How the hell—oh never-fucking-mind," he said as he started the car. He glared at the girl next to him. His agitation subsided a bit. Her hair was shiny and lustrous. Her eyes were bright blue, and her skin color no longer ashen. The wound on her neck had almost sealed completely. A thin line denoted where the knife had slid through her skin, but only small trickles of blood ran down her neck.

Chrissy turned and frowned. "What? What's wrong?"

Derek's face softened. "Nothing is wrong, Chrissy. You look, beautiful," he said in a warm and caring tone. He pulled out of the hotel parking lot and drove to the freeway. Derek glanced over at the young girl. Chrissy beamed a bright smile at him. Her teeth were perfectly white. No roots or decay showed.

"I guess that means I must look—normal?"

"You look better than normal." His throat thickened. He was still to blame for her death in the first place. At least now, looking at her, he wouldn't be reminded of his stupid actions that put her in the ground.

"Stop doing that Derek." She shifted slightly in the seat. "You have to let yourself off the hook."

He entered US 63. Traffic was light for a Monday morning. He hoped when he hit US 79 and US 49, that the traffic would stay light. Derek reached over and turned on the radio. Rock music filled the car.

"Do you ever listen to anything else?"

Derek frowned. "Why? What music could be better than classic rock?"

"Soul music."

He grinned as he searched the satellite radio for a soul channel. "How's that?"

Chrissy smiled. "I like that." She hummed along to a Bill Wither's tune. "My momma loved soul music. She used to dance around the house while she was cleaning." She glanced down at her hands. The cracked and bloody fingers were now gone. She had tried to dig her way out of the box that Josiah kept her in as the carnival traveled around. She smiled at how pretty her long fingers looked now.

"What are you thinking Chrissy?" Derek asked.

"Did your team find the box?"

His forehead wrinkled. "The box?"

"You know Josiah had to keep all the girls hidden from the other carnies."

Derek's shoulders sagged as the memory flooded his mind.

"I remember when he put me in that box. I barely fit. I had to lay on my side with my knees drawn up to my chest. When he opened it up that first night, I remember gulping in the fresh air. The sides had small holes. Allowing a little air to come in, enough to keep you alive, but it was stale air." She paused. "The box smelled like pee, too."

The agents that searched the tent after the incident had relayed the information about the box. One of them had come to the hospital and filled Derek in on what had been recovered from the carnival. Derek had blocked that out until now. "I didn't see it, but I was told about it."

Chrissy sighed. "I hummed all these songs my momma used to sing around the house. It was the only thing that kept me from going crazy." She smiled at him. "Thank you for changing the channel."

He nodded but remained quiet.

"Where we headed?" Chrissy's head bobbed up and down to the beat of the music.

Derek couldn't help but grin. She looked so peaceful and happy. Something he longed for. Peacefulness. "Clarksdale Mississippi."

"Is this where the first girl was found?"

"Yes."

"Do you have any other information?"

It dawned on Derek that he hadn't heard from Agent Marcum yet.

He cocked his head to the side as he glanced at the dashboard clock. "No. Not yet. I'm expecting a phone call soon, though." Derek found himself swaying to the music as he drove. He tried not to smile, but he remembered his own mother occasionally dancing around the kitchen. Except she liked country music. He never liked that kind of music, but he loved watching his mom.

"What are you smiling about?" Chrissy asked.

The sunlight filtered through the window and made the blue of her eyes sparkle. Derek almost ran off the road looking at her. He recovered and slid back into his lane. This time he kept his eyes on the road. "My mom liked to dance around the kitchen. She loves country music." He shook his head. "I really hate country music. I think that is the one thing I am dreading most when I get to Tennessee."

"Oh, my Granny loved country music. She had that back disease. You know, makes you all hunched over...I can't remember what it is called."

"Scoliosis?"

"Yeah, that's it. She ended up in a wheelchair shortly before she died. She still loved her music though. She would knit and sing day in and day out." Chrissy smiled at the memory.

Derek's thoughts shifted to that summer in Tennessee.

Chrissy glanced over at Derek. The atmosphere now heavy and suffocating. She turned towards him. "Derek, tell me what's in your head."

He maneuvered in and out of the sparse traffic. His fingers gripped the steering wheel. So tight he had to shake them out to relieve the cramping. His chest tightened pulling his shoulders into a hunched position. He fought the urge to shut the memory down, but he couldn't stop it from bubbling over. His mind was flooded with the events of the horrible day.

CHAPTER THIRTY

"I was fifteen. We had been in Tennessee for two years. I'm pretty sure it was my second summer there." He swallowed hard. His lips pressed together. "My father worked a bunch. He and my mother, both. My brother and sister were each a few years older than me. They had their own friends. It happened one evening. A fog had rolled in blanketing the valley where our house was located. We lived on a back road, nestled between the mountains."

Derek pushed the hot air out of his lungs. "Mom and Dad were out with friends. They had said they wouldn't be home until late. My brother and sister were spending the night with friends. I was bored." He pulled over into the slower traffic lane and set the cruise control.

"I had my driving permit, and I had this old truck that my dad and I had rebuilt. We had gotten it running the day before, and I wanted to test it out." A heaviness filled his chest. He had to take several short breaths. His chest was so tight, he couldn't fill his lungs completely. He wiped the bead of sweat from his upper lip.

"I was so excited when that truck started up. It was rough. Had a lot of dents and chipped paint. But it was mine. Built it from nothing. Me and my dad. I remember that being one of my greatest accomplishments." He passed a small car. "I figured I could take it out, for a quick spin. The road we lived off had miles in either direction before you came across another house or business. I was just going to go up a few miles, turn around. Go the other direction and then come home.

"I backed it out of the barn and headed up the road. I drove a few miles then turned around and headed back the other way. The fog had grown ten times thicker than when I had pulled out of my driveway. The road winded around the base of a mountain. It had some steep curves, and most of them were blind."

Derek lifted his forearm wiping his sweaty brow. "Are you hot?" he asked glancing over at Chrissy as he turned the AC down. Holding the steering wheel with his left hand, he used his right to fidget with his watch. The tremors started in his fingertips before engulfing his body. "I didn't see her. I wasn't going fast. I wasn't even driving the speed limit, I promise." Derek exhaled sharply.

Chrissy nodded. Silently reassuring him to continue.

"I came around this bend. It was sharp, and it curved to the right, then took an immediate left. It was the windiest part of the road. She was in the middle of the lane. The fog was so heavy I didn't see her." He blinked hoping to clear the wetness from his eyes.

"Even though I wasn't going fast, the impact knocked her onto the shoulder. I pulled to a stop on the edge of the lane. Jumped out and ran to her. I had never seen a dead body before. But there was no mistake she was dead. Her eyes were open, and her neck had been broken. You could tell. It hung to the side at a very awkward angle."

He blew out a breath. "My hands were shaking so bad. I reached out and touched her arm. Kind of pushed her to make sure she was dead. I didn't know what to do."

Derek pulled over to the side of the freeway. He maneuvered as far off the highway as he could by pulling onto the grass, away from passing traffic. His entire body trembled. He stared at his hands. "When I touched her, I got her blood on me. She must have had a cut somewhere on her arm. I don't know. I remember staring at her blood. I don't know how long I stood over her. Just staring at her. Maybe a few moments. Maybe longer, but I was about to get into my truck, and I saw this watch on her wrist."

He twisted the watch. "I still don't know why I took it. I didn't do it to rob her. I think I wanted to make sure I never forgot what I had done. I slipped it off her wrist, and I put it in my pocket. I jumped back into my truck and sped home. I got the hose out and washed my truck. It had so many dents and dings in the bumper and front grill that no one ever saw the damage."

Derek used the palm of his hand to wipe his eyes. "I never said a word to anyone about that night. I didn't know her name or where she was from." The salty tears stung his eyes. They flowed over streaking his face. "I listened to the news every day. Finally, they had a report of a young runaway that had been hit on the road. The news said it looked like an accident. The authorities didn't even know if the person who hit her knew they had hit a person. The news reports also mentioned how bad the fog had been for days, and it was assumed that the person who hit her probably thought they hit a deer or something.

"They gave her name and where she was from. Sheila Raven. She had run away from her home outside Nashville." Derek's throat ache from the swelling lumps. His airway felt as if it was the size of a straw. He sucked in air and blew it out through thin lips. "I never told anyone, I couldn't do it. I hated myself. I hated myself for being a coward and leaving her on the road alone. I cried myself to sleep every night." The tears ran down his cheek. Gripping the top of the steering wheel, he rested his head against his hands. "I didn't mean to hit her. I was a stupid kid. Then I was so scared I would go to jail, and all I could see was my family hating me."

The car rattled as eighteen-wheelers zoomed past. Derek sobbed. "I'm so sorry. I asked her to forgive me every day for months. Then one day, I promised her I would never let anyone who hurt someone get away with it. I didn't know how I was going to do that, I just knew I was going to spend my life making sure people like me didn't get away with hurting others.

"That following summer, I got my driver's license, and I drove that truck all the way through college. It finally died, and I buried Sheila that day." He sat up and wiped his face. He turned towards Chrissy. Her face was soft. Her blue eyes were moist as tears dripped off her chin.

"When did you start wearing her watch?"

"The day the truck died." He spun the watch on his wrist. Sliding it up and down. "I had to get it fixed. I wore it broken for a few days. Then I took it to this old guy who was known for fixing watches and clocks." I asked him to rebuild it. Make it at least water resistant if he could. He couldn't do that, but he sent it off to a place that did it. I rarely take it off now."

"You have to forgive yourself. All the work you have done since then is atonement enough, Derek."

He leaned his head back against the seat. "I want to. I want to let her go. I don't know how."

"I think you do. And you will be able to do it when you're ready."

Derek pulled back onto the road. He increased his speed before he merged into traffic. A mileage sign showed sixty-five miles to Clarksdale. With every mile, Derek sealed up the memory of Sheila. He hoped that one day he would be able to let her go, and forgive himself.

CHAPTER THIRTY-ONE

Mid-morning Monday

Derek took the first exit leading to downtown Clarksdale. Chrissy left the vehicle several miles back. He steered his car towards a gas station. Needing to fill up and figure out where he was going next. As he pumped gas, he scanned the area. He wondered if after this case if he would ever look at gas stations and truck stops the same way again. He replaced the nozzle when his phone rang.

"This is Derek."

"Hey, man. Sorry, it took me so long to call you today. I had to finish up some work on another case," Agent Marcum said.

"Oh, that's fine Kyle. I understand. You have an actual job. Do you have anything on Liza Parks?"

"Not much. She was an only child. She was abducted from the side of the road in Greenwood Mississippi. Reports said her car had broken down right after she left her workplace."

"Where did she work?" Derek asked.

"She worked at a Dairy Queen next to a truck stop. Derek, this is one of the saddest cases I've ever researched. After she was found murdered, her father became an alcoholic. It was a slow descent into the disease, too. I have several reports of him in fights..."

"Fights with who?"

"Anyone, everyone. He never hit his wife. But he took out his anger and sadness on everyone else. He was eventually fired from his job. I found a few articles from the local paper. The community tried to help him. He was killed in a car wreck. He was drunk, but the accident report said it appeared he intentionally ran off a local bridge in Greenwood. Ultimately, they said it was an accident."

Derek heard Kyle speak with someone. He wasn't sure, but it sounded as if someone wasn't too happy with Agent Marcum.

"Sorry about that, Agent."

"Look, if you need to let me go, I understand Kyle."

"No. Don't worry about it."

"What about where she was found? Anything on that?"

"No. She had been dumped near a wooded area, and some wild animals had gotten ahold of her. What was left was very little."

"That had to be another slap for the parents. To know she was ravaged by creatures." Derek sighed into the phone. "What about her mother? Is she still in Greenwood? You think I can talk to her?"

"No. That's another sad part of this story. Her mother suffered a stroke shortly after her husband died. Eventually, she went into a nursing home. She had Alzheimer's. The community took care of her. They took it upon themselves to make sure she was cared for. She died four years ago. A story about her death said that she called out for her daughter daily. She told anyone who would listen that her daughter was coming by to see her. No one ever told the woman her daughter was dead."

"Damn," Derek said.

"However, I got one name for you. One of the nurses that took care of Mrs. Parker is still alive. Her name is Lilly Spencer. She is in her seventies. And lives at a retirement center in Greenwood. She is healthy and very much in control of her faculties."

"No shit? That is great news. Text me her information. I can call her and see if I can speak with her."

"I just did. I'm still working on the truck companies. I got your email regarding your hunch. I think that's a good assumption. Do you have the address of the house outside Vaughn? The farmhouse?"

"Fuck no. I searched everywhere for it. I'm going to pull up the roads I drove and see if I can get satellite images maybe I can track it down that way."

"Okay. As soon as you get it, let me know. I can start searching for its owners. I looked up how far Clovis was to Vaughn; it's like three hours."

"Yeah, but the house is closer to Fort Sumner. I remember that trip was less than an hour. So that would make the farmhouse less than two hours from Clovis."

"That's true. I need a little more to go on."

"Thanks, Kyle. I'll hunt down the route I took tonight. I'll get you something soon. When you get settled in Arizona, I owe you dinner and several beers."

"I'll take you up on that. I've started looking up places to live. If you got any suggestions, I would love to hear them. I'm having a hard time finding something."

Derek smiled to himself. "I might be able to help with that. I just need to check on something first. Give me a few days, and I'll get back to you."

"Sounds good. I'll take any help I can get."

The line went dead without a word. He pocketed his phone and got back in his car. The ten minutes in the baking Mississippi heat had his clothes stuck to him. He cranked up the AC to full blast and pulled away from the gas pump. He parked in an empty spot in front of the store enjoying a few minutes of cool air. Checking the GPS Derek pulled up the best route to get to Greenwood. It was a straight shot down 49E from Clarksdale to Greenwood.

He went into the store to get a few snacks. Not really hungry but wanting something to munch on and something to drink, he picked way more stuff than he needed off the shelves. He didn't want to stop again until he rolled into Lilly's home. He stood in line behind a very large trucker who towered over Derek's six-four frame. He overheard Gigantica and the clerk discussing a massive wreck on 49E.

"Excuse me, where is the wreck?" Derek asked as he set his snacks on the counter.

The large man turned around and smiled. "Just north of the 442 junction. Both sides of the freeway are shut down. A tractor-trailer loaded with chemicals turned over. You going to Greenwood?"

Derek nodded. "Yeah," he said.

"Take 49W, you can cut right over on Highway 82 at Indianola. Takes you right to Greenwood."

"Thank you for the heads up." Derek paid for his items and left. Once in the car he double checked that route. "That's not the way I want to go," he said as he searched the map for an alternate way. Instead of driving to Indianola, he decided to cut across Highway 442. The accident was north of that junction. The route he chose was the next fastest way, and it avoided Moorhead. He didn't think his psyche could handle driving through the damn city again.

CHAPTER THIRTY-TWO

Derek followed Highway 49 out of Clarksdale. By the time he reached the 49E/49W junction the traffic had started to back up. He imagined his route would be heavily traveled because of the accident. He hoped that by taking the smaller state highway 442 that he would miss a lot of the traffic out of Indianola.

His mind drifted to Sheila. He hadn't said anything about that night out loud since it happened. He had to face what he did and forgive himself. But he didn't know how to do that. He twisted her watch, tapping the face. It was a constant reminder of the sin he committed. It reminded him to do the right thing, always.

Lost in his memories, he didn't hear his phone blaring through the speakers until the third ring. He smiled at the caller ID. "Hey, Mom. How's everyone doing?"

"Derek, where are you? I thought you would be here by now. Arizona to Tennessee doesn't take forty damn days."

"Calm down, Mom. I'm making the most of this trip. Doing a little sightseeing on the way."

His mother giggled into the phone. "I'm sorry. I can't wait to see you, that's all. It's been forever. Since you're too busy to come home these days. Everyone is so excited to see you. Your dad wants to know a few days before you plan on getting here. He's planning one of his cookout parties."

"Oh, Mom. I don't want a big party. I want to spend time with you guys, not the whole town."

"You know your Dad. He has it all planned out. The opening weekend of college football. Big party. Any reason to have Joey bring over the smoker and cook up an absurd amount of meat is his idea of a perfect day."

Derek sighed into the phone. Dad's college football parties were notorious. More arguments broke out over whose team was better. But if Derek was honest, he missed them. "I'm not sure when I'll get into town, but I'll have a better idea in a few days or so. I'll let you guys know."

"Betty Sue is excited to see you."

"No. No, absolutely not. You better not have led her to believe I'll take her out or go out on any kind of date." Derek's heart sped up. Betty Sue was the last person he wanted to spend time with. His mind scrounged for an excuse to not even show up.

"Now Derek, Betty is super sweet. She and her husband recently divorced. She has held up well."

"Held up well? What the heck Mom, you make her sound like a good used car."

"Oh, you know what I mean. She isn't fat. Maybe a little chubby. She has all those kids. Now don't go worrying the youngest one is seventeen."

Derek shook his head. His mother already had him married to Betty Sue. She probably had the venue picked out as well. "Mom, I'm seeing someone."

Silence. Nothing.

"Hello, Mom?"

"You didn't tell me that. When did you start seeing someone? Why haven't you told your father and me that? Who is she? What is her name..."

"Jesus Mom, breathe. It's someone I've known for a while. We're taking it slow. When I'm sure of where it's going, I'll introduce you."

"Well, you can still hang out with Betty. You don't have to marry her." She paused. "What's this girl's name?"

"Her name is Elizabeth. I call her Lizzy."

"Oh. I see."

"I'll tell you all about her when I arrive."

"I can't wait to see you, honey. I miss you."

"I miss you too, Mom. Tell Dad I'll have a better time frame of my arrival in a few days. I love you, Mom."

"Love you too. Drive safe baby."

His mother hung up, much to Derek's relief. He didn't want to use Lizzy as an escape girlfriend, but if he didn't say something, he and Betty would be picking out table settings by the time he left to come home.

The turnoff for Highway 442 was up ahead. His GPS barked out orders to stay to the left and take the next exit. As he hoped, traffic decreased dramatically. Derek was betting on a peaceful twenty-five-minute drive until he picked up 49E again.

Moorhead was a few miles south of him. For the rest of his life, if he never had to come back to this part of the world, he would die a happy man. He opened his soda and took a drink. It was early afternoon, and the sun beat down on the road. The extreme heat rising from the asphalt roadway gave the illusions of rippling waves. Derek wondered if he stopped for any length of time if his tires would melt on the hot surface.

He looked down for a moment then glanced back up to see a giant armadillo crossing the road. Derek swerved narrowly missing him. He didn't look in his side mirror before he swerved, relieved when there was no car in the lane. He let out a shaky breath and glanced in his re-view mirror to see if the creature had made it to his destination. He watched as the little guy scampered to safety.

Derek scanned the road keeping a look out for any more critters. He heard a noise from the back seat and assumed Chrissy was playing a trick on him. "Okay, Chrissy. Why are you in the back seat?" He quickly glanced over his shoulder. His brow wrinkled. Again the noise, this time louder.

The hair on his arms and nape stood on end. He hadn't felt unease since the first few visits with Chrissy. This wasn't Chrissy. He stepped on the gas pedal, not sure what or who he was trying to outrun. He shook off the unease and reached for a bag of candy. As he picked it up, a car honked at him as he drifted into the adjacent lane causing the candy to slip from his hand. Sliding off the seat and landing on the floor a few inches in front of it.

Derek assessed the traffic. He quickly reached over and grabbed the bag. As he came up something caught his eye from the back seat. He held the candy in his hand as he glanced in the mirror.

"Holy shit!" he screamed as Josiah Craig reached around the seat grabbing him by the throat. He felt the pressure of something around his neck. Whatever it was it yanked him back against the seat. He smelled the rotting flesh and gagged for air as what felt like a leather strap tightened around his neck.

"I can't believe you would drive by and not say hello Derek." Josiah Craig whispered in his ear.

Derek clawed at his neck. The car veered to the right. Overcompen-sating to keep from hitting a sign, he yanked the car to the left and ran over a small barricade before stopping abruptly in the middle of the grassy median.

When the car jerked to a halt, the pressure around his neck vanished as did the putrid smell. He pulled his gun from the glove box and jumped out of the car. He yanked open the back door. Empty. "Son of a bitch! Where the fuck did you go, Josiah?" He searched all around the vehicle. Traffic whizzed by him. No way he could have gotten away from him.

Derek sat on the front seat. His head hung low. "I'm looking for a dead guy." He pinched the bridge of his nose, sending a burning pain to the back of his head. The bones in his face felt as if they had exploded. Derek stood and screamed. "I hate you, you motherfucker!" He continued screaming at the top of his lungs kicking his tire at the same time.

"What the hell am I doing?" He yanked on his hair. He started to place his gun back in the glove box. Instead, he went to the trunk. He found his holster in his bag and clipped it on the side of his belt. Walking around his car, he didn't see any damage. He eased back into the seat and started the car. Relieved when the engine roared to life. Driving slowly through the grass, he entered the highway increasing his speed.

As his speed inched closer to sixty miles per hour, the car began to violently shake. The steering wheel bounced up and down. "Fuck me. This can't be happening." Derek slowed the vehicle. When his speed dropped under fifty, the car drove normal. The front end pulled slightly to the right, but it didn't seem too bad. However, if he continued to drive, he may do severe damage to his car, if he hadn't already.

He turned on his flashers and kept his speed steady at fifty miles per hour. A snail's pace compared to the rest of the traffic. He saw a sign for the town of Schlatter, Mississippi. The next sign showed lodging and gas was directly ahead. "Oh for Pete's sake, let there be a mechanic," he said exiting the freeway following the signs to the gas station.

Rolling up to the stop sign he could see a mechanic garage a few yards past the station. "Thank you, God." He drove towards the garage pulling in front of the building. He untucked his shirt as he exited the vehicle, covering his weapon.

CHAPTER THIRTY-THREE

Derek stepped into the small mechanic's shop. The cramped waiting area was empty. A TV on the wall played a baseball game. He glanced around hoping the empty room meant his car would be fixed quickly and get him on his way.

"Hey, how you doing?" a lanky man said as he came out of a doorway to the left of the waiting area. "What can I do for you?"

Derek held out his hand. Even with his long legs, the man stood at least two inches shorter. "I'm Derek. I ran off the road onto the median a few miles back. Swerved missing an animal. Now when I get above fifty miles per hour, my car shakes violently. You think you can take a look at it?" He glanced at his watch.

The guy wiped his hands on a rag before shaking Derek's hand. "I can take a look, sure." He opened a door that separated the waiting area from the mechanic bay. "Gerald, would you pull this car around for me and put it up on the lift?"

An older gray-haired man came in and held out his hand waiting for the keys. "Sure. I'll have it up in a jiff."

Derek handed over the keys. "Thank you."

"My name is Cory. Cory Thompson. I own this place," he said leaning against the office door frame.

Derek smiled. "Nice to meet you, Cory." He watched as Gerald lifted his vehicle. Once in the air, the man began his inspection.

"Where you headed?"

Derek peered at the man. "I'm on my way to see my family in Tennessee. I need to make a few stops for work before I headed north."

"Hopefully, it won't take us too long to get you back on the road. Let me go out and see what Gerald has come up with. See if we can get you on your way."

"I'd very much appreciate that." Derek smiled at the man as he walked out into the bay. He studied the pair as they stood under his car. He tried to gauge what the two men were discussing. He squinted as he watched them laugh and joke around. He kept glancing at his watch. "C'mon. Let's get the show on the road already."

Fifteen minutes later, Cory walked back into the waiting room. "Did you hit anything?"

Derek nodded. "Yeah. When I swerved to miss an armadillo, I ran over a small barricade on my way to the middle median area."

Cory motioned for him to follow him into his office. "Have a seat." He sat at his desk. He logged on to his computer and punched in some information. "The damage isn't too bad."

Derek sank into his chair. "Great. But why do I sense you're about to tell me some bad news?"

Cory chuckled. "I don't think it's going to be that bad, but it looks like you damaged the front axle and struts. That's where the shimmy and shaking were coming from as you sped up."

"Is this a major repair?"

"Cost-wise, not too bad. A few hundred dollars. Getting the part, a little more time-consuming."

"What does that mean?"

Cory clicked away on his computer. "I'm guessing from the pristine condition of that car, that you want Jag parts. It looks like it will take me at least two days to get them in. Once I get the parts, it's only a few hours to replace them."

Derek stood and moved towards the door. He could see his vehicle through the bay window. "Two days or more? What the hell am I supposed to do here for two days? Shit."

Cory sighed. "I know this ain't New York, but Schlatter isn't that bad of a place. We have a summer arts festival going on right now. People come from all over for it."

"Perfect. That means I probably can't get a hotel room. If I drive my car, what will happen?"

"You run the risk of seriously damaging it. Not to mention, you can end up in a nasty wreck if either of those parts breaks while you are driving."

Derek's shoulder hung. "This is awesome. Fucking awesome." He turned towards Cory. "Can I rent a car anywhere around here?"

Cory shook his head. "Not here. Probably in Greenwood. As for a place to stay, my sister-in-law runs the B&B here in town. I know she always keeps a room available, even when she is booked. Everything is within walking distance of her place. She's in the heart of downtown."

Derek looked back through the bay window. He watched as Gerald worked on another vehicle.

"Hello, Mr.?"

"Huh? I'm sorry. I need to get to Greenwood for an interview." Derek chuckled. "You know of anyone who will let a stranger borrow a car?" he asked as he plopped down in the chair.

"Is it that important? The interview. You can't do it over the phone?"

Derek had to watch how much information he gave. "I'm a writer. I've been working on a story, and I have a deadline. I need to interview someone in Greenwood."

Cory leaned back in his chair. "I got an old truck. I use it to get parts over in Greenwood. You could use it to go do your interview. When you come back, I'll drive you over to the B&B." He glanced at his watch. "How much time you think you need?"

Derek's jaw hung open. "Why would you let me use your truck? You don't know me."

"I'm a pretty good judge of character. It's barely noon now. I close this place between four and six. You think you can be back by four?"

"Absolutely I can." Derek stood. "I can leave you my credit card, so you know I'll be back."

"I have your sweet car. I'm not worried about you not coming back." Cory reached behind him for a set of keys. "Do you need anything out of your car?"

"Yeah, I'll grab my computer and suitcase. That way when I come back, I won't have to get into it again." Derek followed Cory into the bay. He waited for the lift to lower his car. Once down, he reached in and popped the trunk. He noticed Cory and Gerald talking to another gentleman who had pulled into the station. Derek quickly took his registration and any identifying paperwork from his glove box. He stuffed it into his computer bag then lifted his suitcase from the trunk.

He walked over to the three gentlemen. He nodded at the newcomer as he got back into his car. Derek turned towards Cory. "I really can't thank you enough. I don't think it will take more than two hours."

Cory handed him the keys. "Be back by four. That's all I ask. While you're gone, I'll get you a room over at Catherine's place. I'll also get your parts ordered and see if I can put a rush on them."

"I really appreciate this. Can I buy you dinner tonight for this?"

Cory shook his head. "My wife is making pot roast with mac and cheese." Cory licked his lips. "I have been thinking about that all day."

"I bet. What truck?" he asked glancing around.

Cory walked him over to a 2000 Ford F150. "This one. It might not look like much, but it will get you where you need to go."

"Hey, I'm not picky. I'm super thankful for the ride." He threw his bags in the back seat, then hopped behind the wheel. Derek rolled down the window. "I promise I'll be back before four p.m. Thank you, Cory."

"No worries. See you when you get back."

Derek waved as he drove out of the lot. He pulled up his destination on his phone and headed to Lilly Spencer's home.

CHAPTER THIRTY-FOUR

Monday afternoon

Parking in a visitor spot at the assisted living facility Derek exited the vehicle. In all the mess with his car, he forgot to call Lilly Spencer. He hoped this trip wasn't a wasted one by not arranging the meeting first. He opened the rear driver's side door of the extended cab and stuck his gun in the bottom of his suitcase. He walked past several residents sitting on the porch as he headed to the front desk. "Hi, I'm here to see Lilly Spencer."

"Does she know you are coming?"

"No. I'm hoping she can help me with a story I am writing."

"You're an author?" the nurse batted her eyes at Derek.

A grin filled his face. "I am. I'm hoping she can help with a case I'm looking into."

The nurse's eyes lit up. "Are you a true crime author? Oh, I love watching all those true crime shows."

Derek nodded. "You could say that. Do you think I could speak with her?"

The nurse walked around the desk and nodded for him to walk with her. "I think that Lilly would love to speak with you. She doesn't have much in the way of family here. A granddaughter comes to see her once a month, but she loves to talk and visit."

"This is a nice facility," Derek said.

"It is one of the best senior assisted living facilities in the United States. We have people who come from all over to live here. We have this wing and its sister wing just next door that has suites. Each resident has a very large living space with a small separate bedroom and full bath in their suite. All the meals are taken in the dining room, or occasionally a resident may want to eat in their room. Across the quad, we have a more hands-on living area. In that building, the apartments are smaller and have more medical assistant staff. That is also where our onsite hospice is located."

She led Derek down a wide hallway. Several of the doors to the suites were open. "Most of our residents have just finished lunch. We have afternoon activities getting ready to start. Lilly always goes to the garden after lunch. But she should still be in her room."

The young nurse stopped at a large door. "If I can help you with your story, I get off work at five p.m." She pulled a notepad and pen from her pocket. "Here is my number." She leaned into him and licked her lips. "You can call me, anytime." She winked at him as she handed the piece of paper to him.

"Thank you. I will definitely keep this." He smiled at her as she pushed the door open after knocking.

"Mrs. Spencer? You have a visitor."

Derek walked into a brightly lit suite. An arched window drew the eye to a view of the garden. A small courtyard with several benches sat on the other side of the glass. His eye was drawn to the elderly but beautiful woman sitting in front of the window.

"Shelly, who is this handsome young man?" Lilly said as she turned towards them.

"Lilly, this gentleman is an author. He wants your help with a case he is investigating."

"Oh my. Do come and sit down," Lilly said pointing to the open high back chair across from her.

The nurse walked towards the door. "If you need me, push the button, Lilly." Shelly smiled and nodded at Derek as she left the room.

Derek took the seat in front of Lilly. He was awestruck at the woman's beauty. Her skin was an alabaster color, and not a wrinkle lined her face. Her pale blue eyes were as round and big as saucers surrounded by long eyelashes. Lilly's hair was silver gray with streaks of shimmering highlights. She wore it in a loose bun with tiny curling tendrils framing her face.

"Mrs. Spencer, my name is Derek Reed. I'm investigating a cold case. I'm hoping you can shed some light on it and possibly close it after all these years."

Lilly smiled and sat back in her chair. "Please call me Lilly. Mrs. Spencer makes me sound like I'm a hundred years old. I'm only seventy-three."

"Well Lilly, you don't look a day over twenty."

"Ah heck, you're full of crap. But I'll take it. Now tell me what you think I can help you with."

"Do you remember when Liza Parker went missing?"

Lilly's eyes lit up. "Oh do I."

"Do you think you can tell me anything you remember about the case?" Derek reached into his back pocket and retrieved a notepad and pen.

"I was working here. Funny, I always said I would never live here when I got older. But this is one of the best retirement places. Anyway, I was working here. Liza's mother worked at a bakery in town. I saw her every morning on my way to work. That girl of hers was always doing what she wanted. I remember many conversations with Liza's mother about her." Lilly giggled at the memory.

"My understanding is that Liza was a good kid, maybe a little rebellious. Is that true?"

"Oh boy if that isn't the truth. She got good grades and volunteered here on weekends. She would play cards with the residents. Read to some of them. She was a good girl, just didn't like rules." She reached over and patted Derek's hand. "What teen has ever liked rules?"

He smirked. "I think none ever." He scribbled a few notes. "Tell me what you remember when she went missing."

"I can do a little better than that." Lilly stood and walked towards an armoire.

Derek watched the woman move with grace. She didn't move as if she was in her seventies. Lilly seemed to float across the floor. She opened the cabinet door and retrieved a decorative box. "Do you need help with that?" Derek asked.

"Oh, no. This isn't heavy." She came back to the chair in front of the window and set the box on the small table between her and her visitor. "Since I knew Liza's mother, I kept every newspaper article regarding her disappearance."

She handed a stack of articles to Derek. "They don't really have much information in them. Mostly about the family. If you look at the later ones, you will see how the mother and father fell to pieces over the next few years." She paused, looking at Derek. "It's a sad story. Liza's parents had such hope that she would be found alive. When her body was discovered, they began a slow downward spiral."

Derek skimmed the articles. The first few talked about Liza's disappearance. Interviews with the boyfriend, with the parents, even some of Liza's friends weighed in on her abduction. The news story on the finding of her body was front page material. He paid particular attention to the details, hoping he found one stray clue that would help guide him. He found nothing.

"Lilly, I understand that the father had an accident sometime after Liza's death. What do you know about that?"

Lilly sat back and folded her hands in her lap. "Liza's parents began to drift apart quite rapidly after their daughter was found. Marnie, that was Liza's mother, spent more time at the bakery than at home. I would stop by in the mornings, and she would allude to Frank's drinking." Lilly took a sip of water from a glass on a little table next to her. She rubbed her hands together. "Marnie said he was having a hard time with the murder. I never knew what to say, so I spent most of the time listening." Lilly kept her head down.

Derek smiled. "What are you not telling me, Lilly?"

"Am I that obvious?" she asked, looking up at him.

"Just a little."

She stared out the window. "I went to that bakery every day. I noticed Marnie had trouble remembering even the simplest orders. Everyone attributed her lack of concentration to the loss of her daughter. But I knew it was more than that. I worked here, after all."

"What was going on with the Parkers, Lilly?"

"Marnie exhibited signs of Alzheimer's early on. After Liza was found murdered, Frank planned everything to a tee. He got into fights, was always 'seen' drinking or buying alcohol. But it was all an act." Lilly stood and walked towards the window. "I love this view," she said as she pulled her light pink sweater a little tighter around her waist.

She stood silent for a few minutes before turning around and facing her guest. "Frank knew that Marnie was going to need care. He took out an outrageous life insurance policy. I can't tell you if it was before or after the disappearance of their daughter, but the whole drinking act came after."

"He wasn't an alcoholic, was he?"

"Not in the least. He was a broken-hearted man who lost his daughter and knew his wife was going to live what days she had left with no memory of anything or anyone."

Derek placed the newspaper clippings he was holding into the box. "He set it up to look like he was drinking heavily."

"Yes. He was broken. I don't think he could bear to watch his wife disintegrate in front of him. The life insurance provided everything the wife needed to pay for her care here. He staged the entire thing."

"So his accident wouldn't even be questioned. There may be speculation he killed himself, but with the alcohol, it would have looked like an accident." Derek sighed. "When did you know?"

"About two months after the daughter was found dead. I promised him I wouldn't say anything. I cared for Marnie when she came here. Which wasn't too long after her husband died. She had a stroke, and that exacerbated her condition. I think his death was the final straw in her sanity."

"You never said anything about this to anyone?"

"No. I kept his secret. I cared for Marnie because she needed someone. I made sure everything she needed was here, in this facility. When she died, I felt like I had lost my sister." She sighed. "When I found out he made me a beneficiary when Marnie died," she shook her head, "I had no idea he did that either. I was so surprised."

"Did anyone ever find out about you being the beneficiary?"

"No. Frank had set it up for a lawyer to contact me and keep it confidential. I made everyone think I had a rich uncle who died."

Derek walked to the window. He took Lilly's hand in his. "You're a good woman, Lilly."

"You aren't a reporter, are you?"

Derek shook his head. "No. I'm an FBI agent. I'm on vacation, and I happened to stumble on this case. No one knows I'm hunting down Liza's killer. If I can get enough evidence, I can take it to my boss and hopefully get the go-ahead to investigate it properly."

"It seems I have another secret to keep." She patted his hands. "I won't tell anyone. Do you have anything yet?"

"No. I don't. I'm chasing a thirty-year-old killer."

She smiled at him. "If anything in that box will help you, you are welcome to take it with you."

"Thank you for the offer. I don't think anything in there will help with this case." Derek turned to leave but was stopped when Lilly touched his arm.

"I have a picture of Liza when she worked here. Would you like to see that?"

Derek's ears perked up. "Yes, I would."

Lilly again walked to the armoire. She searched through a drawer and came back to the window where Derek stood. "Here. This was taken not too long before she was abducted." She held out the photo.

Derek smiled at the two. Liza was a young, vibrant, beautiful girl. Her smile was infectious. She had her arm draped over Lilly's shoulder, and her hands made some sort of silly gesture. "May I keep this?"

"You sure can. I have several pictures of us.

Derek placed the photo in his back pocket. He took Lilly's hands in his. "You were a good friend to the Parkers. They were lucky to have you."

"I was the lucky one. Will you promise me, if you find out who killed Liza, will you let me know?"

"I will. If you think of anything that might help me, will you call me?" he handed her a business card. "Please call me any time if I can help you. If you think of anything, please call."

"I will, Agent Reed." Lilly smiled at him and watched him leave her room. She turned back to the window and gazed out at the small rose garden she had planted, all those years ago, when her friend died. She wiped her cheeks and smiled at how beautiful the pink roses looked this time of year.

CHAPTER THIRTY-FIVE

Derek drove into the parking lot of Cory's garage. He hadn't gained any information that would help him find Liza and the other girl's killer, but he was reminded of the goodness that still lingered in this world. He hoped that one day he had a friend like Lilly in his life. One that he could count on. As he parked in the earlier vacated spot, Cory came out to meet him.

"That didn't take you long," Cory said.

"Not at all." Derek held out the keys to the truck. "I can't thank you enough." He shut the rear door of the truck after grabbing his bags. "Do you have my car fixed?" He wiggled his eyebrows at him.

Cory laughed. "You're funny, aren't you?" He led them into the office of the small station. "I did order the parts. I got my guy in Greenwood putting the screws to his supplier. I'm hoping he can work some magic and get them here fast. But it's looking like it will be at least two maybe three days."

Derek leaned his head back and grunted. "Thanks for trying. Does your sister have a room I can stay in for the next few days?"

"She does. If you wanted, you could come to my house, have dinner with my family and me and then I'll take you to the B&B."

"Oh, I couldn't impose like that."

Cory waved his hand. "No imposition at all. Plus, my sister-in-law needs the few extra hours to get the room ready."

"Well then, looks like you have a dinner guest. You sure your family won't mind?"

Cory's brow wrinkled. "Not at all. My wife always makes enough food for a small army. It's just our two kids and us." He stood and moved towards the work bay area. "I need to finish up a few things here, and then we will go. You can wait in here."

"Thanks. Holler at me when you're ready." Derek pulled out his phone and checked his email. Nothing yet from either Jerry or Agent Marcum. He scanned through emails and text messages. "Oh, crap." Derek phoned his mother.

"Honey, are you on your way here?"

"No Mom. I had to stop in a little town in Mississippi. I'm having some car trouble. It may be two or three days before I get on the road again."

"Oh, Derek. Are you okay?"

"Yes, Mother. I'm fine. I need a few parts replaced, but it will take a couple of days to get them. I'll call you as soon as I'm back on the road."

"Alright. I'll let your dad know. He is going to be disappointed. He is so excited you're coming home. Drive safe. Let us know when you start this way."

"I love you, Mom." He hung up before she could respond, afraid she may ask more questions than he wanted to answer. Derek noticed a photo on the wall. He moved to it and stared at it. It was Cory, but he was very young. Maybe eighteen, maybe nineteen. He was perched on the side of a large tractor as he worked under the open hood. Turning his head when he heard the door from the mechanic bay open, he squinted at Cory. "Is that you?" he asked pointing to the photo.

"Yeah. That was on my grandfather's farm. That's where I learned to be a mechanic. I traded in farm equipment for cars. Much easier to work on. Hey, I'm all finished here. You ready to go eat some pot roast?" Cory asked as he grabbed a set of keys from his desk drawer.

"You sure I won't be a bother? I can hang out somewhere near the B&B until she's ready for me."

"Nah, c'mon. Let's get out of here."

Derek followed Cory out to a much nicer Ford F150 and threw his bags into the back seat. He climbed up into the front cab and buckled his seat belt. The truck was hot, and he was grateful when Cory set the AC on full blast. "This is one hot August."

"I think this has been the hottest summer in a long time. I can't wait for fall. Hell, I'll take brutal cold over this. At least I can bundle up with a lot of layers."

"I live in Arizona. I'm used to the heat without the humidity. This, though, is sweltering. I prefer a colder climate myself."

Cory drove off the lot and entered traffic. "I live about ten minutes away. On the other side of town. Schlatter is actually part of the Greenwood micropolitan area. With Greenwood twenty minutes up the road, you get the best of both worlds. A small town with big city amenities when you want them."

Derek watched the countryside pass by. The luscious greenery was such a stark contrast to the desert areas of Arizona. "This area is beautiful. So green compared to where I'm from."

"How long you been in Arizona?" Cory turned down a two-lane county road.

"About ten years."

"I guess being a reporter you travel around a bunch, huh?"

Derek nodded. "Yeah. I do. But I'm not a reporter."

"Oh. What do you write?" Cory pulled into the driveway of a two-story modest house. A golden lab came bounding up to the side of the truck.

"All kinds of stuff, really. Sometimes human interests. Sometimes I cover crimes or court cases. Almost anything." Derek exited the vehicle and left his bags in the truck. He walked around the side as a dog ran up to him and gave him the sniff over.

"That's Goldie. She's harmless."

Two kids came running down the front porch steps. "Daddy!" A little blonde girl screamed leaping into Cory's arms.

"Hey, Babydoll. How was your day?" he kissed her and set her back down. "Hey buddy," he said as he hugged his son. "What did you do today?"

"Hung out with Billy. I'm spending the night tonight and tomorrow. We're going camping."

Cory turned towards Derek. "This is Kayla, my daughter. And this is Bobby, my son. He's twelve and Kayla is five."

Derek nodded at both. "Hello. My name is Derek. Nice to meet you guys."

"Who are you and why are you with my daddy?" Kayla asked.

"Kayla, that isn't very polite," Cory said as he lifted her chin to look at him.

She shrugged. "You said not to bring strangers home. Why is he with you? Do you know him?"

Cory motioned for Derek to follow him. "Kids. You got any?"

Derek smiled. "Nope. Never really wanted kids."

Kayla's brow wrinkled, and she frowned at the stranger. "What's wrong with kids? Don't you like us?"

"Kayla." A young woman said as she walked from the kitchen to the front door. "That is no way to speak to a guest in our house."

She pouted. "I was just asking if he liked kids."

Bobby rolled his eyes at his little sister. "Kayla you're a dork."

"Bobby." Cory frowned at his son. "Don't call your sister names."

"I'm sorry."

"Why don't you two go upstairs until dinner is served. Bobby, make sure you got all your stuff packed."

"Yes, Sir. C'mon, Short Stuff." He yanked his sister by her shirt and dragged her towards the stairs.

"I may be short now, but I won't stay like this forever," Kayla said.

Cory watched his kids run up the stairs. "Derek, this is my wife, Candace."

Derek held out his hand. "Thank you for the invite to dinner. It smells wonderful."

"No problem. Cory said you had an accident. My sister will have the room ready in an hour or so. You can eat, then Cory will drive you over. You'll love it. Her B&B is right in the middle of downtown. Lots to do."

"That's what Cory said. I'm glad to have a place for the next few nights."

They all went into the kitchen. It was a large open area. An eat-in nook set off to the side. The table looked as if it could accommodate six or more people. A long bar ran along one of the walls, with six stools. Derek glanced around impressed with the high-end appliances.

Cory motioned for Derek to sit at the bar. "Can I get you something to drink?" he wrapped his arms around his wife's waist and gave her a hug and kiss. "I missed you."

She swatted him. "I missed you too."

Derek smiled at her obvious embarrassment from the overt affection her husband showered on her. He watched their interaction. Candace smiled and giggled at her husband, then looked away tending to the meal. It was hard not to like these two.

Cory opened the fridge. "What do you want to drink?" he asked Derek as he pulled out a bottle of water.

"I'll take one of those."

Cory handed it to his guest and took another one from the fridge. "Baby, what do I need to do?"

"Go ahead and set the table. I'll put the meat and fixings on a platter. We can serve ourselves." She pulled a large roaster pan out of the oven.

Derek lifted his head and sniffed the air. "Wow. That smells fantastic."

Candace turned around. The corners of her mouth lifted in a sincere smile. "Thank you. I hope it tastes as good as it smells."

Cory finished putting the last of the plates on the table. "You're cooking is always good."

Kayla ran into the kitchen and tugged on Derek's shirt. She held out her wrist.

Derek looked down at the young girl. "What am I supposed to be looking at?"

She pushed her wrist closer to him. "My charm bracelet. My mommy and daddy gave me a new charm for my birthday."

Derek quickly glanced at the piece of jewelry before turning back to the bar. "Very pretty."

She pointed to the bracelet. "This is my new charm."

Derek glanced again at her wrist. "That looks very nice." He smiled at the young girl.

"Kayla, take off your bracelet. You know you aren't supposed to wear it unless we're going somewhere special."

"Okay. I wanted to show it to Daddy's friend." She turned to go upstairs.

"Hurry up and grab your brother, it's time for dinner," Candace yelled out.

Within a few moments, clomps of feet barreled down the stairs. Cory carried the platter to the table and nodded at Derek. "Have a seat."

Doing as he was instructed, he sat at the table. The young girl sat across from him next to her brother. The parents took seats at opposite ends of the table. Derek watched as they took a silent moment before saying a quick grace.

"Lift your plates, kids." Cory put a nice helping of meat, potatoes, mac and cheese, and vegetables on each kid's plate. He then motioned for Derek to lift his plate and filled it as well.

"Thanks," Derek said. He took a bite of the pot roast, groaning as the meat melted in his mouth. The edges were caramelized, while the center was moist and juicy. Each chew of the beef erupted in pure bliss in his mouth, overriding any pain brought on by his injuries. "This is fabulous, Candace."

"Thank you. I'm glad you like it."

"What do you do?" asked Bobby.

"I'm a writer." Derek took a sip of his water.

"Do you write scary stories?" Bobby took a gulp of his milk. Then shoveled in several bites of his dinner.

"Bobby quit stuffing your mouth with food. You're going to choke," said Candace.

"I got to hurry. Billy and his dad are going to come pick me up."

"You can take the time to eat dinner." Cory reached over and rubbed the kid's head.

"Okay." Bobby ate his next bite exaggerating each chew of the food.

"You're a funny guy." Cory winked at his son.

The rest of the evening conversation revolved around what the kids had planned for the last few weeks of the summer. Derek enjoyed listening to the conversations and remembered his own childhood dinners. The scene is reminiscent of the best times he and his family spent together.

CHAPTER THIRTY-SIX

Monday evening

Derek's eyes widened as Cory drove into the circular driveway of his sister-in-law's bed and breakfast. "This place is beautiful."

"It really is. A few blocks in either direction you will find bars and restaurants. Outdoor cafes, and my wife's favorite—shopping."

Derek exited the vehicle and grabbed his bags. "I really appreciate all your help today. And thanks for finding me a place to stay." He glanced around at the property. Even though it was so close to the central plaza of downtown, it was nestled back in a thicket of tall oak trees.

Several rose bushes were in bloom and seemed to be strategically placed around the side of the house. The house was painted a pristine white with crimson red trim and shutters. The front porch was wide with five steps leading up to what looked like a wraparound porch. Potted flowering plants lined each step. Several ceiling fans were placed at alternating intervals down the length of the porch, between a line of rocking chairs. Derek figured a lot of glasses of iced tea were sipped under those fans.

"Listen, I have been stuck a time or two somewhere with no one I knew around. I like giving back to others. Kind of my way of paying for all those sins I committed as a young kid."

Derek laughed. "I don't want to do penance for my sins as a young kid. I'm hoping all those sins will be forgotten."

Cory squeezed Derek's shoulder. "Don't we all, buddy."

As they reached the top step, the front door flew open. "Where's my sister?"

"She's at home with the kids." He glanced at his watch. "Actually, by now it's just Kayla. Bobby is on a two-night camping trip."

"Oh yes, I forgot he had those plans. I don't know how I could either, he must have said, like a hundred times this week, that he and Billy were going camping. Said they were going to hunt for Big Foot."

"As long as they don't catch him and try to bring him home, I don't care what they hunt." Cory motioned to Derek. "Catherine, this is Derek Reed. He is stuck here until I can get his car running again."

Derek held out his hand. "I can't thank you enough for finding a spot for me." The woman was striking. She had long black hair and green eyes. Her slender figure was outlined under a white tank she wore beneath a sheer top. She took his hand in a firm handshake. Nothing but muscle under her slim frame.

She waved them in and closed the door behind them. "Really no problem at all. I had someone check out a day early, so I made up that room. It's at the top of the stairs. Has its own bathroom so you won't have to share."

Derek admired the masculine living space. Dark mahogany wood trimmed all the doorways and windows. The floors were a slightly darker shade. In spite of the dark wood, Catherine had placed enough pops of color around to keep the space from closing in. "This is a fabulous house. Is this all the original woodwork?" He reached out and dragged hand along the rich wood banister held in place by intricately carved wooden spindles.

She led them into the kitchen. "Yes, it is. I considered changing it so it wouldn't be so dark, but I just lightened the paint on the walls instead. I love that dark wood."

"It is gorgeous. You were smart to do that, lighten with paint instead. I wouldn't change anything about this wood." Derek watched as Cory lifted the lid off a pot on the stove. The smell of cinnamon and cloves filled the room.

"Umm, I hope this isn't what you are planning on feeding your guests Catherine. This would not get repeat customers."

"Haha, very funny." She walked over and turned the heat on low and removed the lid. "This makes the whole house smell good. I'll leave it simmering for a few hours. When everyone begins to trickle into the house from their days out, they will be greeted by this wonderful aroma." She turned and smiled at her new guest. "So much better than those air fresheners in a can," she said as she sat at the table.

"It smells wonderful, Catherine," Derek said.

"Did you feed him already?" She asked Cory.

"What is he a dog?" He responded as he bit into a piece of the freshly baked bread from the counter. "Yes, we fed him. Now he has to go for a walk."

Derek chuckled at the exchange. "I'm not hungry. But thank you for asking." He turned and faced Cory. "Thanks again for all this. I'll hang out either here or in town until you call me about my car."

"No problem." Cory bent over and kissed Catherine. He started towards the front door. "Listen, Derek. I might be going fishing early tomorrow afternoon. You want to come if I go?"

Derek shrugged. "I haven't been fishing for a while. I'd love to go. Do you have a time in mind?"

He nodded as he pulled the front door open. "I'm leaning towards, one or two p.m."

"Sounds good to me. I'll be here if you want to go."

"Perfect. Later Catherine," he said closing the door behind him.

Derek turned towards his host. "Where is my room? And do you want my credit card now?"

She shook her head. "I'll get all that from you tomorrow." She removed a key from her front pocket and handed it to him. "Your room is right at the top of the stairs. Number 2. You'll find a little card on the side table with the WIFI login. If you find you need anything, I'll be up until ten or eleven." She started towards a back room when she turned to him. "Derek, please make yourself at home. I have plenty to eat and nibble on in the refrigerator, as well as tons to drink."

"Thank you, Catherine," Derek said as he headed up the staircase. At the top, a small landing wrapped around leading to his room on the right. Unlocking the door, he entered and dropped his bags by the bed. He walked into the bathroom to a spacious area. A single pedestal sink with cabinets next to it lined one wall.

He spun around looking for the tub and shower. "Umm, okay." He almost missed the small opening cut out in the wall across from him. He poked his head in, and a wonderful sight greeted him. He stepped into a cavernous walk-in shower with two shower heads and a bench that ran along one wall. The way the heads were aligned, allowed someone to sit on the bench and relax in the water. "Oooh, nice. I'll be trying that out tonight," he said as he walked back into his room.

Derek checked to make sure his weapon was still at the bottom of his bag. A small desk sat on the opposite wall. He set his computer up and logged into his work email. "Fuck," he grumbled as he read the reminder from his boss to give him at least one or two names of some agents he wanted. "I don't care. Why can't you assign them to me?" he groaned.

"Crap," he said as he took the folder out of his computer bag. Derek glanced over the first person on the list. All of these people were more than qualified. He wasn't looking for that. He wanted to know what made each person tick. The first agent, Agent Charlie Jones, was from California and looked every bit the surfer.

Derek set him aside. The next one, Agent Felicia Rogers, was very attractive. He read through her bio. She was from Marquette, Michigan. "Don't be fooled by those pretty looks," he said reading her combat skill set. Proficient in martial arts she was also an amateur boxer. He scanned the area that asked for personal information like hobbies and special interests. "Ah, let's see who you really are, Agent Rogers." A broad smile crept across his face as he read her answer to the question, *what do you like to do in your spare time?* She had answered, 'I herd cats at the Furball Feline Rodeo.' "Oh yeah, you're a keeper." He chuckled as he marked the sheet and placed it to the side.

Derek had to choose seven agents overall. He now had two. He continued to skim the remaining files and had it narrowed down to six remaining agents to pick from. The two he knew he didn't want in the unit he set aside with red marks in the corner of their bios so he wouldn't look at them anymore. He was going to stop and email AD Fretz this one name but figured he could pick at least one more.

After reading their information for the tenth time, he closed his eyes and picked one. "Franklin Pillard. Now that's a name." He double checked the man's credentials. An agent for over seven years, prior to that he was in the military. Served four years in the Navy. Applied for the Academy upon leaving the service after one tour.

Derek liked that the man was an ammunitions specialist. He also liked that he spent some time in the fraud unit. Tracking down fraud involved a lot of research and compiling information from several outlets. Derek thought that would be a great asset to this cold case unit. He was about to close the folder and email his boss when something on one of the other agent's bios caught his eye.

"Holy shit. That can't be the same kid. How did I miss that?" He stared at the photo of the youngest agent in the group. Michael Flinch. "I'll be damned," he said as he read the kids history. A story he knew all too well. Michael Flinch's sister had been murdered when he was a senior in high school. Derek remembered the case. It was one of his first cases as a profiler.

He leaned back in his chair. That was one of the hardest cases he had as a profiler. A combination of it being his first, and a case about young teenage girls being raped and murdered. Something that never sits well with any law enforcement officer.

Derek remembered some serious mistakes he had made. He was able to correct many as the case progressed and ultimately helped lead authorities to the man responsible for the heinous murders. But not before three other girls had fallen victim. The correlation to Josiah Craig was glaring Derek in the face. Another reminder of mistakes he has made as a profiler.

Michael had been a young athlete and was just days away from signing with a college for a baseball scholarship. After the arrest of the killer, Derek had some follow up work he was doing with the families. The young kid had approached him at one of those meetings. Michael had promised he was going to apply for the FBI and not let another person get away with hurting someone else's sister.

Michael held true to his promise. He used that scholarship to pay for college. After graduating with honors from UC Berkley with a degree in Criminology and an associate degree in Psychology, he contacted Derek and asked for a letter of recommendation. Derek didn't hesitate. He set Agent Michael Flinch's paper with Felicia's and Franklin's, then emailed his boss. "That should buy me a few more days before I have to choose the remaining three agents."

Looking at his watch, he was surprised to see it was only eight thirty p.m. The combination of his injuries, long hours in his car, and chasing a thirty-year-old cold case made the days seem a lot longer. He undressed at the bed, leaving his dirty clothes on the floor. Walking naked into the bathroom he turned on the shower and checked his wounds in the mirror. The gash on his right side was healing nicely. The doctors had used absorbable sutures along with glue. They had explained this particular type of suture would keep the scarring to a minimum.

Derek ran his finger along the line. Still very tender but the pain that once erupted with every touch of fabric was now at a nominal amount. He studied his nose and cheek. Shifting his jaw around he still had an extreme amount of pain. He wasn't about to turn down the meal Candace had made, but as tender as the meat was, each bite had given him microbursts of pain.

A slight amount of swelling still surrounded his nose. But those who didn't know him, would never even notice. The doctors had warned that his nose would take the longest to heal. Any heavy activity would increase that healing time. They weren't lying.

Derek gingerly touched the bridge. He winced in pain which seemed to erupt and reverberate against the back of his skull. He squeezed his eyes shut causing starbursts to pulse. He had to brace himself against the sink. "Damn, that hurts."

Remembering the conversation with the doc, he probably should've left the bandages on his nose longer. Although it was straight, it was going to take that much more time to heal. He walked towards the shower stepping through the curved opening he checked the water. A digital readout allowed the temperature to be manually set and change the flow of water out of the showerhead. "Oh man, I need one of these." He giggled like a girl as the water pulsed out of the two shower heads. Before he immersed himself completely, he heard his door open.

"Hello?" Derek asked as he quickly walked to the bathroom doorway and peered into the room. Empty. He moved to the door and made sure it was locked. He started back to the shower when he grabbed his gun from his bag. Naked, he felt a little stupid, but after his last few days, he felt more secure with it in reach. He placed it on the small shelf outside the opening of the shower.

Stepping into steam, he sighed in extasy. The water pulsed over his back and shoulders. Turning his back to one showerhead, he used the keypad to angle the other one to pulse on his chest. After a few minutes, he reangled the shower to run over his head, careful to keep from directly hitting his face. He stayed in the 101-degree water for thirty minutes before reluctantly shutting it off.

With the towel wrapped around his waist, he walked back into his room. He sat on the bed and turned on the TV. Propping the pillows behind his back, he laid on top of the spread and turned on the evening news.

His eyes drifted shut. The drone of the newscaster enticed him into a peaceful doze. He was almost fully relaxed when a noise caught his attention. He shivered as goosebumps filled his arms. He glanced around the room. Empty. Just him and the TV newscaster. But his body said otherwise.

He reached over to the nightstand expecting his weapon to be at the ready. "What the hell," Derek whispered. Squinting as he looked around the room wondering where his gun was, he sighed. He remembered. "Shit." Glancing through the doorway across the room, there he saw it. Right where he left it, in the bathroom.

CHAPTER THIRTY-SEVEN

Derek swung his legs over the side of the bed. Despite his shivering, sweat beaded on his lip and forehead. His adrenaline spiked as he leapt from the bed and ran into the bathroom. Grabbing his weapon from the shelf, he removed it from its holster.

He tightened the towel around his waist as he put his back to the wall that separated him from the rest of his room. He blew out a sharp breath as he relaxed his shoulders. He stepped out from the wall and entered the bedroom area.

"I have a weapon. If you are hiding in this room, I suggest you come out now," he said aloud as he walked to a closet on the other side of the room. Before reaching the doorway, he positioned himself where he could look under the bed and keep the closet in his view.

"You need to show yourself, now." Derek stepped towards the closet and yanked open the door. Empty. He slowed his breathing and flicked on the light to make sure. He started to turn around when the hair on the back of his neck lifted. His breathing sped up as the weight of someone's stare bore a hole through his back. He closed his eyes and settled his nerves with slow breaths. Forcing his pulse to slow down.

He spun around, with his weapon at the ready. "What the hell?" he said to an empty room. "Quit fucking with me." He kept his weapon out in front of him as he moved around the bed. A noise came from the bathroom he aimed his gun at the doorway, at the same time Chrissy came from around the corner.

"Motherfucker." He gasped. "Can you stop showing up like that?"

Her brow wrinkled as she stared at the crazy half-naked man. "What the heck is wrong with you?"

"How long have you been here?"

"Ask yourself that question," Chrissy said.

The hand holding his weapon fell to his side as he ran his other hand through his hair. "I heard noises. Someone was in here." He glared at her. "Was it you? Were you fucking with me?"

"Yeah. I spend my days trying to figure out ways to fuck with you. Even though you think I'm a figment of your imagination." She sat in the desk chair. "Hmm, if you think about it like that, you're really fucking yourself. Man, you need a hobby."

Derek stomped to the other side of the bed. He yanked a pair of clean underwear and sweats from his bag. He stepped into the bathroom, quickly dressed, and returned to the room. He bent down, and grabbed his dirty clothes, placing them in a pile by the desk. "If it wasn't you, then I'm losing my friggin mind. Because I swear someone was in here," he said checking the pockets of his jeans.

He removed Margaret's ring from the front pocket and placed it next to his weapon on the little table. Removing his phone from one of the back pockets, he placed it next to the ring. He found the photo of young Liza and tossed it on the end of the bed. He sighed with exaggeration as he sat on the edge.

"Maybe so. But it wasn't me." Chrissy stared at him. "You haven't been chewing gum."

"What?" he asked with a scowl.

"Your love of gum. You aren't chewing it incessantly like you usually do."

"It hurts my jaw." He stared at Chrissy. The corners of his mouth twitched. Her wound had a slight trickle of blood. Other than that, she was perfect. She looked so real. He wanted to reach out and take her in a hug and tell her again how sorry he was.

"What is your problem?" she asked raising an eyebrow at him. "Why are you looking at me like that?"

"You look wonderful."

She beamed a radiant smile at him. "That's all you. I keep telling you that." Chrissy rolled the chair towards the bed and looked at the photo. "Who's this?" she pointed to the picture.

"That's Liza Parker. The first girl murdered."

"She's beautiful."

"She was." Derek pulled a t-shirt from his bag and found the tin box. He sat on the edge of the bed holding it in his hands. He picked up Margaret's ring and lifted the lid on the box. He dumped the contents and laid them out.

"What are you doing?" Chrissy asked.

"Something has been bugging me ever since I spoke with Julie Richard's parents." He found the photo the Richards had given him of their daughter Julie in his computer bag. He took Margaret's ring and placed it next to her photo. He placed Lisa's and Liza's pictures next to Margaret's.

He searched through the mementos from the tin box. He had a pink coral ring and a broken charm bracelet. "I know that Julie Richards wore a necklace that was never recovered." He slid her picture to the side. "I know this green ring is Margaret's." He pointed to the young girl's picture with the ring in it. "I have this coral ring, and I know it is Lisa's." He pointed to her picture. Her hand clearly showed the coral ring. He held up part of the charm bracelet. "This broken bracelet must be Liza's."

"Okay, but I still don't understand what is bothering you."

"A few things. First," he picked up Margaret's ring, "I think the killer left this at the grave site, but I haven't been able to figure out the reason." He peered over at Chrissy. "I do not think a ghost left this for me."

"You may never know the answer to that question. What else is bothering you?"

"Killers don't keep things randomly. If they're keeping trinkets, it's for a reason. It seems like he kept certain trinkets over others." He pointed at the collection on the bed. Derek twisted his watch on his wrist. "Okay, the remaining items in this box, aren't worth very much. I mean this coral ring, is not very valuable. The charms on this bracelet aren't that fancy, yet it looks like one was pried off at some point. I think that is how the bracelet got damaged." He pushed the pieces around the bed with the tip of his finger.

"He kept Julie's necklace. See that's just it. At some point, the killer took Margaret's ring, Julie's necklace, and a charm from Liza's bracelet. Those were important to him. They had meaning. But something doesn't seem right."

"What doesn't seem right? He took the items, big deal."

"No." Derek paced around. He tapped the face of his watch. "I'm missing something." He continued to pace. He stopped. "I found the box in the floorboards of the house. He took these items out then hid the box. Only these items were important to him. He buried everything else."

Chrissy spun around in the chair. She pushed off from the side of the bed and rolled across the floor, then pushed off the desk and rolled back to the bed. She did that until Derek stopped her with his foot. "Uhh, sorry."

"That's annoying."

"Uhh, yeah. You're wound tight. I bet you're about to pop a gasket or something. You really should consider chewing through the pain."

He shook his head rolling his eyes. He concentrated on what he had. "Why were they important? I need that. Why did he leave Margaret's ring behind? I'd like to know that and what charm he took." He frowned as he walked the length of his room. "If I could understand why he left the box behind. That is what is bothering me most." He stopped pacing. "It's right in front of me."

Chrissy glanced up. "I don't know why you can't see it."

"See what?"

"The answer to why he left the box and took the items. They're connected, you know?"

He glared at her. "Enlighten me."

"You said killers keep things because they are valuable. Think about what makes them valuable."

Derek faced soured. "If I knew that, I would have my answer."

"Why did you keep the watch?"

"Huh?"

"You heard me. You aren't a serial killer; you kept the watch for another reason. I'm sure Sheila had other valuable items in her bag or on her person. But you didn't take those. You only took the watch. It held importance to you.

"Maybe even then you didn't understand why, but you took it none the less. Maybe you're thinking this killer kept these items because of the relationship to his victims. Or maybe to remind him of these particular victims. But what if it has nothing to do with any of those. Maybe he buried the box after taking these items, for a simpler reason." Chrissy spun around in the chair humming a tune.

Derek started to rebut what she said but stopped. He sat on the edge of the bed. "Holy shit."

She smiled at him. "You see it."

"He didn't need them anymore, and he only took the ones that had monetary value. He discarded everything else. That's it. I found the box because he buried it. He buried the killing, the girls, and everything else in the box. All of this," he waved his hand over the items on the bed, "no longer had meaning to him. It had served its purpose. It's almost as if he was finished and moving on."

Derek shook his head. He banged the palm of his hand on his forehead. "If I'm operating under the assumption the killer left Margaret's ring at her grave, then something made him keep the jewelry. Because Margaret's empty coffin was buried four years after her disappearance. If he kept her ring, why wouldn't he keep the other jewelry?"

"If he kept it, was it a sentimental reminder?" Chrissy asked.

Derek shrugged. "I have no idea. But if he left the ring at the grave, then he had to feel some kind of remorse. He had to know that Margaret's parents had a funeral with no body to bury. Maybe he left it so a piece of Margaret would be buried at the gravesite."

He went to his computer bag and quickly made a phone call. "Hey, Jeffrey, it's Derek Reed." He placed his phone on speaker.

"Hey Derek, do you have some news for me?"

"Not really, but I have a question. Did Margaret's funeral get picked up by local papers, or any other news agencies?"

"Yeah. All the local news channels covered it. I think it was even mentioned on one of the syndicated shows."

"Okay. That's all I needed. I really appreciate it."

"No problem. Call me if you find anything out."

"I will." Derek disconnected the call. He spun around on Chrissy. "The killer had to see the news. That's why he left the ring."

Chrissy smiled at the gleam in Derek's eyes. "Another clue."

Derek nodded. "Yeah. That makes sense. He buried the pictures of the dead girls. He was walking away from it. But for whatever reason, he held onto the more expensive jewelry. Maybe he wanted to make sure time had passed before he tried to sell them. Maybe he just wanted to keep them to give to someone else, but never did."

"And when he saw the news on Margaret, he wanted to do something nice." Chrissy frowned. "Do killers do that? Change their spots?"

"Killers have been known to stop killing. Change their lives. Never kill again. Actually, go on to lead normal lives. That wouldn't be unheard of." The excitement he felt vanished. He hung his head. "It's been right in front of me, staring me in the face. Why could I not see that? How could I have missed all that?"

"You're too close."

He laid back on the bed keeping his feet on the floor. "I'm an idiot."

"No, you aren't. Derek, you're too close and too focused. You need to take all the emotion out of it."

"What emotion? I don't have anything in this case, emotionally-wise."

"You do. You're bringing all the girls Josiah killed into this case. In some manner, you're even bringing Sheila into this case. At least for a bit, leave us out of it." Chrissy leaned over the bed and stared at one of the pictures. "Did you look at this picture of Liza Parker?"

"I glanced at it. Why?"

"She's wearing a charm bracelet."

Derek picked it up. Liza's arm draped across Lilly's shoulder. "Damn, she is. Well, at least I know for sure the broken charm bracelet is Liza's." He frowned at Chrissy. "Crap, if I had seen that, when I was with Lilly, I could've asked her then about the charm bracelet." He reached for his phone, about to call Lilly.

"I wouldn't do that."

He stopped. His brow wrinkled. "Why?"

She tapped her wrist.

He frowned at her, slow to register whatever she was trying to tell him. "Oh, crap." He looked at his watch. It was after eleven p.m. "Thanks." He dropped his phone on the table.

"I'm pretty sure Jeffrey stays up later than Lilly."

"I bet you're right." He cocked his head to the side. "You know the guy who is working on my car, his little girl showed me her charm bracelet tonight. I didn't really pay attention to it. But she had a few charms hanging off it. Why do you guys like them?"

"Why do you ask that?"

He shrugged. "Just curious. Maybe it will give me some more insight into why he took the one charm he did, but not the others. Maybe it will give me some insight into his victims. Hell, I don't know."

She nodded. "I think most little girls like charm bracelets. I had one. I know two of my friends had one. Whenever we got new charms, we showed them off to each other."

"That's exactly what the little girl did. She made sure I saw her charms. Why is that?"

"You are such a guy. Girl's love to show off their jewelry. I think we like the bracelets because they dangle. They clink and make noise when you wear them. They're girly."

He sniggered. "She even said that, the little girl. Wait." He picked up

Liza's photo and held it out in front of him. He angled his phone so that he could get a better picture of her wrist.

He snapped a photo and quickly looked at his phone. He zoomed in on the bracelet. He could make out the charms. He slid the photo around trying to find the best picture of the bracelet. The more he zoomed in, the fuzzier the picture got. He looked at the charms on the bed. "Okay, I can see a soccer ball, a dog, and a pineapple." He shook his head. "Why does anyone want a charm of a pineapple?" he shifted the picture around. "I can't really make out this last charm. The resolution is too fuzzy."

He paced. "Shit. I have to wait to call Lilly until tomorrow." He glanced up. Chrissy was gone. "You could have said goodnight, you know?" he said out loud. He placed everything into the box, including Margaret's ring. Closing it up, he placed it in his bag. He took the photos of Margaret, Liza, and Julie, and put those into his computer bag.

His mind raced. He crawled under the covers not bothering to undress and turned off the little light next to his bed. He laid on his back trying to put all of the pieces he had together. He still had so many puzzle pieces missing. His eyes grew heavier. He was so close. So very close to solving a thirty-year-old mystery.

CHAPTER THIRTY-EIGHT

Derek's head pounded. Thump, thump, thump. He tried to grab it, but his hands were tied. Bound tight by leather straps. "No. Let her go," he mumbled.

"Derek. When will you learn?" Josiah sneered as he slit the throat of the young girl.

"I hate you." Derek choked out the words.

"Then why do you let me live in your head?" Josiah walked casually towards him.

Derek started to gag from the stench. The smell of putrid rotting flesh engulfed him. He tasted bile. The caustic fluid burned his dry, parched throat. He opened his eyes to see Josiah's head covered in maggots. Blowflies buzzed around Derek hovering near his face. He shook his head blowing out long breaths to get them away from him. One landed on his cheek. He rubbed his face on his shoulder as best he could.

Josiah moved within inches of him. "Don't you like the way I look?"

Where Josiah's brain would've been, a thick soupy green and black mixture sloshed around. With every movement of Josiah's head, some of the nasty liquid splashed about. Derek flinched back when some of the sticky fluid splattered on his face. He gagged as the decaying bodily fluid dripped down his cheek.

"Oh, how rude of me," Josiah said as he reached a finger out and wiped the moisture from Derek's face. The flesh from the tip of the finger had rotted and receded back, exposing the bone. Maggots traveled up and down the bone, weaving their way into the layers of exposed flesh.

Derek drew back turning his head away as a maggot dropped on to his chest. He glanced down blowing trying to get the insect to fall off. He looked up to find Josiah inches from him. Josiah opened his mouth to laugh, and a worm crawled out.

The pounding erupted again. He reached for his head, this time his arms were free. "What the heck?" he groaned.

"Mr. Reed?"

He shook his head. It wasn't pounding, the door was. Derek jumped out of bed and stumbled to the door. He yanked it open to find Catherine standing ready to knock again.

"Are you alright?"

He fumbled with his words as he scratched his head. "Umm, yeah. Why?"

"You were yelling."

"Excuse me?" he asked in an uncertain tone.

"You were yelling. Well, screaming really."

He cringed, leaning against the edge of the door. "I'm sorry. Did you say I was screaming?"

"Yes."

"What was I saying?"

"A few things. First, you yelled, please stop. Then you screamed get it off me."

"I'm really sorry. I hope I didn't scare anyone. I must have had a bad dream."

She reached out and touched his arm. "You didn't. I was up here cleaning one of the rooms and heard you. Do you remember what you dreamt?"

He shook his head. He wasn't about to share it with her.

"I have pancakes, bacon, and potatoes from breakfast this morning under the heat lamp down in the kitchen. Come down and eat with me."

He nodded. "Give me ten minutes. I'll be down."

She headed down the stairs. "I'll make some fresh coffee."

Derek closed the door and went to the bathroom. He checked his clothes making sure he didn't have any bugs on him, brushed his teeth, and headed towards the kitchen.

He found Catherine setting the table with a large canister of coffee and two plates. Several bowls filled with various foods lay between the plates. "I'm really sorry about my screaming," he said taking a pancake off the platter in front of him.

"Don't apologize. I have had some bad dreams before. You sure you don't remember what you dreamt?" she asked as she heated some syrup in the microwave.

"Not really. Something with bugs."

"Have you had the same dream?" She smiled when he didn't answer, but barely nodded his head. "You know, my daddy used to say, dreams were our minds way of telling us something needs tending to."

"Your daddy said that, huh?"

"He sure did. You might want to consider it. Those nightmares will only get worse until you deal with what is haunting you. Pushing things down deep never solves anything." She reached up and tapped the side of her head. "Your mind will find other ways of dealing with whatever it is. That can sometimes mess you up even more."

"I have a tendency to shove stuff down deep."

She nodded her head. "Don't we all?"

They ate in silence for a few moments.

Derek took a long sip of his coffee. "This is good."

"I buy it from a retailer in Colorado. Won't buy any other brand."

"Maybe you will share it with me?" he winked at her.

"For a small fee of course."

"Tell me about Cory. He's a really nice guy."

She nodded. "He is a great guy. Cares about people. Genuinely cares for their well-being."

"Have you known him all your life?" Derek refilled his cup with coffee.

"Oh no. He met my sister years ago. Damn, I think maybe twenty-five years ago. When he moved here."

Derek shrugged. "I thought he was from here."

"No, he moved here from out west. I think west Texas or something. To be honest, it feels like he's from this area. He met my sister when she was nineteen. I think."

"Wow. I had no idea they've been together that long." His coffee mugged stopped shy of his lips. "They waited to have kids?"

"My sister had trouble getting pregnant. Took a while. They thought they could only have one kid. Then poof at forty-five she gets pregnant with Kayla. She can't have any more kids, though."

"I'm sorry about that."

"No need to be. They're perfectly happy with the two they have." Catherine filled their glasses of water. "Can I get you some juice?" she asked before she sat back down.

"No. I'm fine. Thank you." Derek savored the potatoes. "These are so good. You could package and sell them."

"I enjoy cooking for my guests, but I don't want to make a living at cooking."

"How long have you had this place?"

Catherine sat back and tilted her head to the side. "This house was my uncles. He died and left it to my mom and dad. When they died, me and Candace got it. She didn't want to sell, but she doesn't have any interest in the B&B. I keep most of the profits, but I set aside some for her. She owns half of the house, but not the business. If I ever sell, I only have to give her part of the house sale price. I would get to keep everything else."

"Do you think you will ever sell?"

She shook her head. "Nope. I love it here, and I make a great living running this place."

One of the guests walked in and asked Catherine for help with something. She excused herself and left Derek alone. He finished his meal and set his plates in the sink.

CHAPTER THIRTY-NINE

Late Tuesday morning

Derek was working at the desk in his room when his phone rang. "You got me, what do you need?"

"Hey, it's Agent Marcum."

"Tell me you got something for me." Derek perked up waiting for the Agent's response.

"No. I'm still working on the truck companies. I wanted to let you know I was going to have to leave the office to help with a case. I won't be able to do any follow up until I get back. But that could be the end of the week."

Derek's heart sank. "I understand. You're still an active member of that unit. Do what you got to do. You aren't in any kind of trouble, are you?"

"No. Not at all. I have to get this case wrapped up before I leave for Arizona."

"Okay. I'll touch base with you at the end of the week," Derek said.

"I'm really sorry. I know you are hoping to solve this case. I'll work on it if I get any spare time."

"Don't worry, Kyle. Do your job. I'll talk to you later."

Derek placed his phone on the desk. "Damn. I hope Jerry comes up with something." He rubbed his temples. The lack of sleep due to the nightmares were beginning to take its toll. He couldn't seem to get a handle on this cold case. He wondered if taking on an entire unit that only handled cold cases was really something he wanted to do. The time spent chasing down outdated clues hoping for a break often felt like a dog chasing his tail. He leaned back in the chair, put his feet on the desk, and closed his eyes.

A knock at Derek's door brought him out of a light slumber. He shook the cobwebs from his head yawning. "Hang on," he called out. He closed his laptop and made sure his gun was in his bag, then opened his door.

"Hey, buddy. You ready to go fishing?" Cory stood in the hallway.

Derek glanced at his watch. "Holy shit! I sat down at the desk and must have dozed off."

"How long have you been napping?" Cory said leaning against the doorway as Derek put his wallet and cell phone in the pocket of his jeans.

Derek patted himself down, making sure he had everything. "I guess about two hours." He pulled his door closed behind him and followed Cory down the stairs. "I haven't been sleeping well. I think it finally caught up to me."

They climbed into Cory's truck and headed down the drive.

Derek admired the quaint neighborhood. Large colonial style homes lined a tree filled street. Large tall oaks provided needed shade from the blistering August sun. "How is my car? You got it fixed yet?"

Cory barked out a laugh. "Man, you're killing me." He drove onto the main thoroughfare. "What the hell? Is everyone taking off early today?"

Derek chuckled. "Degenerates."

Cory smiled at him. "I got sandwiches and snacks in the cooler in the back."

"Sounds good. Where do you go fishing?"

"Not too far out of the city limit, we have a small fishing hole. Not too crowded. Whatever we catch we will throwback. I wanted to take a day to relax. Gerald is covering the garage. He got his son to come up and help him."

Derek ogled the man. As men went, he figured Cory would be considered good looking in most circles. His hair was a little long, but it suited him. His sandy brown hair matched his hazel eyes. He had some muscle but still maintained a slender build. "How long have you lived here?"

Cory turned off the main road onto a gravel one. "Gosh, close to twenty-eight years. Maybe more, maybe less. Too long."

"Catherine said you moved here after meeting her sister."

Cory's brow wrinkled. "What else did Catherine say? Don't believe half of it."

Derek smirked. "Sure."

"Oh, I had a job that kept me traveling a lot. I met Candace during a few of my business trips. After my grandfather died, I decided I had nothing keeping me where I lived, so I moved here."

Derek could see a few trucks on the side of the road. "Are all these people fishing?"

"Probably."

Derek glanced around. "You said it was a small fishing hole," he said as the truck pulled into a clearing. "This is not a small fishing hole. This is a damn lake."

Cory laughed. "I come out here so much, I don't think of it as being big."

"Trust me, it is huge," Derek said looking out over an enormous lake which spilled out in front of them. "We need a boat."

Several boat ramps lined the edges of the lake. There were parking areas filled with a few trucks and trailers. The water had a green-blue color. Not the usual murky brown most lakes seem to have.

"Oh, that would be so nice. I have been trying to talk Candace into it. She keeps saying no. I'm going to get her to agree soon."

"Does it extend out past the jut out?"

Cory nodded. "Yeah. Around that bend is a swimming area. It's roped off to keep boats and jet skis from getting to close. They have a few food trucks that park over that way. A nice beach area. The city carved it out and even imported some sand to make it more—beachy."

"Nice. We have a lot of lakes in Arizona. We have some great swimming holes that you can jump off rocks into a bottomless pit of water. My job keeps me busy. I don't get to them as much as I would like." Derek shifted in his seat. He had to bite his tongue. Almost gave away what he really did for a living. He surprised himself how comfortable he was talking to Cory.

"I used to live in west Texas. I couldn't stand it, way too hot. I don't think I would ever like to live in Arizona."

"You get used to it."

Cory stopped at the edge of a sloping bank. He backed the truck up so that the bed faced the lake. "Let's catch some fish." At the rear of the truck, Cory slid the cooler over. He lifted two beers out and handed one to Derek. "I got soda and water. I only brought a few beers each. But what is fishing if you don't have a beer?"

Derek twisted off the top and took a long pull. "Oh, that does taste good." He sat on the tailgate. Several groups, including a few boy scout troops, were camping at the edge of the lake. "I thought you said this wasn't too popular? This looks like a popular place to me."

"I guess I come out here during the week. Occasionally I have come on the weekends. Then it gets pretty busy. The city makes sure to stock it. You can keep what you catch. But we aren't going to eat it, so why keep it?" He grabbed a pole from the back of the truck. "I really only fish because I find it relaxing. I don't need to keep them."

Derek took the pole that Cory held out to him. He took two grub worms from the container Cory held out as well. Baiting the hook, he cast his line in the water. He sat on the tailgate. Glancing to his left, he noticed a PVC pipe bolted at an angle to the side of the truck. "What the heck is this?" He asked Cory pointing to it.

"I came up with this one day. A buddy and I were tired of holding our lines. A lot of times fishing is waiting. Why not let this hold it for us?"

Derek placed his pole in the holder. "Well, now, this is very handy."

Cory joined Derek and sat on the end of the tailgate. "You married?"

Derek shook his head. "No. I don't ever plan on it either."

"It's not that bad you know?"

Derek's brow furrowed. "For some. Just not for me." He drank his beer. "My parents have been married for almost fifty years. I think." He chuckled. "A long time."

"You dating anyone?"

"Are you asking for a reason?"

Cory smiled. "No. I'm just curious." He had a tug on his line. He spun the reel holding on tight to the pole. After a few tugs, Cory reeled it in. "Empty. Damn bastards took the bait, though."

"How dare they," Derek said taking another beer from the cooler. "I don't have to drive." He raised the bottle and took a sip.

Cory rebaited the hook and cast it back into the water. "I know you said you were heading to Tennessee, you spending a vacation with your family?"

"Yeah. I don't get home very often. Promised my family I would come for a visit. Then I end up here. But I have to say, it hasn't been all that bad to be stuck here."

Cory smiled, taking a bottled water from the cooler. "I'm glad. I tried to talk my wife into moving to Tennessee. But her family is from here."

"Where does your family live?" Derek rummaged through the cooler. He pulled out a sandwich and unwrapped it.

"I was raised by my grandfather and grandmother. My parents died when I was a little kid."

"I'm sorry about that."

"No need to be." Cory sat silent for a few minutes. "My grandfather was an ass. Mean as hell, too. Had a farm out in west Texas. After my grandmother died, he became even meaner." He finished off the last of his beer. "Shortly after her death, I left. I took a job in another city. I wanted the hell out of that damn house. Then I met Candace, and the rest was history."

"Is your grandfather still at the farm?"

Cory shook his head. "No. He died in the late '80s. I sold the farm and never looked back."

CHAPTER FORTY

Cory glanced at his watch. "It's close to four thirty. Before I take you back to Catherine's, do you mind if I stop at my house? I promised my wife I would bring a small chair to her sister, and I forgot it earlier."

"Yeah, no problem at all." Derek helped pack everything up and jumped into the cab of the truck. Cory cranked the AC, and cold air blasted them. "Man, that feels good. Crap it's hot."

Cory wiped his brow with the bottom of his shirt. "I can't wait for fall and winter. Anything to get rid of this heat."

Fifteen minutes later, they drove down Cory's drive. They exited the vehicle and Kayla came out to greet them.

"Hi daddy," she said as she hugged him.

"Hey, Babydoll." He picked her up and kissed her. "Let me go in and talk to your mom. You sit out here on the porch and keep my friend company."

"Okay, Daddy."

Derek sat on the top stair of the porch. He smiled at Kayla who stood staring at him. "Hey, Kayla. What did you do today?"

"I'll be right back." She ran off inside and came back a few minutes later. She plopped down beside him. "I got some of mommy's old photos and made a picture book." She held out a book that had edges tied together with a ribbon.

"Wow. That sure is creative." Derek took it from her. He thumbed through the pages.

Kayla scooted closer. With each page turn, she explained the picture.

"This is my grandpa. He died before I was born. But my mommy talks about him all the time."

"He looks like a smart man," Derek said.

"Mommy said he was."

Derek turned the page. The next picture was of a young girl and boy. It was obviously taken years ago, but he recognized Candace immediately. "Now, that looks like your mommy, only years and years ago."

Kayla looked up at him and smiled. "It is. She's pretty. She's still pretty." She pointed at the photo. "That's my daddy, too."

Derek narrowed in on the photo. Cory had longer hair back then. He stood in front of some sort of work truck. Derek couldn't make out the logo. He and Kayla went through a few more pages until they came to an old house. Derek's hair stood on end. That house looked so familiar. "What is this?" he asked Kayla.

"Oh, that was Daddy's house. I think it was his grandpa's house first."

Derek zeroed in on the picture. It looked so similar to the farmhouse where he had found the tin box. *It can't be,* he thought. He continued to stare at the house. The paint was pristine white, and the shutters had a beautiful yellow on them. He turned the page hoping Kayla had put another picture of the farmhouse in her book. One showing the property from a different angle. He flipped through a few more pages but didn't find any other pictures of the house.

Derek pulled his phone from his pocket and opened the camera. Kayla turned when her mother called her into the kitchen, and that gave Derek a perfect chance to snap a photo. He peered around making sure no one saw him. Satisfied he got it, he pocketed his phone.

Derek continued to stare at the house. He hoped the picture he took would jog his memory and he could remember the town where the house he and Chrissy visited had been. Damn, he needed that town. He wondered if all farmhouses looked the same. Cory's family hailed from west Texas, making this another farmhouse. He looked through the rest of the book as Kayla came up next to him.

"Did you like it?" She asked with bright wide eyes.

"Yes, I did." He handed it to her. "You did a great job on it."

She smiled. "Thanks," she said as she took it and ran into the house.

Cory came out and patted him on his shoulder. "You ready?"

"Yeah. Whenever you are."

Cory carried a small chair and led the way to the truck.

Candace called out from the porch. "I'll have dinner ready when you come back."

He waved at her, and put the chair in the truck bed, then got behind the steering wheel. "What are you going to do for dinner?"

"Catherine is fixing something. I can eat at her place. Maybe go out and have a few beers at the pub up the street."

"That sounds fun." Cory drove out into the traffic.

Derek watched the scenery go by. The picture of the house really had his mind going. "Tell me about your grandfather's house. Where is it located?"

"West Texas. Far West Texas."

"Kayla had a picture of it in her little book."

"That little girl is going to be a photographer. She loves pictures. Especially our old ones."

"I've always lived in a city until we moved to Tennessee. Our place was in the valley. It wasn't a farm, but it was farm-like. Big barn and old house."

"That was a farm," Cory said laughing. He entered the circle driveway of the bed and breakfast. "If I can talk my wife into it, maybe we'll meet you at the pub." He lifted the chair out of the truck and carried it up the stairs to the porch.

Derek smiled as he opened the door. "I'd love it. I'm going to head over around eight p.m. Call and let me know or just meet me at the pub."

Catherine came from around the side of the house. "Hey Cory, I'll take that to the shed."

Cory handed it over and glanced back at Derek. "Sounds good, Derek."

Derek watched as the truck left the driveway. He entered Catherine's place to a loud group of guests. He nodded as he made his way up the stairs. He was almost to the top when he heard Catherine call out to him.

"Dinner will be ready in an hour. Hamburgers and all the fixings tonight," she said.

"Sounds fantastic. I'll be down." Derek entered his room. He sat on the bed and laid back. A few hours in the hot sun and he was worn out. "Being on vacation is not what my body is used to," he said out loud as he yawned. He started to drift off when he bolted up. "Crap, I forgot to call Lilly."

He reached into his pocket and pulled out his phone. He dialed and then laid back down on the bed.

"Hillside Manor."

"Hi, I wanted to speak with Lilly. I dialed her room; how did I get the front desk?"

"If she isn't in her room, she forwards her calls to the front desk. She is out for a while. You want to leave a message?"

Derek sighed. "No. I'll call back tomorrow." He hung up and cursed himself for being so stupid to forget to call her earlier in the day. He looked at his watch. He really didn't want hamburgers. He hoped Catherine wouldn't be too upset with him, but he decided after a cat nap he would go to the pub to eat. He set his phone alarm to wake him in just over an hour.

CHAPTER FORTY-ONE

Tuesday evening

Derek opened his door and peeked into the hallway. He could hear people on the first floor. He crept down the stairs stopping short of the bottom. He craned his neck, peering around the edge of the wall. Everyone was in the kitchen giving him the perfect opportunity to sneak out of the B&B. He didn't have it in him to explain what he did for a living. He didn't want to have to field questions from a bunch of nosy vacationers.

After a ten-minute walk, he entered the pub. Not much of a crowd, but enough to keep Derek distracted. The pub had dark wood plank floors and amber lighting from ball like chandeliers placed in three rows across the ceiling. The walls were decorated with eighteenth-century armor. High back booths lined each wall. Each one covered in a robust red leather. The center floor had several tables and chairs in a haphazardly placed arrangement. A stage sat off to the right in the corner.

The main bar spanned the entire length of the back wall. As he got closer to the bar, he could see the shelves lined with every beer known to man, as well as a wide variety of whiskeys and other grains. There were also several taps with even more variety of beers available. He pulled out a stool and took a seat in front of one of the five humongous TVs.

"Hey, what can I get for you?" The bartender placed a glass of water in front of him on a coaster.

"I'll take whatever you got on tap."

"Coming up." He grabbed a mug from the cooler behind him, and filled it with beer. "I haven't seen you in here before. You visiting our area?"

"Yeah, sort of. Had a small mishap in my car and it's being worked on over at Cory Thompson's place."

"Oh, best mechanic in this area. Probably all of Greenwood too." He reached out his hand, "I'm Ted."

Derek nodded shaking his hand. "Nice to meet you. I'm Derek."

"What are you doing out this way?"

"On my way to Tennessee, family. But I had to see someone in Greenwood. Then, of course, the car thing, and I'm here." He took a long drink of his beer. "How did you end up here?"

"Born and raised. Too stupid to leave. Or too lazy."

Derek chuckled at the man's response. "Tell me, what do you have to eat here?"

Ted placed a menu in front of Derek. "Our sandwiches are great."

"Yeah? Give me the best one." He handed the menu back to Ted.

The bell above the door chimed. Ted looked up. "Hey, Cory. Were your ears burning?"

Derek turned around. He smiled and waved over Cory and Candace. "You guys decided to come out."

"Kayla wanted to go see aunt Catherine, so we decided to meet you here and have a few beers. We won't stay long."

Derek nodded. "I'm grateful for the company. Let's get a table." He motioned to Ted. "Put their drink on my tab."

"You got it. Cory, what do you guys want?"

Candace's brow wrinkled then relaxed. "I'll have a glass of white wine."

"Tap will be fine for me," Cory said as he pulled out a chair for his wife.

Derek sat across from Candace. Cory sat next to him. "I'm glad you guys came out."

"Well, you have Kayla to thank for that. She overheard us talking and said she would love to see her favorite aunt," Cory said.

Candace leaned in. "Her only aunt."

Cory nodded. He squinted at Derek when his food showed up. "I thought you were going to eat at Catherine's."

Derek slunk down in his seat. "I didn't want hamburgers. I snuck out and walked here." He sipped on his beer. "You think she will want to kill me?"

Candace giggled. She shook her head. "You don't have to worry about Catherine. She has learned over the years not to get offended by her guests. She doesn't care if you eat or not. She still cooks."

"I didn't say anything before I left." Derek took a bite of his sandwich. "Oh, this is good."

"They have the best sandwiches here." Cory reached over and took his wife's hand.

"That's what Ted said. He wasn't lying either," Derek said as he continued to eat his meal. He watched the interaction between Cory and his wife. He could tell how much they loved each other by the way they stared at one another.

A few people came over to the table and spoke with Cory. Derek could tell the man was quite popular. It seemed everyone that entered or left the bar either spoke with Cory or waved at him. He noticed Candace leaned a little into her husband. He reached for his sandwich to take another bite when his hands began to tremble.

His pulse sped up, and his mouth instantly went dry. Derek held his beer in one hand and placed the other on his lap. His knee began to bounce under the table. He wiped his clammy palm on his jeans. It took a few minutes for the breathlessness to subside. "Umm, that is a beautiful pendant. Where did you get it?"

Candace's fingers touched her neck. "It was one of the first gifts Cory gave me." She squeezed Cory's hand. "When Cory and I met he wasn't living here, yet. We had seen each other a few times when he drove through here. When his grandfather died, and he moved here, we started dating full time." She lifted his hand and gently kissed it. "We didn't have the money for an engagement ring. Cory gave me this." She lifted the pendant off her neck. "It was the perfect symbol of our love. I never take it off."

Cory raised an eyebrow smirking at Derek. "I gave her a diamond ring several years later, she takes that off all the time. I think it's because this doesn't look like a wedding or an engagement ring. She can keep all her boyfriends and not scare them away."

Candace smacked him on the shoulder. "I do not." She took a sip of her wine. "Plus, all my boyfriends are perfectly fine with me being married."

Derek couldn't take his eyes off it. He smiled at the story. "Is it an emerald?"

She nodded. "Yes, and it is surrounded by diamonds."

Derek tried to inhale, his throat constricted, closing in on itself. He heard his chest thumping and hoped no one else could hear it. He stared at Cory. *It couldn't be the same necklace. There's no way this could be Julie's pendant.* When Cory glanced over at him. Derek smiled. "Nice. Very nice. Where did you get it?"

Cory stiffened. He looked at his wife then back to Derek. "Hmm..." His mind raced searching for an answer. "It used to be my grandmother's. When I went back to the farm after my grandfather died, I found it going through their things. I only kept a few of their belongings."

"At least something good came out of that." Derek took a bite of his sandwich. He questioned the accusations rattling around his mind. He had no evidence that this family man could be responsible for the rapes and murders of several girls. Especially not based off one piece of jewelry that could be purchased almost anywhere. *Get a grip, Derek.* He thought to himself. After a few more bites of his sandwich, he pushed his plate to the side, his appetite gone. "That was good. I just seem to be full." He drank the rest of his beer. Trying not to stare at Candace's neck.

Cory raised an eyebrow at Derek. His reaction to his wife had him questioning Derek's motives. "I do have some good news for you. Well, sort of good news."

"Oh, yeah? What's that?" Derek asked.

"Gerald called me this evening and said a portion of your parts order came in. He said my guy from Greenwood said the other one would be at the shop by mid-morning tomorrow. Your car should be ready by late afternoon."

"Oh, that's fantastic. Call me when it's ready, and I'll get a ride over to the shop tomorrow afternoon." Derek smiled at Candace. He couldn't take his eyes off the necklace.

Candace drank the last of her wine. "Are you going to drive out tomorrow or stay and leave the following morning?"

Derek sat back in his chair. "I'll probably leave early the next morning. No sense leaving so late that I have to find another hotel within a few hours." He continued to study the pendant.

Cory squinted at Derek. He followed the man's stare and noticed he continued to look at his wife. He stood and reached out a hand to Candace. "You ready to go?"

Candace's forehead wrinkled. "Why?"

"I guess being in the sun today has made me more tired than I thought."

"Uhh, okay. I guess so, then." She stood. "You want a ride back?" She asked smiling at Derek.

"Yes, that would be great. Let me pay the bill." Derek moved towards the bar.

"Are you sure you don't want to stay a little while longer? You don't have to rush out on our account," Cory said pushing his wife towards the door.

Derek straightened and faced Cory. "No. I'm sure. I would love a ride back." He paid his bill and followed Cory and his wife out the door.

CHAPTER FORTY-TWO

Cory drove into Catherine's driveway. They weren't even out of the vehicle before Kayla came flying out the front door.

"Whoa, girl. Where you going?" Candace asked her daughter as she jumped off the second to last step while her mother exited the truck.

She bounced up and down from foot to foot, then spun around in a circle. "Ooh, I helped Aunt Cathy make cookies tonight." She tugged on her mom and dad's hand leading them up the porch steps. "You got to come see them. C'mon, c'mon."

"Okay, okay. We're coming," Candace said laughing as she let her daughter drag her through the house.

Derek entered the house behind Kayla and her parents. A few guests sat in chairs sharing drinks and conversations. He nodded as he walked past. In the kitchen, a few more people gathered around the large table. Kayla led her parents to the bar. Several plates of cookies lined the top. Each decorated with various colors of icing.

Candace smiled down at her daughter. "Did you make these?"

Kayla nodded. "Yeah. I mean with the help of Aunt Cathy."

Catherine walked over to the table. "She did most of it. I just made sure she didn't burn down my house."

Derek took a seat at the table and accepted the cup of coffee that Catherine held out to him. "Thank you."

"Did you like the pub?" Catherine asked.

Derek grinned sheepishly. "Sorry. I guess I should've said something."

She patted his shoulder laughing. "Oh, sweetie. You owe me no explanation. The pub has great sandwiches."

Kayla came over to Derek. "Look."

"Look at what?" he asked.

She held out her wrist. "My Bracelet. I got to wear it tonight."

His eyes widened. "Oh," he said. "Didn't you show it to me already?"

"Yes, but I don't think you paid attention. This is the new charm I got." Between her tiny fingers, she held a charm.

Derek pulled her wrist closer and studied it. A heart with a diamond right in the middle of it. "Wow, Kayla. This is very pretty."

"It's a real diamond. My mommy said so. It even has my nickname on the back."

He flipped it over and saw the name Babydoll. Derek winked at her.

"My Daddy said it was a very special charm and I had to make sure I never lost it." She held up her wrist and shook it. "I love the way they jingle."

Cory walked over and picked her up. "Are you harassing my friend again?"

"No Daddy. I was showing him my pretty bracelet."

"You have cornered him every time you see him. How about you give him a break?"

"Okay." She laid her head on his shoulder.

"You tired Babydoll?" Cory asked as he rubbed her back.

"A little."

"Hey Candy," Cory motioned towards the door. "Let' get our princess home."

Candace hugged her sister. She nodded at Derek. "If I don't see you before you get on the road, I hope you have a safe trip." She gave him a quick hug and followed her husband out the door.

"Thank you," Derek called after them.

His phone rang at that moment. "Excuse me," he said to Catherine as he walked towards the stairway. "This is Derek."

"Derek, this is Lilly."

"Lilly is something wrong?" he unlocked his door and stepped inside.

"No silly. I'm returning your call."

Derek scratched his head. "How did you know I called? I didn't leave a message."

"Maggie, from the front desk, told me a young man called for me. You are the only young man I know. I assumed it was you. It was you wasn't it?"

Derek smiled at the uncertain tone in Lilly's voice. "Yes, Lilly. It was me."

"What did you need? Do you have some information for me?"

Derek searched his computer bag for the photo of Liza. "I was looking at the photo you gave me, and I was hoping you could tell me about the charm bracelet Liza is wearing in the photo."

"Let's see. She had just gotten it. It didn't have many charms, I think four. A soccer ball, a dog or cat, I can't remember which. I think a pineapple."

"Why a pineapple?"

"Oh, my goodness, Liza ate pineapples every day. It was her favorite fruit."

"Okay. What was the last charm on the bracelet?"

"Her favorite one. Her parents had given it to her for her birthday. It was a silver heart with a diamond in the middle." She giggled on the phone. "I remember when she showed it to me. Liza was so excited. 'It's a real diamond,' she said. It was small, but you would've thought it was three carats."

"Thank you, Lilly. That helps me a lot."

"I'm so glad I could help you. Call me if I can do anything else for you. I need to go. I'm playing bridge with the other girls, and tonight is high stakes."

Derek chuckled at the vision of these women playing high stakes poker. "Thanks again." He started to hang up when she called out to him.

"Derek, Derek? Are you still there?"

"Yeah Lilly, I'm still here. What's wrong?"

"I forgot to tell you. The charm has an inscription on the back. Liza's dad had the nickname he used to call her inscribed on it."

"What was the name, Lilly?"

"Babydoll. She used to love it when he called her that, too. Well, anyway. That's it. You call me if you find anything out."

Derek fell into the desk chair. He blew out a sharp breath. "I will Lilly, I will." He hung up the phone. His heart pounded in his throat. Opening his bag, he pulled his camera out and removed the SD card from it.

Plugging it into his computer he tapped the desk with his fingers. "Hurry up," he said. Finally, he accessed the photos on the card. He scrolled through them until he found the old farmhouse. Then he opened the photo gallery on his phone, Derek found the picture he had taken of Kayla's photo book.

Enlarging the farmhouse photos, he compared the photo on his phone. "It's like two different properties," Derek said as he searched for something that would show that these photos are of the same homestead. He searched each photo. "C'mon there has to be something here."

Studying the photo on his phone, he noticed a dream catcher in one of the front windows. Cropping the photo so that the resolution wouldn't get fuzzy, he narrowed in on the dream catcher. It was faded from the sun, but he could make out the design.

Derek then found the best photo on his computer of the front of the house he had visited. His heart rate sped up. "Why didn't I see that when I was there?" he asked out loud. He used the mouse to pull up the window in question. It had half of a dream catcher in the window. Zooming in on the design, he was able to match the top half of it to the one in the photo on his phone. "Son of a bitch!"

Derek paced his room. "The pendant, maybe a coincidence. The house, possibly a coincidence. Right? Tons of people throughout the region have dream catchers. But the charm, no fucking way." The pounding of his pulse echoed in his head. He started to call Agent Marcum but remembered he was out of the office. "I can't run this search on anything that will leave a trail until I'm sure." He rummaged through his computer bag until he found what he was looking for. He dialed the number.

CHAPTER FORTY-THREE

"Jerry here."

"Jerry, this is Derek Reed."

"Derek. I was going to call you tomorrow. Although I don't have much. Kainetorri is still working on the companies. He has it narrowed down to three that were in the area."

"I need you to ask your friend to get some information on a guy. Everything he can find."

"Did you find a suspect?" Jerry asked.

Derek heard the rattle in the man's voice. "I don't know, Jerry. But I got a gut feeling on this." Derek didn't want to give his reasons away for the gut feeling, on the off chance he was utterly wrong and about to ruin a man's life for nothing.

"Give me the name."

"Cory Thompson. He runs Cory's Garage here in Schlatter, Mississippi. I need you to get your friend to get me all of the property he has owned. I know his grandfather had a farm." Derek hesitated. Cory had said he grew up in West Texas. "Check for property in and around the Duran and Vaughn New Mexico area. I'm looking for him to have inherited a farm and farmhouse back in the '80s."

It took a minute for Jerry to respond. "You think this is our guy?"

"Jerry, I don't know. I do know that I have seen a few things that could be absolutely nothing more than coincidence. However, I just don't buy into shit like that. If my hunch is right, this man is our killer. I don't mind saying this, I hope I'm wrong."

"What the hell? How can you say that?"

"I have sat with this man and his family. He is a good man. A loving husband and father. He has two beautiful kids. How the fuck am I going to tell them, oh, by the way, your dad is a rapist and a murderer?"

"I get that. But if you need to remind yourself of why you are doing this, you pull out the photos of those four girls. I don't care if this man has turned into a fucking saint. If this is our guy, he needs to be held accountable."

"I know that. Fuck I know that. But it isn't black and white. People make mistakes all the time and change."

"That may be so, but you don't get to rape and murder four or more girls and walk away from it, just because you're a good man now. Or a good husband or father."

Derek paced his room. "I know that, too. I wish I hadn't met him and spent time with him."

"Where are you anyway? How did you find this guy?"

Derek sighed. "My car broke down. I got stuck in this town outside Greenwood, Mississippi. He's the mechanic working on it."

"Wow. Thirty fucking years later, you happen to have found a tin box at an abandoned farmhouse, and then your car breaks down in the one city that the killer lives and works in. I think you have someone or something else directing your path, son."

"No. No, I don't. How quickly can you get something from your friend? My car is going to be done tomorrow. I'm scheduled to leave the following day. Can he get us anything in the next twelve hours?"

"As soon as we hang up, I'm calling him."

"Call me with whatever you get. But email it to me, too."

"You got it." Jerry paused. "Derek?"

"Yeah?"

"You're a hell of an investigator."

"Call me as soon as you hear something."

"Will do."

The line went dead. Derek stared at his phone. How would he tell Cory's kids if this ends up being true? How do you tell a family, a community, that the man they've known all their lives is a rapist and a serial killer? For once in his life, he hoped this guy wasn't the killer.

He heard a noise behind him and spun around to find Chrissy sitting in the desk chair.

She smiled at him. "Looks like your closing in on your guy."

He cocked his head to the side. Something seemed slightly different. He moved closer and stared at her.

She slid the chair back until it bumped into the desk. "What is wrong with you?"

He wiggled his finger at her. "You look different."

She glanced at her arms. Looked down at her clothes. "What? How do I look different?"

Derek stepped back. "I don't know. But something is off. Something is different."

"Is that good or bad?"

He shrugged. "I don't know for sure." He tilted his head to the side. "I don't think it's bad. If that makes any sense."

"I guess it does." She slid the chair across the floor.

A grin filled his face. "I know what it is."

"Know what—what is?" Chrissy asked.

"You're wound. It's completely gone. You look like nothing ever happened to you." Derek's expression softened. The corners of his mouth turned downward.

"It's not your fault. You have to know that."

He glanced up. "I'm starting to understand that."

Chrissy glanced at his notes on the desk. "What's your next move in this cold case?"

"I wait."

"Why not confront him?"

Derek sat on his bed. "You can't do that. You get one bite of the apple. One chance at surprise. I'm going to have to wait to see what Jerry's friend comes up with. Then, I'll know how to proceed."

"What do you mean?"

"I really have no evidence. Everything I have is circumstantial, and a good lawyer could get him off easily. A great lawyer could help him walk away with millions of dollars and my career. But, if I can tie him to the tin box and all the trophies, as well as the property, I may have a shot at getting somewhere."

Derek rubbed his face. But stayed away from his throbbing nose. He sighed. "Nothing ties directly to Cory. Any lawyer could say someone else put those things in his house. The jewelry isn't one of a kind. Hell, I can't even imagine how many other women are wearing this same pendant or charm bracelet."

Chrissy nodded. "You have all this evidence, but it isn't worth squat."

"Basically. Unless I can use it to get him to confess. If I can make him think what I have is enough to get a warrant and an arrest, I may be able to get him to admit to everything."

"And what if he doesn't confess, then what do you do?"

Derek shrugged. "I don't know. I honestly don't know."

CHAPTER FORTY-FOUR

Wednesday morning

Derek awoke early. He snuck down to the kitchen and found the largest coffee mug in the cabinet. There were muffins and bagels under one of the warming lamps. He grabbed a few of those and a small bottle of orange juice. He didn't want to face Catherine knowing he was trying to figure out a way to blow her and her sister's world apart. Back in his room he ate watching the news and checking his email. He was about to shower when his phone rang. He glanced at the screen and gathered his nerves before he answered.

"Hey AD, what's up? Did you get my email with the three other agents I picked for the new unit?"

"Yeah, I got it. But that isn't why I called."

"Oh. Why did you call then?" Derek picked at the chocolate chips in one of his muffins.

"Guess who I got a call from?"

"I have no idea. The President?"

"Don't try and be funny. Why don't you tell me about the case you have Agent Marcum working on," AD Fretz said.

Derek had ten seconds to decide if he should lie or tell his AD everything. Lying would be so much easier. "I asked for his help with something."

"What is that, Derek? Aren't you supposed to be on vacation? Not working on FBI matters?"

"Well to my credit, this case has nothing to do with the FBI. Hell, the FBI didn't even know about it."

"Derek, do you like your job?"

"I like it very much."

"Then quit bullshitting me and tell me what the fuck you're working on."

Derek sat up straight in the desk chair. "Okay. I'll tell you everything. At the beginning of this trip, I was sightseeing, and I found an abandoned farmhouse. Inside that house, I found an old tin box. Like a lunch box. I didn't open it until I got to my hotel that evening. When I did, I found photos of murdered girls and trophies that the killer had taken from the girls." He continued to tell AD Fretz the rest of the case. Everything that he had uncovered up to this point. When he finished, he sat and waited for the hammer to fall. He expected his AD to say you're fired, don't come home. But when he didn't say anything, Derek wondered if he was arranging for him to be picked up and institutionalized.

AD Fretz breathed out slowly. "Let me get this straight. You're telling me, you've been following a cold case from thirty years ago, and you have managed to find the killer, all because your car broke down in the same city he now lives?"

"Uhh, yeah. But when you say it like that, it sounds so far-fetched."

"And if it sounds far-fetched to you, what the hell do you think a good lawyer is going to do with this when your suspect sues the government for harassment?"

"I haven't harassed him."

"Maybe not yet, but when you start digging into his past with no warrant or even cause for a warrant, your ass will be strung out to dry."

"I'm not doing that though." Derek picked one of the chocolate chips out of his muffin and ate it. He took a gulp of his now cold coffee.

"I don't understand, how are you going to research this man and find out if he owns this property?"

"That sheriff, Jerry, he has a buddy who is going to find out everything on this guy. If he can tie the property to him and match up work records that put him in every city the girls were abducted from and dumped in, we will have enough to get a warrant."

"Wait, wait a second. You have some sheriff using a buddy to snoop out a guy's past? Are you fucking crazy? Do you not care about your career at all?"

"Wait, hear me out, he said this guy has done work for you guys, the FBI."

"Who? What is this guy's name?"

"Oh hell, umm, fuck it some Italian name...umm, Kainetorri. Yeah, that's it, Kainetorri. I don't know his first name."

"Are you shitting me? This sheriff that you just met knows Giovanni Kainetorri, of Kainetorri Securities?"

"You know who this guy is?" Derek asked with a tad bit more excitement than he should have.

"He is the father of Damien Kaine, a Lieutenant out of the Vicious Crimes Unit."

Derek rubbed his temple. "Am I supposed to know who that is?"

"Have you been living under a rock for the last six months?"

"AD, I don't know who you are talking about. Tell me."

"Agent Dillon McGrath, she's dating Damien. They brought down that cartel group, along with Senator Lockhart and his father. Her family was murdered when she was twelve, and that same killer came back and killed her grandparents, and damn near killed her."

"Oh. I had no idea that was the same family." Derek paused on the phone. "That's a good thing, right?"

"It isn't bad. Derek, why can't you just go on vacation like every other person in this country, and not get into anything?"

"I have wondered the same thing. Listen, AD, let me finish this out. Let's see what the Kainetorri's come back with." Derek paused. He swallowed hard. "I can't let the families of these girls get this close to solving their cases and walk away without seeing it through."

AD Fretz sighed into the phone. "Twenty-four hours. I will give you twenty-four hours. If the Kainetorri's don't give you anything that will back up this treasure trove of circumstantial evidence, you will walk away. You will not mention this man's name in conjunction with any rapes or murders. Am I clear?"

"Yes, Sir. You are perfectly clear," Derek said.

"I mean it, Derek. If you can't tie him to these girls, that's it. He's off the radar. Again, am I clear?"

"Yes, AD, you are clear. I will let it go. I promise."

"You call me when you find something out. I don't care what the time is. If this does come back to this guy, I will have to call Director Sherman and fill him in. But I refuse to do that without evidence to back this theory."

Derek started to say something when the line went dead. He held the phone out and looked at the screen. His AD had hung up on him. At least he didn't fire him. Now he had to hope he heard from Jerry soon.

CHAPTER FORTY-FIVE

By eleven Derek still hadn't heard from Jerry. His stomach growled, he had to get something to eat. He ventured down to the kitchen. Peeking around the corner before walking in, he saw a buffet set up with all kinds of sandwich makings. He quickly put together two sandwiches. He grabbed some fruit, chips, two sodas, and a bottle of water then headed right back up to his room.

Once inside a wave of relief washed over him that he didn't have to speak with anyone. Especially Catherine. He pushed down the guilt that tried to creep up his spine and take up residence in his head. He wasn't doing this to hurt Catherine or Candace. Let alone the kids. But if Cory killed these girls, Derek couldn't let him get away with it. No matter how much he liked the man.

He glanced around expecting Chrissy to show up. He was surprised she hadn't visited yet that morning. If for no other reason than to scare the crap out of him. He turned on the TV while he ate. He hated baseball but hated talk shows more. Baseball won out.

After eating, he flipped through the channels as he paced his room. The walls seemed to close in on him. If he hadn't heard from Jerry by one p.m., he would call him. "Ugh, I can't stand this." He checked his phone. No missed calls, no missed messages. He flopped down on the bed and propped his back and head up.

He slowed his breathing trying to shut his brain off. Relaxing into the soft pillow, he began to doze. Memories carried him back to the carnival tent. He smelled the stench of stale piss and blood. He wasn't tied this time, and he was alone in the tent. Derek walked around the table where he remembered Chrissy lying. A quick vision of her flashed before him. He squeezed his eyes shut. "Not this time," he said as he leaned against the table, blocking the vision.

A sound erupted behind him. Josiah walked into the tent smiling at him. The gums surrounding his teeth had rotted away, and the roots were decayed strands of black string. Beetles and maggots weaved their way in between the rotting teeth.

Josiah dragged another girl behind him. She was bound and gagged.

Derek couldn't see her face. "Let her go."

Josiah's maniacal laugh filled the tent. Two of his teeth fell to the floor. The right half of his head was nothing more than a bowl. One eye socket was caved in, and the other held a cloudy gray eye. Flesh hung off his arms, pieces of it falling to the floor around him.

"I said let her go." This time Derek took a step towards the rotting man.

"And what are you going to do about it, Derek?" Josiah asked as he raised a long sharp knife above his head. He started to bring the knife down in a slashing motion across Derek's neck.

As the blade sliced his skin, Derek heard the shrill scream of the young girl. No, not the girl, something else.

Derek blinked his eyes as the dream receded and the fog cleared. The shrill sound was his phone. He leapt quickly from the bed, almost knocking it off the desk. "Derek here." He panted trying to catch his breath.

"Hey, this is Jerry."

Derek inhaled a deep breath and exhaled slowly. "Please tell me you got something."

"Oh yeah. I got something. I sent you a detailed email. But I'm going to break it down for you over the phone."

Derek sat at the desk. He had to work at keeping his hands from trembling. At least once, he almost dropped his phone. "Hey, I'm going to put you on speaker phone."

"No problem. You ready?" Jerry asked.

"Yeah. I'm ready. Tell me what you got."

"Your guy owns a house outside Vaughn, New Mexico."

"Wait, he still owns it?" Derek remembered Cory telling him he sold the property right after his grandfather died.

"Yes. He still owns it. He worked for a company called Morty's Mobile Mechanics. Morty's was one of the companies that worked that stretch of area where each girl was from. Kainetorri found one other company operating in the area as well. Cory began working for this company when he was nineteen. But here is the kicker. Guess where they operate their headquarters out of?"

"Where?"

"Clovis."

Derek's mind raced at lightning speed. "That puts him around each of the girls. But that doesn't mean we can prove it."

"No. But it is more than I ever had. More than any other investigator."

"Did your friend find out anything else?"

"Yes, he did."

Derek heard Jerry shuffle some papers around. "What is it, Jerry?"

"Cory's parents died when he was young. Like five or six."

"He mentioned that."

"The police report stated that the grandfather said he came over and found them dead. He said the house had been ransacked. But the reports of the crime scene say that it didn't look like that at all."

"I don't think I understand."

"I called up one of the officers listed in the original report. He's in his seventies, but he remembered the case well. He said he had the impression the house looked like a staged robbery. It didn't have the feel of a home invasion. He tried to get his superiors to investigate the grandfather, but they never did. The man had a lot of money and a lot of clout in the community. They listed it as a home invasion gone wrong."

"Does he think the grandfather killed Cory's parents?" Derek dragged a hand down his face. His nose erupted in pain.

"He does. Based on his interview with the kid. The boy had said he was asleep in his room and woke up after he heard what sounded like gunshots. The boy stated when he came out into the hallway, he saw his grandfather coming out of the parent's room.

"The grandfather said he had the times confused. The grandfather had stated that the boy, Cory, had come out of his room after he found his son and daughter-in-law dead, not after he heard the gunshots. Of course, the investigators had no reason to suspect otherwise, but later the events started to not match the stories."

Derek couldn't believe what he was hearing. Cory had mentioned that his grandfather was mean as hell but having to live with a man you believed killed your parents had to fuck with a kid. "Oh shit. You realize if this ever made it to a jury, that a good lawyer would use the grandfather as the scapegoat for any deviant behavior. If it even gets that far, because we have no evidence."

"I know. But its more than we had years ago."

"One more thing, did your friend tell you anything on Cory's garage, does he own that?"

"Yeah, after his grandfather died, he came into a lot of money. I guess that's why he didn't have to sell the farm. He bought that garage shortly after that. Paid cash for it," Jerry said.

"Okay. I don't know if this is enough to get my AD on board, but I'm going to call him now. Let him know what we have."

"What do you think you're going to do? I mean, if he isn't on board with you proceeding?"

Derek dragged his hand through his hair. "I don't know. I'm not leaving here without exhausting every avenue. One way or another, I will know before I leave, if this man is a killer."

CHAPTER FORTY-SIX

Derek took a few minutes before calling his boss. He pulled up the email Jerry had sent him. He read through it making a few quick notes. As he scanned what he had, he knew this was going to be an uphill battle. He had to find a way to convince his AD that he could either get Cory to confess or prove that he is innocent and walk away. He dialed AD Fretz's number.

"AD Fretz."

"Hey boss, it's Derek."

"Really? I should fire you just for calling me that."

"You are my boss, right?" Derek chuckled into the phone.

"You are my problem child. I assume you're calling because you have some news."

Derek fiddled with the edge of his notepad. "I do. I spoke with Jerry."

"Mmhmm. Go on."

Derek gave him the run down. "Everything points to him."

"That may be true, but proving it is another story."

"I know that. But I have a plan."

"Oh, no. What are you planning on? Derek, hang on."

Derek could hear a muffled conversation with someone who came into the AD's office. He examined the notes he made one last time before giving his boss a plan of attack.

"Okay, Derek. Tell me your plan."

"I pick up my car today. I was planning on staying through the night and leaving in the morning. I'm going to take Cory out to dinner and lure him into a false sense of security. If he is the killer, which I'm going to approach this as if he was, I'm going to try to trip him up and get him to admit to it."

"How the hell do you plan to do that?"

"I'm an interrogator. I'll figure something out." Derek opened his water bottle from lunch and took a long drink.

"Derek, if you're going to trick him into giving you a confession, you better stay within the law. If you do something that won't hold up in court, then you ruin any confession you might get."

"I know, Sir. I won't do anything to jeopardize a chance to close a thirty-year-old case."

"I trust your judgment, Derek. This could go left at any moment. I'm assuming you have your weapon on you, as well as your credentials?"

"Yes, Sir. I do."

"Okay. If anything comes of this meeting tonight, I want to know immediately."

"I will keep you informed," Derek said.

Derek laid his phone on the desk and went into the bathroom to splash cold water on his face. It had been several days since he had last taken his pain meds, and the achy thump pounding behind his eyes reminded him of that fact. He inspected his nose by turning his head from side to side. To him, it looked a little swollen on the bridge. He splashed more water on his face just as his phone rang.

He bolted to the desk. "Derek here."

"Hey Derek, it's Cory."

"How's your day going man?" Derek walked back into the bathroom and dried the water off his face. He threw the towel on the shelf next to the sink and headed back to the desk.

"Going pretty good. Gerald is finishing your car. You can head over here anytime. I know you are anxious to get your ride back."

"Great, I will catch a cab and see you in a bit."

"Okay, see you when you get here."

Derek hung up. He fished his gun out of his bag and clipped the holster on his pants at the small of his back. He was wearing a short sleeve button up shirt, he checked the mirror to make sure the shirttail covered his weapon. Satisfied it wouldn't be readily seen, he stuck his FBI credentials and his wallet in his pants pocket and headed downstairs to find a ride to the shop.

CHAPTER FORTY-SEVEN

Derek exited the cab in the parking lot of Cory's Garage. He walked into the waiting area and lingered for a few minutes. He waved through the bay window at Cory and Gerald. They stood under his car that rested on the lift. He squinted wondering why it was still being worked on.

He smiled at Cory as he walked into the room. "Hey, I thought you were done."

Cory waved him into the office. "We are. Gerald wanted to make sure you didn't have any other damage. Didn't want anything else to go wrong once you got on the road." Cory sat behind his desk and opened a drawer. He pulled out a large book, leaving the drawer open. "I need to fill out a few things. By the time I'm done, Gerald should be finished."

"Cool," Derek said as he sat across from Cory. He watched as he made some notes and scribbled on a piece of paper. "I really can't thank you enough for all your kindness, Cory. You have restored my faith in mankind."

Cory frowned at him. "Right," he said chuckling. "Hey, like I said before, I have been stuck in some places, with no one around. I consider it paying it forward. You know, payment for all my past sins."

Derek barely nodded. "I have a few sins I need to do that for."

He pulled up something on his computer. "You never really said what you were working on, just that you write all kinds of stuff."

"I'm working on a true crime story at the moment." Derek watched his reaction.

Cory shifted in his seat. "Really? Like for a book?"

"Yeah. I have a book I'm working on regarding cold cases."

Cory stopped what he was doing. His fingers hovered above the keyboard. "Can you share, or is it top secret?"

Derek chuckled. "No. Not at all. I have been researching a case from the '80s. Along a highway corridor, several girls were abducted, murdered, and later dumped."

Cory sat up straight and placed his hands in his lap. "Wow. That's a hell of a case. Have you gotten anywhere with it? Found anything out yet?"

Derek nodded. "I have been able to get a bit further than the police who investigated each murder."

"A thirty-year-old case. Man, that has to be hard to track down evidence from that long ago."

"It is. That's for sure. Most of the families have either died or moved away. Several families fell apart after these girls were found dead." Derek noticed that Cory flinched a bit when he mentioned the state of the families. "Covering cases like this takes its toll."

"That's hard. Having to deal with parents of dead kids. I don't know that I would be able to do that."

"It makes you thankful for those people you have in your life."

A strange silence settled between them. Derek wondered where he should go next in the conversation. He was walking a tightrope. Had to give Cory enough information to pique his interest but not give all the cards away.

"Have you found any evidence to help the authorities narrow in on the killer?" Cory asked.

"Yeah, by luck, really. I was visiting the grave site of the last girl murdered, Margaret Shelling, I found a ring on the tombstone. At first, I figured someone had left it behind. However, after speaking with some of her family members, I was able to establish it was hers. And none of them had seen it since she went missing."

"No way?" Cory's eyes were wide and slightly glossy. "What are you doing with it?"

"I have some contacts in the FBI, I contacted them and asked them to send it out for DNA testing."

"Can they find anything on something that old? From that long ago?"

Derek noticed Cory fidgeted in his seat. "If they can find a big enough sample to test. You would be surprised how much DNA we leave behind just by handling items." Derek pulled out his phone and typed out a text. "I'm sorry. I had to respond to that. It was my editor. They are waiting for the first ten chapters of this book."

"Oh. Are you on a deadline?"

"Yes. A strict one, too. This little stopover has thrown a monkey wrench into my vacation plans."

"You still heading out to Tennessee?"

"I was planning on it. I'm supposed to be at a meeting with law enforcement regarding some new guidelines on how to handle cold cases. They have asked me to speak at a conference back in Arizona." Derek's phone rang. "Gimme a sec. I have been waiting for this call." Derek answered the call but didn't leave his chair. "Hey Agent Marcum, how's the FBI treating you?"

"Derek, this is Jerry, you asked me to call you, what's up?"

"Oh, hey yeah, no this is perfect timing, I got a few minutes. Have you found out something on the DNA test?"

"What the fuck is wrong with...oh shit, you're there with him aren't you?"

"Of course. No, I understand. But the fact that you got enough DNA to test is a great start." Derek smiled at Cory and gave him a thumbs up.

"I can't wait to hear this story. Is he reacting to what you're saying to me?"

Derek studied Cory as he conversed with Jerry. A thin line of sweat had formed on the man's upper lip and beaded around his hairline as well. "Yes. No, call me anytime, as soon as you have results. I'm hoping we can get something that points us in the direction of a suspect. Or even a person of interest. Okay, I look forward to hearing from you." Derek hung up and glanced up to see Cory glaring at him.

"Was that news about the ring you found?"

"Yeah, it was. They found enough DNA on it to test. Said they were going to have the results in less than a day, two days tops." Derek smiled at him. "This is the break I've been waiting for."

"Doesn't the person have to have been put into the system for you to get a match? My wife watches those crime shows all the time."

"Yeah, but you can get into the system by other ways than committing a crime. The best scenario, our guy committed other crimes. But if not, if he has a family member that has been incarcerated, we can get a hit off that. Or if they were involved in a crime like you were when you were little. You know with your parents being murdered. See, the authorities would take everyone's DNA to make the appropriate eliminations from the crime scene."

Cory became more agitated. He scooted his chair closer to the desk.

Derek watched him as his breathing increased. He was about to say something regarding the box he found at the house when Gerald walked into the office. He turned towards the older mechanic. "You about...."

A loud bang brought his attention back to Cory. Derek turned to see Cory held a gun pointed directly at him. "Whoa, Cory. Put down the weapon. You don't want to do that." Derek stood and pushed his chair out, allowing him to take a step back toward the wall.

Gerald froze. "Cory, what the hell are you doing man?"

Derek glanced at Gerald, then back at Cory. "Cory, this isn't what you want to do. Think of your family." He slowly moved his right hand towards the small of his back, making sure to not draw attention to his movements.

"I'm not going to jail. I'm a different man now. You know that." Cory's hand holding the gun shook. "I can't go to prison. I built a new life." His chin trembled. "Derek, I'm not the same man."

Gerald's head swiveled between Derek and his boss. "Cory, have you lost your fucking mind? Why would you go to prison?"

Derek didn't take his eyes off Cory. "Gerald, I'm asking you to not say anything."

"What the hell is going on?" Gerald's voice quivered.

"Cory, you can't live with this secret any longer." Derek's hand now rested on the grip of his gun.

"I told you, my grandfather was a nasty man. He abused my grandmother and me. She tried to protect me, but when she died, he took all his hate for my dad out on me. He made me the killer I was back then."

"I know, Cory. I know what kind of man your grandfather was. I know you aren't that man anymore. But the families of these girls need answers. They need closure. Tell me where Margaret is. Please, Cory."

Cory leaned against the wall, still pointing the weapon at Derek. Occasionally he would shift it to Gerald. Tears spilled over running down his cheeks. "I didn't mean to kill her. I really didn't. But she was going to tell what I did to her at the farm. I had just met Candace, and I came back to the farm to bury my grandfather and sell that damn place. It was an accident."

"I understand that. And now you want to do what's right." Derek pulled his gun from his holster and moved his hand to the side of his leg. "Cory, I'm Agent Derek Reed, with the FBI. Let me help you do the right thing."

Cory shook his head. "You said you were a writer. Did you come here to arrest me?" His voice took on a shrill tone. "You tricked me to get close to me?" he lifted the gun. "How could you?"

"No. No. Actually, I was on my way to Greenwood to talk to Liza Parker's family. She was the first girl you murdered."

"I don't remember their names. I'm not the same man." He wiped his eyes. "How did you find out it was me?"

"Cory, you kept the jewelry. I saw Julie Richards' necklace around your wife's neck. You gave the jewelry to your wife and daughter."

He shook his head. "I'm not the same man," he screamed.

"Cory, I believe you. I know you want to do the right thing now. I see how you are with your kids. You're a good husband and a good father. Give Margaret's family the chance to bury her. Tell me where Margaret is. Help me bring her home," Derek pleaded.

"How did you find the ring?" he asked.

"What?"

"Margaret's ring. How did you find it?" he shrieked.

"It was sitting on her tombstone."

"No. No, it wasn't. I buried it at the grave. When I found out they buried an empty coffin, I left the ring in the dirt. How did you find it?"

Chills ran up Derek's spine. "I guess it was unearthed by the ground's crew. Tell me where Margaret is. Please."

Cory sobbed now. He couldn't catch his breath.

"Cory, take a deep breath. I know you are a changed man. I know you want to do what's right. I need you to tell me where Margaret is buried," Derek demanded.

A still and calmness came over Cory. He lowered his weapon. "I love my wife and my kids. I need to tell them how sorry I am."

Derek raised his gun. "That's good Cory. Put your weapon on the desk. Let me help you. We can tell them together."

"I'm not the same man I was back then," Cory's breath hitched. He used the back of his hand to wipe his eyes.

"I know that Cory. I know you're a good man now. Please, tell me where you left Margaret. She needs to come home."

Cory looked down at his hand that held the gun. He started to put the weapon on the desk. His hand stopped, hovering above it. He looked up at Derek. "I'm sorry. I never meant any of it to happen." Tears ran down his cheeks. "You can find Margaret where it all began." He lifted the gun and put it under his chin. "Tell my wife and kids I love them."

"NO! Cory!" Derek shouted as the gun went off. Cory's brain spattered upward covering the wall and the picture of the farmhouse.

CHAPTER FORTY-EIGHT

Two days later

Derek stood with AD Fretz on the edge of the back porch. Cory's farmhouse in Vaughn was crawling with FBI agents, crime scene techs, and local law enforcement.

"How did the families of the girls react to the news their daughter's cases were solved?"

Derek watched as CSTs scoured the property looking for Margaret's body. "Relieved. Happy. If you can be happy about something like that."

The AD reached over and squeezed his shoulder. "You did a good thing, Derek. Solving those cases. You gave the families the closure they need."

"Not Margaret's."

"They still have something. They know that Margaret's killer won't hurt anyone again." The AD turned towards Derek. "You have to be prepared for the fact that we may not find her. We have been looking for her for hours now."

"Cory said she was where it all began. It has to be this farm." Derek watched as several CSTs went down into the storm cellar. It was large enough to hold freshly harvested foods and canned food, but it also served as the family storm shelter. "I have to find her. She has to be buried with her parents. They deserve to be together."

A flurry of activity centered around the shelter. Derek's gaze followed a few CSTs that came out and returned with a smaller sonar reader. He grabbed one of the tech's arms. "What's going on?"

The tech's eyes widened. "One of our guys noticed a disturbance in a dirt wall behind a shelving unit. We are checking to see if that's where he buried. We don't want to dig the area out without scanning first. Give us a few minutes, and we should have an answer for you."

Derek's heart raced. He shifted his weight from foot to foot. He tapped the face of his watch. He didn't know if he could stand the wait any longer when he heard the shouts. He glanced over at the AD.

A CST poked his head out of the shelter. "We found her. We got her, Agent Reed."

Derek pulled his phone out. He had the number programmed. It rang only once before the gentleman on the other end answered.

"Please tell me you found her."

"We found her, Jeffrey. We're bringing your cousin home. We're bringing Margaret's body home."

CHAPTER FORTY-NINE

Three days later

For the second time, Derek stood at Margaret's grave. This time the coffin lowered in the dirt held her body. Jeffrey and the AD stood on either side of him.

"I can never thank you enough, Agent Reed. You brought my cousin home. Where she belongs." Jeffrey said as he patted the agent on the back. "My family, we just can't ever do enough to repay you for this."

Derek turned to the man. "There is no need to repay me. I wanted to bring Margaret home. She needed to come home. I wish it was years ago. Maybe her parents would still be here." He reached into his pocket. "This was hers. It helped solve this case."

Jeffrey held out his hand. He gasped when Derek dropped a little ring into his palm. "Oh my God. I thought I would never see this again." He held the tiny ring between his large fingers. He brought it close to his lips and kissed it. Then gripped it tight in his palm. "Thank you, Agent Reed. Thank you for this." The man turned and walked to where his family was waiting.

The AD waited for a moment before speaking. "I'm going to give you a few minutes alone. I want to talk to you before you head to the airport." He patted him on the shoulder as he walked away.

Derek nodded. "I only need a few minutes, that's it."

"Take your time. I'll be over there." He nodded to the covered area off to the side.

Derek watched him step away leaving him alone at the edge of the grave. The coffin had been lowered but not covered yet. "I hope you rest, Margaret. I'm sorry it took so long to bring you home."

"She will rest now," Chrissy said.

He looked over at her. Her hair blew in the light wind. Wispy tendrils danced around her face. Chrissy's eyes were bright blue, and her lips were full and pink. "You're a beautiful young girl, Chrissy. I'm glad this is how I will remember you from this point forward."

She smiled at him. "What about Josiah?"

"What about him?"

"Is he still bothering you?"

Derek shook his head. "Not anymore. I took back my power."

She beamed a smile at him. "Look at you. It's about time. Just saying."

"Yeah, it was. I carried him around long before he died. It was time to let him go."

"It's time to let someone else go. Are you ready?"

He nodded. Without saying a word, he undid the watch clasp and removed Sheila's watch from his wrist. The tears flowed down his cheeks dripping off his chin. He knew it was time to bury her for good. To let her go. "I've carried her with me since that night in Tennessee."

"I know you have. It's time though. You both need to move on, and you can't do that holding on to the past."

"I hope she forgave me." He glanced at Chrissy. His chin trembled. "Do you think she forgave me?"

She reached out and touched his arm. "I believe she has. Have you forgiven yourself?"

He nodded. "I'm trying Chrissy. I really am." He threw the watch into the grave. It landed between the dirt wall and the coffin. Derek kicked some dirt over the edge to cover it. He wiped the wetness from his face and stepped back from the edge.

Chrissy smiled at him. "You did a good thing, Derek. You're a good man. Don't you forget that."

He smiled back. "I probably still need reminding every once in a while."

"Don't worry. I'll be there when you need me."

He reached out to touch Chrissy's arm when she vanished into a thin wisp of smoke. He turned and walked to his AD who now stood alone under the tent. "Hey, boss. You ready to go?"

They strolled towards the parking lot.

"When does your flight leave out of Albuquerque?"

"Late tonight."

"You need the rest of your vacation. Under no circumstances are you to do anything remotely like investigate a case. Do you understand?"

Derek crossed his heart. "I won't. I promise."

The AD followed alongside his agent. "Everyone was quite impressed that you solved this case, Derek. You have proven yourself the right agent to run the Legacy Unit."

"I wasn't trying to prove myself for anything. I needed to move through what happened to me in that tent. I think this case did that."

The AD grinned. "You still have to finish out your sixty days. Don't even try to get out of that." He laughed at Derek's groan. "Is your family glad you're finally going to show up?"

"Yes, they are. My dad has the entire week planned out."

"You're only staying a week?"

"If you ever meet my mother and father, you will understand why."

AD Fretz's brow furrowed. "Who was the girl you were speaking with at the grave? And where did she go?" The AD glanced around. "She was there a minute ago."

Derek stopped abruptly and turned towards the AD. "What girl?" His gaze narrowed in on his Director.

AD Fretz frowned at him. "The pretty young brunette. Looked about twenty. You seemed like you were having a pretty intense conversation with her. How do you know her? Is she related to Margaret?"

Derek's mouth fell open as his posture stiffened. A flush of adrenaline tingled through his body. He grabbed the AD's arm. "You could see her?"

The End.

If you liked this book, please leave a review wherever you purchased it.

Other books by Victoria M. Patton
Damien Kaine Series
Innocence Taken
Confession of Sin
Fatal Dominion
Web of Malice
Blind Vengeance
Series bundle books 1-3

Derek Reed Thrillers
The Box

Short Stories
Deadfall

ABOUT THE AUTHOR

Victoria M. Patton is forced to share her home with a husband, two teenagers, three dogs, and a cat. If she isn't plotting her escape, she uses her Search and Rescue/Law Enforcement skills from the Coast Guard and her BS in Forensic Chemistry to figure out the best way to hide all the bodies and write amazing stories about the murders. If she has any free time, she drinks copious amounts of whiskey and binge watches Netflix. Check out her blog www.whiskeyandwriting.com where she tries to help new authors navigate the indie publishing world. Contact her at victoria@victoriampatton.com. She is on most social media outlets, type in her name, you'll find her.